Lone Wolf in Lights

Also by Stacey Kennedy

The Devil in Blue Jeans

Visit the Author Profile page at Harlequin.com for more titles.

STACEY KENNEDY

Lone WOLF in Lights

 HARLEQUIN

ISBN-13: 978-1-335-57485-5

Lone Wolf in Lights

Copyright © 2024 by Stacey Kennedy

Harlequin Enterprises ULC
22 Adelaide St. West, 41st Floor
Toronto, Ontario M5H 4E3, Canada
www.Harlequin.com

Printed in U.S.A.

For Survivors

Dear Reader,

Lone Wolf in Lights explores emotional healing in the aftermath of intimate partner violence, cyberbullying and the loss of a loved one to homicide. Please always read with care.

Be gentle with yourself!

Stacey Kennedy

Prologue

Willow Quinn's laughter mingled with the crackling of the campfire as she leaned back on her palms. The Montana sky stretched above her, an obsidian canvas dotted with stars that seemed to twinkle in time with the strumming of the guitar being played by Decker, a homegrown cowboy of Timber Falls. The cowboys from Timber Falls Ranch lounged around the campfire. Beside her, the flames from the fire illuminated Aubrey Hale's shiny blond hair and cast a soft glow on Charly's warm light brown eyes. A tightness in Willow's chest unwound at the peace on her best friends' expressions. They'd moved to Timber Falls to start over after their lives fell apart, one way or another, and they'd done just that.

They weren't just surviving anymore. They were thriving.

As Decker strung a melody from his guitar, Gunner Wood's voice rose, soulful and rich, weaving through the night air. He'd returned home from Nashville as his album failed to deliver. Willow didn't get it—his voice was a dream.

His song was of open roads and wild hearts, the kind that made you yearn for something more—a song that felt like freedom. Willow closed her eyes, letting the music envelop her, each note a balm to her heart that still bled if she paid attention to those wounds.

"You know," Charly murmured, breaking the comfortable silence, flicking her brown curls over her shoulder, "sitting here makes it feel real. Moving into Jaxon's house—" a gorgeous ranch-style house set next to a barn on the ranch that raised and sold quarter horses "—it's like I've finally come home. Like, somehow, I should have always lived here."

Willow smiled. "I'm starting to think when we first came to Timber Falls all those years ago, we should have just stayed." They had arrived at the small town a stone's throw away from Yellowstone Park on a backpacking trip after graduating college. They'd made a pact then that if they weren't satisfied with their lives by twenty-eight years old, they'd move back to the town and open a bar to fix their lives before turning thirty. Seven years later after they'd made that pact, they'd fulfilled that promise, and it'd been their forever home for a couple of months now.

Aubrey's blue eyes sparkled as she lifted her nearly empty glass. "I couldn't agree more."

Even Willow knew that since leaving her abusive ex-boyfriend, Niko, and her life in Portland, Oregon—working for a marketing company—behind, her definition of home had shifted. It was no longer a place to tread lightly. Home was starting to feel safe again, a refuge with friends who were more like family, surrounded by wilderness instead of the hustle and bustle of a busy city.

Tightness in her chest unfurled as she stared into the dancing fire, the scent of pine and campfire smoke filling the air. Here, surrounded by the people she loved and the vast beauty of the ranch, she could almost believe in the possibility of a life untouched by fear, a future where her heart could trust again.

A loud bark of laughter drew her attention, but as her gaze swept over the familiar faces illuminated by the flickering flames, she realized Charly and Jaxon were no longer among them. She couldn't fight her smile. Charly was wildly in love, and they often silently vanished. No one asked questions.

"I'm going to whip up another batch of sangria," Aubrey said, rising to her feet. "Need a refill?"

Willow nodded. "Definitely, thanks." She watched as Aubrey walked away, her silhouette merging with the night until she disappeared into the house. The laughter and music continued around her, but as the minutes ticked by, the sudden awareness started to fill her that she was alone in the midst of cowboys she didn't really know.

She hated the lingering trauma that Niko had left on her— the long scar on her cheek a constant reminder—but there was no outrunning it. She wrapped her arms around herself, the warmth from the fire no longer sufficient against the chill that had nothing to do with the night air. She stood abruptly, the log she'd been sitting on rolling back slightly at her departure. "Excuse me," she murmured to no one in particular.

She moved swiftly across the ranch, the open field spread

out before her, bathed in moonlight. As the sounds of the campfire and Gunner's voice dimmed behind her, she exhaled slowly.

The horses greeted her approach with soft snorts and the shuffle of hooves. When she reached the fence, she grazed the soft fur of one of the horses, the dark brown horse. Here, in the quiet presence of these gentle creatures, she let the discomfort fall away.

"Hey there, big guy." She brushed her fingers across his soft nose. The horse leaned in closer, and she wished she'd brought him an apple.

His ears perked forward when the soft crunch of boots came behind her. She straightened, and quickly glanced over her shoulder.

Eli Cole smiled. "It's just me."

The alarm quickening her heart slowly faded. Jaxon's good friend, and Timber Falls cowboy, Eli had a presence about him that had screamed *calm* from the very day she'd met him. He moved with a grace that belied his size, a quiet strength emanating from him.

"Everything okay?" he asked. His strong green eyes drew her in, and in them, there was no judgement—only kindness, but something that she could relate to—deep personal pain. Eli's younger sister's life had been darkened by abuse too.

"I'm okay," she replied with a smile. Her gaze swept over him, taking in the rugged outline of his jaw, the tousled dark hair sticking out from beneath his tan-colored cowboy hat and the faintest hint of a smile playing on his lips. There was no denying it. Eli was gorgeous.

"Hope you don't mind the company." He stopped at the fence, leaning against it.

"Not one bit." She smiled, not sure what it was about Eli that made her feel so...comfortable, considering around most men now, she felt like a mouse who'd scatter at one look. But Eli, from the day she'd met him, felt like a friend. A good one.

"Seems like you found a buddy," he said, gesturing to the horse.

Turning back to the horse, she brushed over his nose again. "He's a cutie. Gentle."

"He is," Eli said, running a hand over the horse's neck. "Horses are honest. They don't hide their feelings or try to be something they're not."

Her lips curved into a smile as she thought about how Eli always seemed to have the perfect answers, especially when it came to calming her worries.

"Would you like to go on a ride sometime?" he offered, a playful challenge lighting up his eyes. "I promise you, there's nothing quite like feeling the world fall away beneath you when you're on horseback."

Her heart skipped a beat, and it had nothing to do with the idea of riding a horse. The same beat that happened every time she was around Eli. She could easily believe he was simply being kind, asking her to enjoy an outing as a friend, but she knew better. They had off-the-charts chemistry, something that at one time in her life she would have gobbled right up. But she couldn't go *there* again. She was in her self-care-single era. "Maybe some time we could all go out," she said, quickly looking to the horse again. "Although since I don't know how to ride, just doing this might be the safer option."

Eli chuckled, low and deep, possibly at her sidestepping his offer. "Nothing wrong with that." Then his laughter faded to his smooth voice. "Being with horses can heal even the most broken things."

She looked his way, drawn to the pain in his voice. Charly had told her that Eli's sister had been murdered by her ex-boyfriend. So that pain that Eli suffered, so visibly raw, was something they had in common.

"So, even if you don't ride," he countered, "come here and just be with them. This place saved me when I thought nothing would save me."

Willow's breath caught in her throat, her own scars suddenly throbbing with fresh memory. She couldn't take her eyes off him. Eli just seemed to see her wounds but didn't pity them.

He glanced sideways, his intense gaze meeting hers. "Horses... I don't know...they've just got this way of making everything in here—" he placed his hand on his chest "—better."

The world seemed to vanish around her, and all the reasons she told herself that she did not want a relationship again went silent. All that remained was this sweet way Eli seemed to understand her. She only saw his heart too. "I'm sorry for what happened to your sister," she whispered, "and that you needed a place that made everything better."

Eli swallowed deeply. "I'm sorry for what happened to you too."

Willow felt his words resonate within her own battered soul. Because he meant them. She saw it bleeding on his face.

Then she was moving without thought, drawn by something she could not control or stop.

One step. Then another. Until his strong body pressed tightly against hers. He lifted his hand slowly.

He gently caressed her cheek. "You're looking at me like you want me to kiss you, Willow." A pause. Then, "Is that what you want?"

"Yes," she whispered, surrendering to the yearning that had been building since their eyes first met. It wasn't just permission; it was a plea for a touch to feel...*safe*. It was a hope that his kiss would fix all the things another man broke in her heart.

His lips met hers tentatively at first, a gentle exploration that quickened her breath. Then, as if fueled by the sheer force of this magical thing between them, he deepened the kiss. Her hands found their way to his chest, feeling the solid beat of his heart against her palms. His arms wrapped around her, strong and sure, and she melted into him, falling into the warmth carrying through her.

When suddenly the sound of a loud cough broke through the silence. Her eyes flew open, the haze of desire lifting as reality slammed into her. She pulled back from Eli's warmth, ignoring the cold void that filled the space between them.

"Sorry to intrude," Jaxon said, emerging from around the barn, his hand loosely intertwined with Charly's, "but this is the only route back to the fire."

Willow gasped, mostly in shock that she'd allowed herself

to momentarily lose her mind and let Eli kiss her, and suddenly shoved Eli—hard.

Caught off guard, he went soaring back, landing on his ass. "What the hell?" he groaned.

"Oh no." Willow reached out to help him before stopping herself. She glanced at Charly then Jaxon, her face burning red-hot. "I'm so sorry," she eventually muttered, as Jaxon laughed hysterically.

Charly's mouth pressed tight like she was fighting her laughter. She tugged on Jaxon. "We'll just...um...meet you back at the fire," she said.

Eli finally pushed himself off the ground, right as Charly's laughter filled the night air.

Willow couldn't laugh. She could feel every muscle in her body tense. The kiss—intense and raw—had been an unexpected leap into vulnerability, a momentary lapse in her defenses.

"This... This was a mistake," she gasped, as Eli took a step toward her. "That shouldn't have happened." She couldn't trust her judgement about men. She wasn't ready for this.

Eli's expression shifted, confusion and hurt flickering across his features before he masked them with a practiced indifference. "My mistake," he said, the gruffness in his voice belying the careful control he was trying to maintain. "That's on me. I'm sorry, Willow."

"It's fine," she insisted, forcing a smile. "That was...we're drinking..."

With one last look at Eli, whose eyes held a storm of questions she wasn't ready to answer, she turned on her heel and walked briskly back to the others, Gunner's low, smooth voice drawing her forward.

She took a quick glance over her shoulder, her chest squeezing tight, as she saw Eli standing alone in the shadows, and her heart broke for another reason now.

One

Three months later...

Aisle by aisle, Willow led her best friends Charly and Aubrey through the maze of Christmas decorations that transformed the modest hardware store of downtown Timber Falls into a winter wonderland. She was totally *not* thinking about that kiss with Eli all those months ago. The scent of fresh pine and cinnamon mingled in the air, wrapping around her like a cozy blanket as she perused shelves filled with glittering ornaments and garlands. Timber Falls might have been small, but the town didn't skimp on holiday spirit. And with Christmas only a month away the holiday season was descending on the town.

"Check these out," she said, gesturing toward a display nestled between snow globes and festive candle holders. Strands of twinkling lights blinked back at her. She reached out, fingers grazing the delicate bulbs. "Wouldn't these look amazing strung up behind the bar?"

Charly's warm brown eyes brightened. "Oh, definitely."

Aubrey agreed with a nod. "Totally. Super cozy."

Willow couldn't suppress the flutter in her chest. Christmastime always warmed the chill in her bones. "Let's grab a few boxes." They had bought The Naked Moose, Jaxon's old dive bar, when they'd first moved to Timber Falls and modernized it with a little big city flair turning it into a cocktail lounge. Charly handled the business end. Aubrey was a chef and created the cocktails. Willow handled the marketing, and she couldn't wait to sprinkle the place with Christmas magic.

While Willow and Aubrey added the boxes to the cart, Charly moved further down the aisle. "What about these?" She held up a set of hand-painted ornaments that captured the rustic charm of Timber Falls. "Imagine them hanging around the bar."

"Yes. Love them," Willow agreed, and Charly placed them in the cart.

They continued on, stopping at the garlands of pine and holly.

"Oh, and these are a must-have." Charly looped one around her neck, pretending it was a feather boa, and flung a grin over her shoulder.

Aubrey snorted, always the most sensible one of them.

Willow chuckled. The happiness in Charly's eyes was a soothing balm, a striking contrast to the last year where Charly's heart had been broken by her cheating ex-fiancé. She'd left him behind in Phoenix. But his passing away three months ago had been unexpected and difficult, and Willow was grateful Jaxon, Charly's boyfriend, had been there for her.

"How about instead of wearing decorations we can drape these along the top of the bar?" Aubrey asked, selecting a garland that shimmered with tiny frosted berries.

"Always no fun," Charly grumbled, setting her garland back down. "Fine. But don't forget the mistletoe."

Aubrey begrudgingly tossed one into the cart.

Willow shook her head at her friends before stopping at the end of the aisle. Her breath caught in her throat. Row after row displayed unpainted wood ornaments, ready to be made into something beautiful. "Now this is exactly what I've been looking for."

Charly and Aubrey joined her, their expressions softening. "These are perfect for your Empowerment Elves group," Charly said.

The idea had come to Willow a month ago, while talk of the annual Timber Falls Christmas market hit the town. Empowerment Elves was a support group for women who needed a safe space and a friend, where they could heal their battered hearts while making crafts that they could sell at the Christmas market to raise money for the local women's shelter, Haley's Place.

"You're right," Willow said, her emotions thickening her voice. "These are exactly what we need." This group she envisioned would be more than a gathering; it would be a lifeline—a place where women could stitch their wounds closed with threads of friendship and understanding. And it gave Willow a purpose she'd needed to move forward from her trauma.

Charly wrapped a comforting arm around Willow's shoulders, determination lacing her words. "Let's get enough for the first night and then we can go from there." She gave a reassuring smile. "The bar will cover the first night."

"You sure?" Willow asked. She'd planned on doing some fundraising but hadn't gotten that far yet and had dipped into her savings.

Aubrey took Willow's hand, squeezing tight. "We've got your back, Willow. Always."

Willow leaned into their warmth. "I never doubt that. Thank you. I love you guys."

"And we love you," Charly said, kissing Willow's cheek.

Aubrey gave a firm nod. "Even more than margaritas."

Willow laughed. That was saying a lot. They all had a slight addiction to a good margarita.

With every item they added to their cart, Willow felt another piece of her armor shatter. And even though her ex-boyfriend Niko's shadow and the trauma of the abuse still lingered in the corners of her mind, she hoped the light she was building here was strong enough to keep the darkness away. Because that was better than hiding away at home.

"You know," Aubrey said after placing a few ornaments in the cart. "You should talk to Walt." He owned the hardware store that had been in his family for a couple of generations. They'd gotten to know him very well since they'd moved to town, always in the store for one thing or another for both the bar and their house. "I bet he'd be willing to help out with the craft nights."

"You think?" Willow hesitated, studying Walt, who stood behind the counter.

"Absolutely," Charly chimed in. "He's nice, and it's for a good cause. Go talk to him. You've got this."

With a deep breath searching for all her courage, thinking of the money they could raise for the shelter and all the women they could help, Willow stepped forward. "Okay," she said, more to herself than to her friends. When she reached Walt, she cleared her throat. "Hi, Walt."

"Hi there, Willow!" His response came easy. He was in his early seventies and had the warmest smile. "Can I help you find something?" he asked.

"No, I'm okay thanks," Willow said, nibbling her lip. She'd never been good at asking for favors. "I actually have this idea, and I'm hoping you might be interested in being a part of it."

Walt leaned forward, his expression open, an encouraging nod prompting her to continue.

"I'm putting together a craft group at the bar," Willow began. "It's specifically for women who've survived trauma. A place where they can come together, create something beautiful with their hands, and find support in each other's stories."

Walt's eyes softened, the lines on his face deepening in understanding.

Beginning to feel more confident, she continued, "We'll be making ornaments, garlands, wreaths—things we can sell at the Christmas market. All the proceeds will go to Haley's Place, the local women's shelter." She took a big deep breath and then added, "And we're looking for donations."

"How wonderful," Walt said warmly, reaching behind him to an empty box. He turned away and began pulling items from the shelves of a mix of art and Christmas supplies. "Consider these a donation to your cause." He offered her the box.

"Thank you so much," she said, her voice steady despite the storm of emotions within her. "This... This means more than you know."

"Anything to help get your group up and running," Walt replied, his smile creasing the corners of his eyes. He reached into the pocket of his apron, producing a well-worn notebook, then opened up a black leathered book on the counter and began writing with names and numbers. Tearing off a sheet, he handed it to her. "Here are the contacts for the other hardware store owners not too far from us. They're good folks—they'll want to support you."

Willow accepted the list, her gaze scanning over the handwritten details. She felt a thread of connection tugging at her, binding her to this community, which was slowly feeling more and more like home. "This is wonderful. Thank you, Walt," she whispered again, her throat tight. "Truly, it means the world to me—and to the women who will come to craft night."

Walt waved off her thanks with a modest chuckle, his eyes crinkling at the corners. "It's Timber Falls's way. We look out for each other here."

Late in the afternoon after a long day at the ranch, and seated in a booth at The Naked Moose, Eli's gaze lingered on Willow as she gracefully moved through the busy bar. Despite the challenges the bar faced in its early days with the locals not pleased by the lack of small town in the bar, the place now buzzed with lively conversation and laughter during the dinner rush.

On the other side of the table, Gunner tapped his fingers along the surface, in sync with an unheard rhythm, most likely a new song he was working on. Gunner hadn't mentioned it, but Eli knew he was determined to make new music that would wow his record label. Meanwhile, Jaxon finished off his last chicken wing, leisurely observing the crowd with a nonchalant air that Eli couldn't help but admire.

Willow, with her curly strawberry blonde hair flowing down her back and her warm green eyes fixed on her customers, was like a vibrant spark in the cozy atmosphere.

She focused on everyone else. He couldn't take his goddamn eyes off her. He hadn't been able to from the moment they'd met.

The cowboys in the bar all tipped their hats in her direction. What was once a hesitant community now warmly embraced the trio of best friends who had turned The Naked Moose into a local gem.

From his spot, Eli couldn't help but feel drawn to her. As the cold grip of winter took hold of Timber Falls, he attempted to suppress the feelings he felt for her. But even with his efforts, that flame still burned fiercely.

He gripped his beer bottle tightly, trying to ground himself against the memories threatening to consume him—memories of a kiss that burned too hot and bright, threatening to break through the walls he had carefully constructed around his own damaged heart.

Shifting uncomfortably, he caused the worn leather of the

booth to creak under his weight. It wasn't just the whiskey that kept him coming back night after night; it was something inexplicable that drew him to her—a pull he desperately fought against. He reminded himself that a man haunted by demons had no right to dream of a woman so sweet, especially not someone like Willow whose own past was built on strength forged through pain. But the memory of their lips meeting months ago still burned in his mind, a sensation he tried to push away but couldn't.

As a retired bull rider, he was more familiar with defeat and dirt than a soft, sweet woman. Yet, she stood there, her laughter ringing out above the noise of the bar, and all he could feel was...need. To bring her close, to see that smile aimed at him, to feel her warming the coldest parts of his heart. It all swirled inside of him, awakening emotions that he had long suppressed under layers of guilt and remorse.

"Damn it," he muttered under his breath, tearing his eyes away from her. He needed to get a grip, to maintain the distance she'd asked for after that kiss. But even as he commanded his thoughts to obey, they rebelled, tracing the curve of Willow's smile, the light in her eyes when she looked at him, the softness of her skin against his...

Stop, he growled silently in his mind.

Gunner slapped a hand on the table, drawing Eli's gaze. Gunner's tousled blond hair caught the dim light of the bar, his blue eyes narrowed. "You're scowling at the table. What's eating you?"

Eli hesitated, his throat tightening around words he had buried deep. But these were his friends, the closest thing to family he had left, and if there was anyone he could trust with the chaos of his mind, it was Gunner and Jaxon.

Before he could muster a response, Jaxon chuckled. "He's got that lovesick puppy look. Willow's got you good, huh?"

"It's not about Willow," Eli lied breezily, not ready to go there yet, focusing on the other problem. He ran a hand through his hair. "Tomorrow is the anniversary."

Gunner's voice dropped. "Miranda's?"

"Yeah," he admitted. The murder of his baby sister.

Jaxon's eyes softened. "You need us to go with you?"

To the cemetery was left off. Eli shook his head. "Nah, I'm all right. Just on my mind."

Right then, the air shifted, and Willow closed in on the table, her presence full of light as she carried another round of beers. Her smile, warm and unguarded, seemed to reach down in his chest. She slid the frosty bottle toward Eli, and as he reached out to take it, their fingers brushed—a fleeting touch that sparked between them.

A blush spread across her cheeks. Eli felt the sensation echo down his spine, the simple contact igniting sizzling longing within him.

"Looks like you could use another," she said.

"I could, thanks." He gave a firm nod.

A curl of her hair fell over her shoulder as she cocked her head. "Anything else I can get you?"

He felt the tingle of her lips on his again. "Can't think of anything," he answered.

"Okay," she replied softly. "Just give me a holler if you guys need anything."

Then she moved closer to the side and Charly took her place next to Jaxon, sliding onto his lap with excitement in her sparkling eyes. "Did you tell them the news?" she asked Willow.

Jaxon wrapped an arm around Charly's waist. "No, she hasn't. What is it?"

"It's just an idea I had," Willow said with a small shrug.

"Don't downplay it," Aubrey chimed in as she approached the table. "Willow came up with this great concept to host craft nights for women who need a safe space and a good friend. They'll make wreaths, ornaments, cards—all kinds of Christmas items! Then they'll sell them at the holiday market to raise money for Haley's Place."

Willow's cheeks turned a deeper shade of red. "It's just a way to bring together people who have been through similar experiences and also raise funds."

"You're doing something amazing here," Eli spoke up before he could stop himself. Her gaze connected with him, feeling like a punch to his chest. "It's a fantastic idea."

"Thank you," she replied, giving him a warm smile.

Aubrey added, "She could use some help too. Especially with getting supplies and everything ready before the holiday market in a few weeks."

"Say no more," Gunner said enthusiastically. "I've got two strong arms at your service."

Jaxon agreed with a nod. "Count me in for heavy lifting as well. And we'll need Eli's truck," he added with a wink at Eli.

Eli shot Jaxon a look but didn't protest. Ever since that kiss, he kept a careful distance from Willow, for both their sakes.

"It's settled, then," Charly declared excitedly. "Operation craft night is a go."

"Yup, all settled," Jaxon said, glancing at Eli. "Right, Eli?"

He nodded, looking at Willow. She held his gaze and the intensity crackled between them. "Of course, I can help."

Willow gave a small nod. "Thank you. We've got tonight covered, but I have another box of donations at a craft store in Wolf Springs."

The larger city was forty minutes north of Timber Falls. He wracked his brain, knowing there was no way he would survive a forty-minute car ride with her, drawing in her sweet scent. He came up with an alternative that kept them both safe. "I'll be out that way later this week," Eli said. "I'll grab it on the way back."

Willow's lips parted, and for a moment he thought that was disappointment in her expression, but he couldn't be sure.

"Excellent," Charly said, kissing Jaxon on the cheek, then sliding off his lap. "You guys are the best. Drinks are on the house today."

Eli exhaled a slow, long breath. Another day he'd managed to not unravel and pull Willow straight into his arms.

Now all he had to do was forget about that goddamn perfect kiss.

Two

The next morning, Willow's fingers danced over the keyboard as she sat in the dining room of the light blue house on Quiet Oak Road that she'd bought with Charly and Aubrey. Their home resembled a setting from an old Western film, complete with floral wallpaper, a grand foyer featuring a polished wooden staircase and generously sized windows that welcomed natural sunlight throughout the day.

The once-elegant dining space, with its vintage charm and hardwood floors, had transformed into an impromptu office for her and Aubrey now that Charly had moved into Jaxon's ranch. The bar didn't open until eleven o'clock, so morning work sessions were a routine now. Two monitors perched on the rectangular table before her glowed with graphics, as Aubrey sat across from Willow lost in her own work.

Over the last hour, she'd created and scheduled a few social media posts for not only the bar, but also the Empowerment Elves group, hoping to gain some interest.

The shrill ring of her phone sliced through the silence. She reached for the device, swiped the screen and pressed the phone to her ear. "Hello," she answered.

"Hi, Willow, it's Janine from Red Deer Crafts," came the cheerful reply, punctuated by the subtle background hum of a bustling store. "I've got fantastic news for you."

A spark of excitement ignited within Willow, causing her to sit up straighter.

"We've managed to put together a weekly large donation box for Empowerment Elves," Janine announced.

Willow's heart swelled. "Janine, that's incredible! Thank you so much."

"Of course, we're thrilled to help." Janine's voice was warm. "We believe in what you're doing. You can pick up the first box this Thursday. Is that all right?"

"Thursday works perfectly. I'll be there," Willow confirmed. The way everything was falling into place left her in awe. She never imagined she would receive this much support, but it only deepened her affection for Timber Falls. "Thank you again, Janine. This means the world to us."

A quick goodbye later, she ended the call, placing the phone down.

"Whoa, look at that smile," Aubrey teased from across the table. "I haven't seen you this lit up since...actually, I've never seen you this lit up."

"I feel lit up." Willow playfully tossed a crumpled-up Post-it note at Aubrey. "It's just...it's really happening, isn't it? We're making waves here in Timber Falls, Aub." Taking the leap to move here and purchase the bar had been a huge gamble, but the confirmation that it was the right choice brought sweet satisfaction.

Aubrey's smile stretched wider. "Oh, you are making waves. You're going to change lives, one craft at a time."

Willow's chest warmed. "I hope so." Even if it meant one woman would feel less alone, it would all be worth it.

"Now, get back to conquering the world," Aubrey said with a laugh. "I'll handle the bar inventory."

Willow nodded and reached for her mug, the steam from the hot coffee curling up, and took a slow, grounding sip. The warmth was a balm to the morning chill that lingered in the corners of the room, when the ringing of her phone again cut through the silence of the dining room.

"Busy girl," Aubrey said with a grin.

Willow winked, reaching for her phone again. "Hello?" she said.

"Hi, is this Willow? Willow Quinn?" The voice at the other end was tentative.

"Yes, this is her," Willow confirmed, setting her mug down with a gentle clink against the vintage table.

"Hi. This is Amie—Amie Jenkins. I heard about Empowerment Elves through your social media post, and, well, I'd love to join if you're still accepting new members?"

"Of course, Amie, We'd be thrilled to have you on board," Willow replied. "We've got our first crafting group this afternoon at three o'clock if you'd like to come."

"Really?" Amie said, her relief practically palpable through the phone. "That's wonderful. I'm really looking forward to it."

"We'll see you this afternoon, then," Willow affirmed, adding Amie's name to the growing list on her screen.

"Thank you," Amie said. "See you then."

The call ended and Willow smiled, reaching for her coffee again, staring at her list of women who would join the crafting group later that afternoon.

"Look at you, Miss Community Hero," Aubrey said.

"Hardly a hero," Willow demurred, but Aubrey's grin only widened.

"Stop it. I've seen the way people talk about Empowerment Elves. You're not just creating Christmas crafts, Wills—you're building something."

"Maybe so," Willow conceded. "Doing something—doing this—it's like I'm finally moving forward," Willow confessed. "And that is better than looking over my shoulder every second or expecting the worst. I'm looking ahead, making plans."

"Exactly," Aubrey said, nodding vigorously. "And that's a wonderful thing."

Willow nodded. She had secured donations from three stores, and *that* was a wonderful thing. She glanced out the window, to the ice covering the tree branches, spotting the small car she shared with Aubrey. "I'm going to have to make a few trips to get all the donation boxes."

"Or," Aubrey chimed in, with a grin that hinted at mischief, "you could just ask Eli to swing by with his truck."

The mere mention of Eli sent a rush of warmth cascading through Willow's veins. She shook her head, attempting to dispel the image of Eli's piercing gaze that seemed to look right through her defenses. "Stop it," Willow chided. "I'm not—I'm not ready for...*that*."

"Girl, Eli's truck," Aubrey emphasized with an exaggerated sigh, rolling her eyes. "Just the truck. And maybe those muscles when he's loading up boxes. But that's it. Purely logistical."

"Logistical." Willow snorted, and promptly ignored Aubrey's laughter and focused back on her work.

Late in the morning, the roar of the engine reverberated through the cab as Eli maneuvered his truck along the country roads of Timber Falls. His grip on the steering wheel was firm, knuckles white with a tension that mirrored the turmoil brewing deep in his gut.

As the truck slowed to a stop near the entrance of the cemetery, the gravel crunching beneath its weight, Eli killed the engine and sat for a moment. He drew in a deep breath, and with a heavy sigh, he grabbed the flowers off the seat, pushed open the door and stepped out into the chill.

He felt the cold seep through his jeans and flannel shirt, prompting him to pull his winter jean jacket tighter around him. His boots crunched on the snow-kissed grass as he approached the wrought iron gates, each step measured. He moved between the rows of gravestones, each marker a silent testament to lives that had rippled through the small town that had raised him.

He stopped before a simple headstone with the inscription "Marianne Cole." His mother's resting place. "Hey, Ma," he murmured. He placed the flowers in the holder. His fingers lingered on the cool granite, tracing the letters of her name, each curve and line etching a memory into his heart. "Miss you," he breathed out, the words carried away by the cold wind that rustled through the bare branches overhead.

He rose, moving to the gravestone next to his mother's. The grave marker before him bore a name that echoed in his soul. He knelt. The bouquet in his hands—a vibrant splash against the muted tones of the cemetery—trembled slightly as he placed it beside the headstone.

"Hey, sis," he whispered. He missed his mother deeply, but his sister had died young. Too young. Only twenty-three years old.

Her absence left an ache in his chest that never left him, even if he'd learned to live with it.

A warm touch on his shoulder startled Eli, and he looked up into the kind light blue eyes of Betty, an eighty-year-old widow with tight purplish-gray curls. Her presence was as comforting and familiar as the town itself. She was a long-time resident and a nosy one.

"Betty," he acknowledged. "Didn't see you there."

She chuckled softly, her hand still resting lightly on him. "You were a million miles away, Eli. It's good to see you here though."

Betty had been a constant in Timber Falls, involved in everything from bake sales to school fundraisers while he was growing up. Her heart seemed to have enough room for the whole town, and Eli had always admired her for it, even when his own world had been falling apart.

"Your mother and sister, they'd be proud of you, you

know," she said, not needing to look at the graves to know whom he mourned. "You've kept on going, kept on living. That's all any of us can do."

Eli nodded, the weight of her words settling deep in his chest. It was a simple truth, one he wrestled with every day. "Are you visiting your husband…" Eli began, then hesitated. He knew grief was a private thing, yet Betty wore hers like a locket, open for those who needed to see they weren't alone.

"Ah, Henry," she sighed, her gaze turning toward a well-tended plot adorned with a simple headstone. "Yes, it's my day to see him." She reached into her coat with a mischievous glint. "You know, I keep a little secret close to my heart on these chilly visits."

Eli raised an eyebrow.

"Here," she said, producing a gleaming flask from the depths of her pocket, winking as she did so. "A bit of warmth for the soul—Henry's favorite way to fend off the cold."

The corners of Eli's lips twitched upward. He took the flask, feeling its cool metal against his calloused hands.

"Betty, you're full of surprises." He chuckled.

"Life's too short for predictability," she quipped back, her smile as infectious.

With a nod of gratitude, Eli unscrewed the cap. The rich aroma of aged whiskey flirted with his senses before he brought the flask to his lips, taking just enough to feel the liquid fire trace a path down his throat.

"Henry had good taste," he admitted, voice softened by the burn.

"Only the best for the best," Betty replied, accepting the flask back and taking a long sip.

Eli took a slow breath, the air icy as it filled his lungs, and watched Betty replace the cap on her flask with a practiced twist. Her hands, though aged, were steady and sure—a stark contrast to the tremble that had claimed his own only moments ago.

"Henry would've liked you," she said. "He always appreciated someone who could respect a fine whiskey."

"Sounds like a man of good character," Eli replied, the corners of his mouth lifting in a half smile.

"Best I ever knew," Betty affirmed, tucking the flask back into her coat. "He'd sit out on our porch, glass in hand, and tell stories until the stars came out. It was…comforting."

The word resonated within Eli, stirring memories. He glanced at the twin graves of his mother and sister. The warmth from the whiskey was a temporary shield against the cold truth of loss, but now, as the alcohol's embrace faded, the past crept back in.

"My mom loved telling stories, too," he found himself saying.

Betty nodded, her eyes reflecting an understanding that only those who have loved and lost could offer. "They stay with us, in the stories we share, the memories we cherish. Grief has a way of isolating us, but it's through these moments we remember that we're not alone."

Eli felt something within him shift—the protective walls he'd meticulously built around his pain began to crumble under the gentle assault of Betty's words. "Thank you," he said, his gaze lingering on his sister's headstone. "I think I needed to hear that."

"Anytime, sweet dear." Betty's smile was kind, wrapping around him like a blanket. "And when the pain gets a little too much, a sip of whiskey always warms up the soul."

He chuckled with her. "I'll remember that."

Three

Just past three o'clock in the afternoon, Willow weaved through the tables in the bar. Her gaze fell to the booth where Eli had sat earlier during the dinner rush yesterday. Late last night at the bar, she'd heard from Charly that it had been the anniversary of his sister's murder. She'd wanted to call him, to comfort him, but she didn't want to blur the lines. The kiss had already blurred them enough. She glanced down to the small snowflake cutout clutched in her hand, as Eli filled her mind—those strong green eyes that seemed to see right through her defenses, that slow drawl which wrapped around her thoughts and refused to let go. A shiver, not from the chill filling the bar as the door opened, traced her spine.

She wanted to get back to what they were before the kiss. Friends, without the awkwardness. But here she was somehow wanting him close and actively avoiding him at the same time.

"Focus!" she muttered to herself, forcing her attention

back to the task at hand. With each piece of glitter or added cutout to her card, she tried to stifle the warmth Eli ignited within her—a warmth she hated that she no longer trusted.

She couldn't afford another Niko, couldn't risk the painful grip of hands that once promised love but delivered only bruises and broken promises. The memory flared, sharp and sudden, and her breath hitched. It wasn't fair to compare Eli to Niko, yet how could she trust her own judgement when it had failed her so catastrophically before?

Her gaze swept over the cluster of women who were diligently bending over the crafting items set out before them. Two bottles of wine sat in the center of the table, with glasses half-full. Gentle music played in the background, a soothing mix of country and soft rock.

She drew in a deep breath and said, "As it's our first crafting group, I want you all to know that here at The Naked Moose, with myself, Charly and Aubrey, it's a safe place for all of you," she murmured, folding the paper. "A place where we can share our stories." She grabbed the small scissors. "Sometimes, it takes just one person to say, 'I understand' for the world to feel a little less heavy." She glanced from face to face. "I want you to know—I understand."

Across from her, Tammy, a middle-aged woman with tired eyes and a tentative smile hesitantly set down her glue stick. "It's just…when you've been told so often that your feelings don't matter, it's hard to believe they do."

Every head around the table nodded agreement.

"Here, they matter," Willow assured her. "Your feelings, your stories—it all matters."

Another woman, Alison, younger, with sad blue eyes and dark curly hair, looked up from her half-finished card. She took a deep breath. "I'm scared all the time," she confessed, her fingers trembling as they traced the edge of the cardstock. "Scared he'll find me, scared that I'll never be able to trust again."

"I often feel that same way too," Willow responded gently, reaching across to squeeze the woman's hand. "I'm sure we all do."

Again, everyone nodded in agreement.

The air seemed to shift, charged with raw honesty.

"Every day is a struggle to remember who I am," Eileen, a twenty-something woman with sharp features and icy blue eyes, chimed in, stronger than the last. "But coming here, making these crafts over the next few weeks, I'm hoping it's like piecing myself back together."

"And that's what we're doing, isn't it?" Willow said with a nod, feeling the same way herself. "It's all about putting ourselves back together, piece by piece. And maybe, just maybe, we're helping someone else do the same with every craft we make."

Heads bobbed in agreement.

Amie said, "I remember the night I knew I had to leave Buck," she began, tucking her long chocolate-brown hair behind her ear.

Willow paused, a ribbon of emerald green satin slipping from her fingers, her attention fixed on Amie. She felt the familiar clench in her chest, the echo of her own past wrapping around her tight.

"Every day was like walking on shards of broken glass,"

Amie continued, gray eyes glistening with pain. "That night, the glass cut too deep. I saw my reflection in his eyes—not a person, just...an object for him to use and break."

A collective silence settled over the group, and Willow knew that look all too well—the one where you cease to exist in someone else's eyes. The memory of Niko's cold indifference flashed in her mind, a stark reminder of the woman she once was.

"Leaving Buck was the hardest thing I've ever done, but also the most important." Amie's voice broke before she swallowed deeply and said strongly, "Because now, I get to be here, with all of you, crafting a new story—one where I'm not the victim."

Tears nearly blurred the edges of Willow's vision, but she refused to let them well. She smiled at Amie. "Thank you, Amie, for sharing your story," she added, reaching across the table to squeeze Amie's hand. "This space, this group—it's for stories like yours. For all of us to find our voices again and feel safe doing so."

Amie smiled in return. "It feels good to talk about this."

"Good," Willow said, knowing that she'd been so lucky to have her supportive parents and Charly and Aubrey to help her get back on her feet when she barely could even kneel.

Over the next hour, the stories of heartache and resilience soon shifted to laughter, and Willow's heart swelled with each one.

Until the last of the Christmas cards were nestled into their plastic wrapping, and pride soon filled her. "I can't thank you all enough for coming today. I'll see you all tomorrow at the same time." Since she handled the marketing for the bar, she knew that a large portion of their profits came from parties celebrating women, ranging from divorce parties to birthdays. So, when there was an opening in their schedule, Willow made sure to fit in the crafting group as well. "Does that work for everyone?"

"Wouldn't miss it," Amie said, and the others around the table agreed.

"Great," Willow said with a smile. "I'm going to take a picture of all our cards for social media," she announced. "If you'd like to be in the photo then please stick around. If you're not comfortable, that's okay too."

Amie glanced around uncertainly, but after a moment's hesitation, she offered a warm smile and stepped forward. "I'll stay," she said.

"Okay," Willow said, and then to the others. "See you all tomorrow."

Once the other crafters filed out of the bar, Willow asked Charly, who stood behind the bar, "Do you mind taking a picture of us, Charly?"

"Not at all," Charly responded eagerly as she walked over and took Willow's phone to capture a shot of her and Amie in front of the colorful display of Christmas cards, holding a few of them up.

"Thanks," Willow said to Charly, taking the phone back.

Willow wasted no time in sharing the photo on social media, eager to spread the word about Empowerment Elves.

"Well, I guess I'll see you tomorrow," Amie said.

Willow nodded. "You will. Take care."

After Amie disappeared through the door, Aubrey took a seat on the stool at the bar and said, "That seemed to go well."

Willow agreed, "It went better than I expected. I'm so proud of this."

"You should be," Charly said. "You should be proud of *you*."

Willow simply smiled in response. Doing something felt better than just existing with the painful memories and her feelings. Helping others felt like the purpose she'd been searching for to make sense out of all that had gone so very wrong.

She busied herself with tidying up to get ready for the cowboys that always came in for a drink after their long workday at the ranch. The Naked Moose, usually brimming with boisterous energy, now held a sacred silence—and Willow felt a similar sweet silence in her heart.

Done good, kid, she imagined her dad would say. She missed her parents who lived in Ann Arbor, Michigan, where she and Charly and Aubrey all grew up, but they understood what brought her to Timber Falls, and they were coming for Christmas.

As she folded up the tablecloth, her phone buzzed from within the pocket of her apron. She retrieved the device, swiping to reveal a comment on the post she'd just made.

Her heart stuttered at the comment.

Willow Quinn is a lying bitch! You think you're helping our community with your support, but you're just out to destroy entire families by false claims of abuse. Timber Falls sees through your lies.

The words hit her like icy needles. Shock rooted her to the spot, her breath catching in her throat as she reread the comment.

Lying bitch.

Destroy entire families.

Lies.

"Willow?"

She gasped and lifted her head, surprised to find Charly and Aubrey staring at her.

At whatever showed on Willow's expression, Aubrey sneered, "Who do I have to kill?"

Charly rolled her eyes. "Stop being dramatic. What is it?"

"I don't... I don't know," Willow replied, handing Charly her phone.

Charly glanced at the screen, glared and announced, "Sorry, I was wrong. You were right." She turned to Aubrey. "You get the shovel. I'll come up with a solid alibi for us."

Four

The following morning, Eli's breath fogged in the chilled air of the arena as he guided the colt through a precise pattern. He'd worked for Jaxon's father every summer growing up, training horses and working the ranch. He'd moved briefly to Seattle, opening up a carpentry business, but his heart wasn't in it. He'd come home to Timber Falls briefly before following his dream to compete as a bull rider on the rodeo circuit. Only that dream never happened, his sister's murder did. His only regret was that he hadn't stayed in Timber Falls when he'd returned from Seattle.

He should have stayed. For Miranda.

The colt's sleek black coat gleamed under the dim overhead lights, its breath matching Eli's in visible puffs. Due to the winter's bite that seeped through the walls, Eli was wrapped in layers—a heavy jacket hugging his shoulders, and thick deer hide gloves.

Across the arena, Jaxon and Gunner were lost in their

own rhythms with their horses. At any given moment, they each had at least six young horses in training. After being weaned, some of the horses were sold while others remained for in-house training. All three of the men had been taught everything they knew by Jaxon's father. He had established a strong reputation for breeding top-notch quarter horses, and Jaxon was carrying on the tradition after his father's passing. Eli felt honored to be a part of such a legacy. His bull riding dreams a faint memory now.

The creak of the gate cut through the muffled thumps of hooves on the sandy floor, drawing Eli's gaze. Charly stepped inside, her presence a warm contrast to the cold. Her brunette hair was tucked beneath a woolen cap.

"Hey guys," she called out, her voice carrying across the arena. "Mind if we chat for a quick second?"

Eli slowed his horse to a walk, heading in her direction.

Jaxon trotted over, dismounting with ease, wrapping an arm around Charly and giving her a proper kiss. "What's up?" he asked.

Charly glanced at Eli and Gunner before speaking, her brow furrowed. "I wondered if you'd heard anything yet about the comment about Willow," she said.

Eli's heart lurched at the mention of Willow's name. He nudged the colt toward her, needing to hear more. "What comment?" he asked.

Charly's concerned gaze met his. "Someone made a nasty post about her on the bar's social media."

"Saying what?" Eli pressed.

"That she's a liar and making up stories about abuse," Charly continued, her words like ice shards in Eli's chest.

"Damn that's harsh," Gunner muttered, resting his arm on the horn of the saddle. His usual sly grin was nowhere to be seen, replaced by a scowl that mirrored Eli's sudden fury.

"They're accusing her of being a liar?" Eli's voice was a low growl, the reins tight in his grip. That was a venomous lie aimed at someone who'd already endured too much pain—he could feel his stomach knotting in response.

"Yeah." Charly gave a soft nod and then slowly shook her head. "I have no idea why anyone would post that, but I definitely want to be one step ahead of this. I don't want it to get worse."

"We won't let that happen," Jaxon said, tugging her closer. "I hadn't a chance to ask Eli or Gunner yet, but I asked some of the cowboys earlier. No one has heard a bad thing about Willow."

"Okay," Charly said, nibbling her lip. She glanced from Eli to Gunner. "You'll ask around too?"

"Of course," Eli replied, and he meant it. "Is Willow okay?"

Charly's eyes softened in the way they always did when she talked about Willow. The love that she and Aubrey had for Willow was a living, breathing, beautiful thing. "Truthfully, not really."

Eli's jaw set.

"We'll get to the bottom of this," Jaxon promised.

"I'll call if I hear anything," Charly said, and then with a final kiss to Jaxon, she left the arena.

Eli's mind raced. The urge to hunt the prick that hurt Willow burned in his gut. "Willow doesn't deserve this," he said, more to himself than to his friends, his body rigid atop the horse that now sensed his disquiet and began backing up.

Jaxon answered anyway, "No, she doesn't."

Eli's hand tightened around the leather reins, and the colt threw up his head. "Damn it," he growled under his breath, dismounting the colt so as not to feed the horse his tension. "We can't let that kind of poison spread."

Jaxon nodding solemnly, while Gunner removed his tan-colored cowboy hat and brushed a hand through his tousled hair, his expression grim. "Nobody's going to believe that crap. Willow's a good one. Everyone knows that."

"Reputation's a fragile thing in a town like Timber Falls," Eli responded. "It ain't just about her safety. It's what people believe. Lies like these—they fester, poison everything." He pulled the reins over the colt's head. "Besides," he continued, "this isn't just some petty online jab. Willow's been through hell and back. She's building something good, something real for people." His jaw tightened as he thought of Willow's un-wavering strength, her resilience. "How fucking dare some-one try and hurt her and this group."

"Agreed," Gunner added, his voice a low growl.

Eli pulled his cell from the back pocket of his jeans, opened the app and read the comment for himself. His grip tightened around the phone, his fingers shaking with rage. He could feel the anger bubbling up inside of him.

"We need to do something about this," he said, his voice tight with emotion. "We can't just let her be attacked like this."

Gunner and Jaxon nodded in agreement, their own anger palpable in the air.

Eli's hand shook as he scrolled through the poster's account, finding nothing but blank posts. "Looks like a throwaway account," he said, his voice thick with anger. "Fucking coward."

Gunner asked, "Any followers of the account?"

"No," Eli said. "No profile picture either."

Gunner shook his head in clear frustration. "This makes no sense. Who would do this to her?"

Eli felt the weight of the moment settle on his shoulders. He knew what she was up against—the whispers, the judgement, the narrowed eyes. He headed for the gate leading back into the barn.

"Where are you going?" Jaxon called.

He growled, "To fix this."

He handed the horse off to the newest Timber Falls cowboy, Casey. "He's done."

Casey took the reins and headed off to untack the horse and put him back out to pasture, whistling as he went.

Eli's boots crunched on the snow-covered gravel as he strode away, his gaze fixed on the dented up old pickup that had seen more miles than he cared to count. The early morning sun cast a warm glow over the dashboard as he fired up the engine, its familiar rumble picking away at the tension in his shoulders.

The drive into town was a silent one. Eli's thoughts, however, were anything but quiet. They buzzed nonstop, swarming with images of Willow's warm eyes and the Empowerment Elves she'd cleverly crafted.

The pickup rolled to a stop down the street from the Timber Falls Gazette, its old stone building standing stark against the clear blue sky. He exited his truck, and as he walked down the road, surrounded by the rustic charm of the two-lane street with quaint shops on either side, people moved out of his way.

He pushed through the glass door, the bell jingling overhead announcing his arrival. The office was quiet with the news channel being played on the television screen. But it was Sally, seated behind her cluttered desk adorned with a small potted cactus and scattered papers, who drew his immediate attention.

"Hey, Sally," he called.

Sally looked up, her face breaking into a smile that was both familiar and comforting. Her eyes, a soft brown, held the kind of understanding that shared pain evoked. Sally had been his sister's best friend.

"Well, well, isn't this a good surprise," she replied, her pen coming to a rest beside the open notebook on her desk. "What brings you by?"

He approached, taking a seat in the chair in front of her desk. "I was hoping you could help me."

Sally's brows rose. "With?"

"A friend of mine, Willow—she owns The Naked Moose with Charly and Aubrey."

Sally smiled. "I've met them all."

"Good—that'll make this easier." He mirrored the smile. "Willow has got this Christmas craft group going called Empowerment Elves…" He caught her up on what the group was all about and the comment on the bar's social media account.

When he finished, a shadow of pain flickered across Sally's features, a mirror to Eli's own heartache. She remembered too well the loss. "Of course, I'll help in any way I can," she said, her voice soft yet steady. "What a wonderful cause."

He agreed with a nod. "Thank you, Sally. Means more than I can say."

Sally paused a moment, curiosity brimming in her eyes. "You know," she began, swiveling slightly in her chair, opening her drawer, "there might be another way to drum up some more financial support too."

She sifted through its contents until her hand emerged clutching a glossy piece of paper. She turned back to him and extended the flyer. "The annual Timber Falls Rodeo is next weekend," she said, her tone casual but laced with intention. "Winner takes home five grand."

Eli's gaze fixed on the bold letters emblazoned across the flyer, a rush of adrenaline coursing through him. His fingers twitched as if already feeling the tug of a rope, the thud of hooves against dirt, but he held himself still.

"Five thousand could sure cover a lot of Christmas miracles," Sally added, watching his reaction closely.

He leaned forward, elbows resting on his knees, eyes tracing the lines of the flyer. The thought of entering the rodeo lit a fire in his belly, one that had been doused years ago when he'd hung up his spurs for good.

But could he?

Should he?

"Sounds like a lot of money for a good cause," Eli murmured. The possibility of getting in the ring again sent shivers down his spine. He could almost hear the roar of the crowd, feel the beast beneath him bucking for freedom.

"Look, no pressure," she said softly, willing him to meet her gaze. "It's just an option. There are other ways we can help Willow raise money for the shelter. Hopefully I can do the story justice and donations will come in."

"You will kill it, like always," Eli said with a smile. "Thank you. For this." He gestured to the flyer. "And for writing the story."

"You never need to thank me, Eli" she said.

Eli gave a final nod and headed for the door, feeling the stir of something akin to hope fluttering in his chest.

Later that afternoon, Willow moved with a sense of purpose around The Naked Moose. She carefully arranged the tables into a long row. She sorted through an array of craft supplies, setting out scissors, glue guns, and ribbons, all the while thinking of that thoughtless comment and hating how much it got inside her head.

She was fanning out stacks of colored paper and jars filled with buttons and beads when the door swung open, jangling the rustic bell above. Sally Carter, the local reporter for the *Timber Falls Gazette*, entered with a vibrancy that she always had when she came into the bar. Her eyes sparkled with an energy that was as infectious as it was genuine, her notebook clutched in her hand.

"Hi, Willow, hope I'm not too early," Sally chirped.

She'd called a few hours ago to inquire about Empowerment Elves and asked if she could write a story on the group. "Perfect timing, actually," Willow replied. After the comment, Sally's interest was the bit of good news she needed. "I'm just finishing up with the setup."

"Mind if I take a look around? It's amazing what you're doing here," Sally said, her eyes sweeping over the half-full box of Christmas cards from yesterday's event.

"Of course, make yourself at home." Willow watched as Sally moved to the box.

She leaned in to examine a pile of cards. "These are beautiful. The personal touch really shines through."

"Thank you," Willow responded, tucking her hands into her jean pockets. "Every piece crafted here carries a story—pieces of bravery and resilience."

Sally nodded, scribbling notes. "I can't wait to share this event. The community needs to see the strength gathered around these tables."

Willow agreed, but did grow curious. "Can I ask how you found about what we're doing here? Through social media?"

"Eli asked me to do the story."

Willow's heart skipped a beat. "Eli asked you to do this story?" she repeated.

"Yep," Sally confirmed with an enthusiastic nod. "He thinks what you're doing here is pretty amazing. Said it deserved to be in the spotlight."

An unexpected rush coursed through Willow's veins. She found herself momentarily speechless with gratitude threatening to spill over. "I…wow, I didn't expect him to do that."

Sally's lips curled into a knowing smile. "It's not just about the story for me either. I was best friends with Eli's sister, you know. This—" she gestured around the room lined with glitter, glue and courage "—this cause is close to my heart too."

Willow returned the smile. "Then this story is in the right hands."

"Absolutely," Sally replied. "Let's make sure everyone hears about the incredible work happening right here." She glanced around. "Is this where the magic happens?"

"Every bit of it," Willow replied, casting a proud glance around the room.

Sally leaned in, her eyes scanning the array of supplies on the table. "And the community's been supportive?"

"More than I ever imagined," Willow said, leaving out the horrible comment from a likely troll. "Local businesses donated materials. I can definitely give you their names."

"Please," Sally said.

Right then, the door opened, ushering in a draft of crisp mountain air and a half dozen women. Laughter and soft greetings filled the space, making Willow's skin tingle with anticipation.

"Everyone, this is Sally. She's doing a story in the *Gazette* about Empowerment Elves," Willow announced, gesturing toward the reporter with an affectionate smile.

"Hi, Sally!" chorused the Empowerment Elves, each member radiating a mix of excitement and curiosity.

"Can't wait to see what you all create," Sally responded.

"Let's get started, then," Willow declared.

As the women gathered around the tables, the room pulsed

with an electric enthusiasm, and Willow turned to Sally. "Thank you for telling our story and getting the word out there. It matters more than you know."

"Thank Eli." Sally gave a knowing grin. "This was all him."

Willow just smiled, but those guards protecting her heart shattered a little.

Hours zoomed by as the craft group finished up. Sally left, then everyone else did too.

The sun had set hours ago, and The Naked Moose pulsed with life, along with the strum of Gunner's guitar. On stage, Gunner sat on a stool with a microphone in front of him, his fingers dancing over the strings, weaving melodies that wrapped around the bar like a warm embrace. His voice was rich and low, and set hearts on fire, given all the women staring at him with love in their eyes. Willow still found it hard to believe his record label had told him to leave Nashville to write new music. She thought his old music was better than anything she'd heard, even if she wasn't a huge country music lover.

She watched from behind the bar, the soft glow of the neon lights behind her as she poured another round of drinks. The hum of conversations and laughter mixed with the music made her smile, regardless of the comment still remaining heavy on her mind.

Her hair was pulled back in a loose ponytail, a few strands framing her face. She moved with practiced ease, her eyes scanning the crowd for empty glasses and signals for refills.

The atmosphere was infectious, even to her, who had seen countless nights just like this one. Yet, there was something invigorating about the way people came together under their bar—strangers becoming friends, worries dissolving away.

Gunner's voice suddenly silenced as did the strings of his guitar. His blond hair fell into his eyes as he grinned, his charm palpable even from across the room. She couldn't help but laugh. The ladies loved Gunner.

Except for Aubrey.

He seemed to get right under her skin. And Willow hadn't quite figured that one out yet. Aubrey barely acknowledged his existence. Willow figured Aubrey was about as done with men as Willow was.

Right then, her cell vibrated in the back pocket of her jeans. She lifted the cell phone, a sense of cold fingers wrapping around her spine.

"Willow, we need more whiskey at table nine," called Aubrey, but her voice seemed distant, muffled by the sudden rush of blood in her ears.

With a flick of her thumb, she unlocked the screen, and her breath caught as she realized she hadn't read the text wrong. Stark against the backlight, words formed a jagged sentence, a venomous message that branded itself onto her mind: **Keep telling your lies, bitch!**

For a moment, time stopped. Her grip on the phone tightened, knuckles whitening as she read the text again, hoping she had somehow misread it. But the hateful words remained unchanged, their threat echoing in the hollow of her chest—they knew her phone number.

Her pulse hammered in her temples as dread unfurled within her. Her eyes darted across the bar, searching for a sign, any clue that might reveal the identity of the sender. Could it be Niko? Her stomach twisted at the thought. He had every reason to hate her, every reason to destroy her from behind bars. Or was someone in town screwing with her?

She scanned the faces in the crowd, scrutinizing each one. Laughter erupted near the pool tables and couples swayed to Gunner's voice. Yet she couldn't shake the feeling that someone was watching her.

Panic began clawing at her insides. It had been long months since she last felt this level of fear, months since she fought tooth and nail to put Niko away and protect herself from his violent interpretation of love. And now, with a single message, those walls she'd meticulously built seemed to crumble when suddenly, her gaze snagged on a pair of piercing eyes that cut through the chaos.

Eli's rugged features etched with concern. His gaze held hers and held fast. In that steady gaze, she found something unexpected—*relief.*

He navigated the crowd with determined strides, a path clearing before him as if the crowd sensed the urgency emanating from him.

She felt the warmth of his calloused hand before she saw it, the touch grounding her. "Eli," she whispered.

"Come with me." His words were gentle but insistent. Without waiting for her response, he wrapped his fingers around hers, firm and reassuring.

Eli led her through the throng of people, every step away from the stage where Gunner still sang a country ballad. Her hand trembled within his grasp, yet the strength of his hold promised safety, as confusing as that was.

His hand was a lifeline as he led Willow out the back door to the alleyway's far end, away from prying eyes and too-close walls. The night air, crisp and cool, brushed against her hot skin.

"Willow," Eli said softly, as he flipped over a milk crate and helped her sit on it. "Breathe with me, deep and slow."

She obeyed, focusing on the rhythm of his breathing. In-hale. Exhale. She followed the rise and fall of his chest, calming the erratic pulse that hammered at her temples.

"Better?" he asked after a few moments, his thumb brushing the back of her hand in a soothing motion.

She nodded, the knot of panic in her stomach loosening ever so slightly. "Yes, better," she affirmed, her voice still a whisper but steadier now. "Thank you."

Eli's gaze held hers, unwavering. "Can you tell me what happened in there?"

The concern etched in the lines of his face, the steadiness in his eyes, all spoke of protection. Willow felt the connection between them pull taut, a thread laced with something more than just shared experiences.

"It was a text," she started, the words spilling out. She unlocked her phone and lifted it to him.

Eli's jaw set into a hard line. Until he met her eyes again and his expression softened. "Do not believe what this person is saying." His voice was a low rumble, filled with unwavering conviction. "And they sure as hell don't get to threaten you and hide behind a damn screen."

The bar's raucous laughter and Gunner's voice filtered out into the night, but here in their quiet corner, she could only stare into the warmth of Eli's eyes.

"I'm trying not to let this affect me," she whispered, the coldness of fear slowly melting away under his warmth. "I've been trying to forget my past, to start over here, but these messages…they're dragging me back to a place I thought I'd escaped, and I hate that." She drew in a sharp breath, shaking her head. "I'm not that scared person anymore."

"That text would rattle me," he said firmly. "Every word in that message was meant to break you, but they don't know you." His eyes blazed with an intensity that burned away the panic. "You're stronger than they'll ever be, and we'll find out who's doing this."

"How?" she asked.

"Leave it with me, all right?" he implored. "I'm going to help you and we'll stop them."

She blinked up at him, and *somehow*…she believed him.

His thumb brushed over the back of her hand in a soothing gesture, and it occurred to her in that moment that he'd come there tonight to see how she was doing. Here was a man who knew pain, who carried his own scars, offering her a safe shelter, after she'd totally and outright pushed him away.

"Okay," she breathed out.

"Let's head back inside," he suggested, releasing her hand but not the invisible thread that had woven itself between them. "Do not let them ruin your night."

He said it so adamantly that it brooked no argument, and

she lifted her chin and reminded herself, "I won't ever let anyone ruin my night again."

"Atta girl." He grinned.

Then went to open the door. "Wait," she called. When he turned back to her, she added, "Thank you for talking to Sally today for me. For writing the story about the group."

"You don't need to thank me," he said.

She closed the distance, hoping her gratitude showed on her expression. "I do. It really meant a lot. Thank you."

Softness reached his typically hard eyes. "You're welcome, Willow." He whisked the door open.

And as she headed back inside, she focused on that gratitude and not on the way her body flushed at his tender, low voice.

Five

Early the next morning, Eli's boots carved a relentless path across the worn floorboards of his living room. The quaint log house on Timber Falls Ranch, usually his sanctuary, now felt uncomfortable with his spiraling thoughts.

Each time he turned on his heel, the image of Willow—those striking green eyes clouded with fear—haunted him. Willow, with her strength etched into every curve of her body, didn't deserve to be looking over her shoulder. Not in Timber Falls, not anywhere. And yet some coward had made it so, hiding behind malicious words cast out into the digital world, targeting her like she was nothing more than prey.

His hands flexed by his sides, turning into tight fists. "Dammit," he muttered under his breath. He thought about Willow's past, the way she'd fought tooth and nail to rise above it, to run The Naked Moose without so much as flinching at shadows of old fears. She was trying to build something for herself and other women to crawl out from their painful memories. And Eli? He couldn't stand to see that light flicker out because of some spineless prick.

He stopped pacing, standing stock-still as a statue, his jaw set in a hard line. He'd done his best to keep a careful distance. She wasn't ready for a relationship and he wouldn't pressure her. But he couldn't take it anymore.

He *could* protect her. In more ways than one. And he would protect Willow, come hell or high water.

"Enough is enough," Eli resolved, seizing the truck keys on his way out the door. He didn't bother to lock the door behind him.

The truck roared to life as his hands gripped the steering wheel, leather worn smooth from years of working the ranch. Through the windshield, Timber Falls Ranch lay before him.

The engine hummed a steady rhythm beneath the hood, mirroring the pulse that thrummed through his veins. His jaw set, thoughts of Willow ignited a fire within him that no amount of whiskey could douse. Every malicious word aimed at her only fueled the flames, and now, as he drove, those flames burned even hotter.

He passed long country roads, but Eli saw none of it. Each mile eaten up under the tires of his truck brought him closer to making this right again for Willow. A sigh of relief escaped him when he drove into downtown and parked at the curb. He got out of his truck and strode into the Timber Falls Police Station.

"Morning, Eli," greeted Jenny, the receptionist in the police station. Her voice was as warm and familiar as it had been back in high school when they'd shared classes and occasional small talk.

"Hey," he replied with a nod, offering a smile. "How things been?"

"Can't complain," she said with kind blue eyes crinkling at the corners. "What can I do for you?"

"Is Detective Harris in?" he asked. Harris had been the lead detective on his sister's homicide case.

She nodded. "He's in his office. Go on back."

"Thanks."

"Anytime," she replied, as he turned toward the corridor leading to the detective's office.

The protective impulse toward Willow burned deep as he walked, steeling himself for the conversation ahead. Eli knew he was stepping into deeper waters with each stride he took, but there was no turning back. Not when it came to Willow. Not when every fiber of his being screamed to stand by her side.

Eli rapped his knuckles against the solid oak door. A gruff voice called out from within, "Come in."

Pushing the door inward, Eli stepped into the sparsely decorated office that carried a scent of coffee and old files. Behind a cluttered desk sat Detective Harris, his dark hair cropped close to his scalp, lines etched around his eyes from years of squinting at crime scenes under harsh suns and dim flashlights.

"Harris," Eli greeted him.

"There's a face I wasn't expecting to see today," Harris said, rising from his chair, offering his hand. "Been too long."

"Too long," Eli agreed, the corner of his mouth twitching upward. He took the seat across from Harris after returning the handshake, noticing the family portrait that claimed pride of place on the detective's desk. The baby was a new addition, or at least new since Eli last visited.

"Your sister's case," Harris began, as he sat back down, "never sits far from my mind."

Harris was once a stranger, but he'd become a friend during those tough days. More than anything, Harris had been kind to Eli's mother, and Eli would never forget that. "Appreciate that," Eli replied, his throat tightening for a moment before he shifted the conversation away from the pain of the past. "How's the family? See you have a new baby."

"A daughter," Harris confirmed, the weariness in his eyes giving way to a spark of pride as he glanced at the family photo. "Heidi. She was born a few months ago."

"Good to hear. Congratulations," Eli said genuinely. "And Sarah?" His wife. "She still teaching over at the high school?"

"I don't think she'll ever leave." Harris chuckled. "She's got the patience of a saint, dealing with those teenagers day in and day out."

"I'm sure they appreciate her," Eli said, allowing himself a brief smile before leaning forward, elbows resting on his knees. His mind churned with images of Willow, her usually vibrant green eyes clouded with fear, her delicate hand trembling in his.

Harris expression firmed. "Now, what can I do for you?"

"Something's come up, and I hoped you could do me a favor," Eli began. "Someone's been messing with one of the new owners of The Naked Moose, Willow Quinn. She's a good friend, and it doesn't sit right."

"Details, Eli. I need details." Harris grabbed a notepad and his pen hovered above, ready to capture every word.

"A couple days ago, an anonymous account posted a comment on the bar's social media page saying that Willow is spouting false claims of abuse in her Christmas-crafting support group at the bar. They're making crafts to sell at the Christmas market to raise money for the shelter, Haley's Place." Eli's jaw tightened at the memory. "Last night she got a text—so this person now has her personal phone number."

"Are they threatening her?" Harris asked.

Eli's hands clenched into fists, released, then clenched again. "They're calling her a lying bitch. She's scared—that's enough of a threat."

"Understood." Harris nodded, his demeanor professional yet tinged with empathy. "What do you need from me?"

"Her ex-boyfriend, Niko Sanchez, is violent." He'd heard Charly mention his full name to Jaxon once, and he had never forgotten it—would *never* forget it. "He should be locked up in Portland, but I need to make sure he's still there. Need to make sure he can't get to her."

"Got it." Harris nodded. "You think he's behind this? Trying to attack her character?"

"I honestly don't know if it's someone local, but I wouldn't put it past him," Eli admitted, the muscle in his jaw ticking. "And if he's out, Willow could be in real danger."

"Leave it with me," Harris assured, his eyes meeting Eli's

with a resolve that mirrored his own. "If Niko's behind this, I'll find out."

"Thanks, man." Relief threaded through Eli. "Willow... she's a sweet woman. She doesn't deserve this."

"Say no more, Eli." Harris's words were firm, laced with a promise. "I'm on it." He leaned back in his chair, sending it squeaking beneath him as he crossed his arms. "I'll need Willow to come in and sign a consent form for me to look into her phone records and her social media," he said.

"I'll ask her if that's what she wants to do and can bring her in," Eli offered.

"Good," Harris said. "But let's focus on her ex-boyfriend and see where that leads us for now."

Eli rose and clasped Harris's hand firmly. "I owe you one," he said.

"Think nothing of it," Harris replied, releasing Eli's hand. "It's what we do here—keep each other safe, keep the town whole."

Eli was aware that he wasn't the sole person haunted by his sister's memory. He knew the case had taken a toll on Harris too, as the police had no clue about the abuse Miranda had been suffering.

Harris reassured him, "Don't worry too much. These incidents are usually harmless and just a result of trolls being trolls."

"That better be the case," Eli responded sternly.

Clearly, his tone was too harsh as Harris raised an eyebrow. "Stay out of this, Eli. Understand?"

Eli nodded and left the office, unable to keep that promise.

★ ★ ★

The bar's opening was only a couple of hours away, and Willow's fingers were numb despite the gloves she wore, making her wish she had to get to work now. But Aubrey was laughing, the sound bright against the crisp air, as she handed Aubrey another string of Christmas lights. "Make sure it's tight," Willow instructed, her breath visible in the chilly air.

"Like my abs after all those planks you make me do?" Aubrey quipped, her curly blond hair peeking out from under a knitted beanie as she reached up to secure the lights along the porch railing.

"Exactly," Willow said with a grin. They'd been decorating for forty-five minutes now, and with every bulb, it began to feel a little more like Christmas.

The quiet, rhythmic snapping of the bulbs hitting against the wooden beams paused as an engine's rumble sliced through the silence. Willow turned to see a familiar truck rolling up to the curb, the vehicle's rugged appearance a mirror of its owner's tough exterior. She felt an odd flutter in her chest, a mix of anticipation and nerves, a reaction that was solely reserved for Eli these days...even if it shouldn't be.

"Looks like trouble on four wheels," Aubrey observed, her tone light but teasing, following Willow's gaze to where Eli's truck had come to a stop.

He emerged from the driver's side and closed the door with a thud that seemed to echo in Willow's ears. His powerful eyes locked onto hers, and there was something about the set of his jaw, the purposeful way he moved toward them that made Willow's pulse quicken.

"Hey," he called out in that gravelly voice that always seemed to resonate a little too deeply within her.

"Hey, yourself," Aubrey replied, stepping down from the porch with a knowing look in Willow's direction. "Looks like you've got company, Wills."

Willow nodded, brushing a stray lock of hair from her face, her gloves making the gesture awkward. She watched Eli approach, the lines of his jacket straining against his broad shoulders, a clear sign of the strength that lay underneath. She hoped her smile didn't look as nervous as she felt. Eli had a way of unsettling her, of stirring things inside her that she'd thought were long buried.

"Everything okay?" she asked, trying to keep her voice steady and casual.

"Can we talk?" His gaze held hers, earnest and insistent, and Willow found herself nodding before the question fully settled in the air between them.

"I'll...ah...give you guys a second," Aubrey said, giving Willow's shoulder a supportive squeeze before retreating into the house without another word.

As the door shut behind Aubrey, Willow turned back to Eli, her hands now tucked into the pockets of her coat to ward off the cold. "Is everything okay?" she asked again.

He closed the distance and leaned against the porch railing. "I went to the police station today and met with a detective I know, Detective Harris. He's willing to look into the comment and text a little deeper, but he needs your consent."

"Consent for what exactly?" Willow asked.

"A formality really, but necessary to let him look into your social media accounts and phone records. We'll need to go into the station and sign some documentation."

She didn't miss the *we'll* he added there. "Okay, we can go tomorrow before work," she whispered, the reality of the situation settling upon her shoulders like a heavy weight.

"Good," he said with a firm nod. "I asked the detective to look into Niko and to make sure he has no part in all this. I hope I wasn't overstepping there."

A heavy weight on her shoulders that she hadn't known was there lightened slightly. "You weren't, thank you," she told him honestly.

"Your safety is the most important thing right now," Eli said firmly. His presence was a force, the intensity in his eyes impossible to ignore. "I was thinking..." He paused, as if weighing the weight of his words. "What if I acted as your boyfriend for a while?"

Her breath hitched in her throat.

"Boyfriend?" Willow finally managed after a long moment. It wasn't just the suggestion, but the man behind it— Eli Cole, whose rugged exterior housed a tender core she'd glimpsed only in fragments.

"Listen, I know it's an unusual situation," he continued, the timbre of his voice grounding her fluttering thoughts. "But it could help throw off whoever is behind this. They might think twice if they see you're not alone, that you have someone watching out for you." He paused to inhale deeply. Then added, "It also improves how folks see you. A lot of old-minded people in town respect the idea of somebody having a partner. It's messed up, but it's true."

"Would you be okay with that, though?" she asked him. Was she okay with pretending?

"Willow," Eli said, his gaze unwavering. "Whatever we have to do to stop this, we do."

She nibbled her lip, her eyes searching his. Was this insanity? Possibly. But Eli was a strong force, and maybe knowing she was with him was all that was needed to get this person to back off.

Real dating? No, she wasn't ready. But fake dating? What could go wrong?

A seed of hope began to sprout. Could this charade actually work? She needed this person to back off. One anxiety attack was enough to remind her of that. "How on earth will we ever get people to believe we're in a fake relationship," she countered, though the protest sounded weak even to her own ears.

"Willow," he said, a smile tugging at the corner of his mouth, "they'll believe it because I want them too. Because we'll make them." His confidence was magnetic, pulling her toward the idea despite her reservations.

"Protecting my reputation with a lie?" she mused aloud, the irony not lost on her.

"Sometimes," he said, stepping closer, close enough for her to feel the warmth radiating from him, "a little deception can stop any rumor or small-town talk in its tracks."

"Could it work?" she whispered, more to herself than him.

"Let's find out," Eli said, offering his hand, a silent vow hanging between them.

Willow hesitated, the weight of the decision pressing down upon her. But there was something in Eli's eyes, a fierce determination mingled with an unspoken promise of protection, that tipped the scales.

"Okay," she agreed, placing her hand in his, feeling the rough calluses of his palm against her skin. "Before we do anything," she started, pulling her hand away, "we need rules. Boundaries. If we're doing this...this facade, we need to be clear on what's okay and what's not."

Eli nodded. "Agreed. So, what are you thinking?"

"Firstly," she said, dusting off snow from the porch railing with her index finger, "no surprise physical affection. If you're going to... I don't know, hold my hand or something in public, I want a heads-up."

"Fair enough," he replied, shoving his hands into his jacket pockets as if to show his compliance. "What else?"

"Second," she continued, "this doesn't go behind closed doors. We're a 'couple' to the world, but when it's just us, we're just...us."

"Understandable," he murmured, nodding again. "No playacting in private."

"Communication," she insisted, meeting his gaze squarely. "If either of us feels uncomfortable or wants out, we say so. Immediately."

"Communication is key," he echoed solemnly. "I can do that."

"And..." A hesitant pause hung in the air. "We end this after New Year's, regardless of how things seem. It's a deadline. Nonnegotiable."

"Until New Year's," he agreed, his voice softening ever so slightly. "That gives us what, a little over a month?"

"Right," she confirmed, her lips pressing together in a thin line.

"Anything else?" Eli asked, his eyes searching hers for any signs of doubt.

"Lastly, no more kisses like that one kiss," Willow declared, the words slicing through the chill air like a blade. It was more for herself than for him.

Eli's chuckle held no humor, only a somber acknowledgment of the gravity behind her words. "No more kisses like that one kiss," he repeated, solemn as an oath.

"Are we clear on everything?" she asked, needing to hear it all laid out.

"Crystal," he responded, extending his hand once more—not as a vow this time, but as a pact between equals. "Partners in crime."

"Partners," she echoed, shaking his hand firmly.

"Meet me tomorrow at Sparrow Catching at eight thirty," he said, and then headed to his truck.

Was this a date? *No*, she quickly reminded herself. It was a fake date. Totally acceptable.

Her fingers trembled as she closed the front door behind her, watching Eli's truck drive out of the driveway.

"Everything okay?" Aubrey's voice sliced through the stillness, laced with concern.

Willow met her friend's gaze. "Eli proposed something… unconventional."

Aubrey's eyebrows knit together, her stance shifting as if ready to pounce on whatever threat loomed. "What kind of unconventional?"

"A fake relationship," Willow confessed, the words hanging between them.

"Fake relationship?" Aubrey's astonishment resonated in the space, her sunny disposition momentarily clouded. "To… what? Why?"

"Apparently, it's to shield me from mean comments, protect my reputation in town." Willow laughed.

"Does he think this is some sort of game?" Aubrey crossed her arms, her protective instincts flaring.

"No, it's not like that." Willow sighed, trying to articulate the reasoning behind the madness. "He's just offering to stand with me in hopes that whoever is doing this—oh, and he's got a detective looking into this and Niko to make sure he's not behind it—will back down if they think I'm dating him. Because, you know, he's big and scary." She grinned.

Aubrey pursed her lips. "Charly should hear this," she decided abruptly, reaching for her phone. The device chirped to life, its speaker filling the room with the promise of solidarity.

"Hey, you two. What's up?" Charly's voice, warm and soothing, flowed from the phone.

"Willow has news," Aubrey said before Willow could even draw breath to speak. "Eli wants them to pretend to be a couple."

"Wait, pretend?" Charly's confusion mirrored Aubrey's earlier reaction. "Is that wise?"

"Exactly my point," Aubrey chimed in, her curls bouncing as she nodded emphatically.

"Rules are set. Boundaries established," Willow interjected. "Open communication. No romance. It ends after New Year's."

"Okay, so we're seriously considering this?" Charly's tone was equal parts skepticism and intrigue.

Willow sighed, and then told Charly and Aubrey every single thing that Eli had said during their talk and explained why she'd gone along with it. She needed—for her mental health—for this person to back off.

When she finished, Aubrey still didn't look convinced, her eyes softening with concern. "Willow, I've seen the way Eli looks at you. There's caring there, maybe more."

"Care doesn't erase the past," Willow replied. "You both know what I've been through. I can't just jump into something real because it's convenient."

"But it's Eli," Charly interjected gently. "He's been through his own hell. He understands what it means to rebuild from broken places."

"Look, I know you're both worried," Willow said firmly. "But the fake relationship—it's just a shield. Nothing more. We've set boundaries. It's all been...negotiated." Willow stepped back, wanting this conversation to be over. "Right now, this is about protection—mine and The Naked Moose's. I can't afford any more rumors or whispers."

"Okay," Charly conceded. "We trust you to know your limits. Just remember we're here for you, no matter what happens."

"Thank you," Willow murmured. "It actually feels good to have a plan, instead of having a breakdown in the bar." A genuine smile tugged at the corners of her lips. "I'm not going down without a fight," she declared, the determination in her voice ringing clear.

"Never thought you would," Aubrey replied with a grin.

Six

The following morning, Eli's gaze swept over the local breakfast hotspot, Sparrow Catching, from his spot in a worn leather booth. The diner always came with comfort and hearty laughter, full of the town's morning risers: cowboys with shirts rolled to the elbows, young mothers desperate for some adult conversations and elderly patrons who made this diner their morning routine. His gaze flicked over the familiar faces, each one etched with their own stories, their own secrets.

He traced the wood grain of the table with a calloused finger, the ridges and grooves as familiar as the lines of his own weathered palm. The bell above the entrance chimed, and he glanced up, heart hitching just slightly at the sight of Willow stepping into the diner. Her hair cascaded in waves down her shoulders, bright like the sun, much like the spirit that hid behind those striking eyes of hers. Eyes that now darted around the room, betraying her nervousness.

She clutched her purse like a lifeline, her knuckles white, as her gaze finally locked with Eli's. A subtle nod from him—the barest dip of his chin—was all it took to spur her forward. As she moved through the diner, heads turned, whispers fluttered around the space.

"Will they buy it?" The question whispered off her lips, barely audible over the voices carrying through the restaurant, as she stopped in next to the table.

The diner was full of gossipers. Betty included.

"Oh, they'll buy it," Eli said, a smile tugging at the corners of his mouth. "Timber Falls loves a good love story—even if we have to write it ourselves."

He rose from the booth, a deliberate motion that stilled the surrounding clamor of Sparrow Catching. The patrons, mid-sip or bite, paused as he stepped into Willow's space. His eyes fixed on hers, and without hesitation, his hands found their way to her waist, pulling her gently but firmly into him.

"I'm going to kiss you now," he murmured, just loud enough for her alone to stay in line with the boundaries she'd set out. Then, after receiving her nod of approval, and full of purpose, he pressed his lips to hers in a kiss that spoke more than any words could convey. It was a performance, yes, but the heat that hit him spoke of this connection with her he couldn't outrun, blurring the line between fake and reality.

The breakfast crowd at Sparrow Catching drew in a collective gasp, forks clattered against plates and cups landed a touch too hard on saucers.

His lips curved into a smile against Willow's, as he whispered, "We're quite the convincing couple, aren't we?" The words were meant for her alone, a reminder of the pretense they had carefully constructed. A show. It was all about perception, but as Eli gazed down at the woman in his arms, he knew this wasn't all for show.

He'd been craving those perfect lips, and he couldn't fight the satisfaction that he'd had them again.

"Best performance this town's seen in a while," Willow whispered back, her voice steady despite the pinkish hue of her cheeks.

As they parted, Betty, who adored Willow from what Eli had seen, shuffled toward them. She was in the bar often, and Eli was sure that Betty adopted Willow as her honorary granddaughter.

"Willow, dear!" she exclaimed, coming to stand by their booth with a gleam in her eye. "How could you keep this wonderful news from me? When were you planning on telling me about this handsome beau of yours?" She rested her hands on her hips, surveying them both with grandmotherly scrutiny. There was no mistaking the twinkle of gossip that danced in her eyes.

"Hi, Betty," Willow said, her tone warm, "I didn't say anything because it's new."

"I see," Betty said, studying them intently. "I must say, you two make a lovely picture. How did this all come about?"

Before Willow could respond, Eli interjected smoothly, "Let's just say life has a funny way of bringing people together when they least expect it."

"Life and a bit of matchmaking, I suspect," Betty quipped, her eyes dancing. "Well, I won't pry any further." With a knowing nod, she blew Willow a kiss. "So nice to see you, sweet dear. I'm so pleased to see you happy like this." She set her smile onto Eli. "Goodbye, handsome."

Eli just grinned at her.

"Bye, Betty," Willow said, as Betty retreated to her seat, leaving behind a trail of lingering glances and hushed conversations that buzzed like bees around a hive when she returned to her table of five women.

Eli chuckled. "Any doubt now?"

Willow shrugged. "Yes. A million of them."

He understood and didn't feel the need to comment. "Holding hands for the show?" he asked, offering his.

Willow nodded, sliding her slender fingers into his.

As they settled back into their seats, they soon placed their orders and began fixing their coffee. It wasn't long before Jenna, the owner and beacon of warm welcomes, approached their booth with plates in hand. The smells of hearty breakfast fare—sizzling bacon, fluffy eggs and golden-brown toast—wafted toward Eli.

"Here you go, two Sparrow Specials," Jenna announced with her trademark grin, sliding the dishes onto the table. Her eyes flickered to their interlocked hands still resting on the tabletop, a silent question hanging in the air like the steam rising from his mug. "So, what's the special occasion?"

"Just enjoying a good start to the day," Eli replied.

Jenna nodded, her smiling knowing. "Well, if you need anything else, just holler." With a final wink at Willow, she sauntered off.

Eli turned his attention back to Willow, whose hand shook

a little before letting go of his as she reached for her fork. That couldn't do, not only for the ruse, but seeing her unsettled left a bad taste in his mouth. That last thing he wanted to do was make her feel uncomfortable, and he realized that this was likely her first meal with a man in a very long time, and she'd been clear—she did not want a relationship.

Grabbing the saltshaker, he broke into the past, a place he rarely visited. "Now that we're dating, guess you should know a thing or two about me," he said with a smirk.

She laughed softly, meeting his gaze. "Yes, I guess I should."

He sprinkled the salt and then reached for the pepper shaker. "I grew up here in Timber Falls with my mom and my sister. My dad wasn't in the picture, and still isn't. But for me, Jaxon and Gunner, it was adventuring every day, whether we were fishing by the creek or building forts in the woods."

Willow's expression softened, her eyes brightening.

"Jaxon was always the levelheaded one, planning our next adventure. And Gunner—" Eli chuckled "—he could charm the birds from the trees with his guitar, even back then. We had a great childhood."

"Sounds like it," Willow said.

Eli paused, taking a forkful of eggs before continuing. "And then there was bull riding. It's a beast of a sport. You've got to have grit, balance and a touch of madness." Willow laughed, and the sound warmed something icy in his chest as he continued. "I started older than most, because a company out in Seattle had seen some of my carpentry work."

Her brows lifted. "You're a carpenter?"

He nodded. "Really, it was something I did on the side while working for Jaxon's father on the ranch—just some passion projects—but the CEO had come to town and had been impressed by some live edge furniture I'd done. He offered to fly me out and give me a job." Eli took a quick sip of his coffee before continuing, "I had nothing really going on, so I jumped on it. I lasted three weeks before moving back home."

"You didn't like it?" she asked.

"Hated it," he replied. "The big city wasn't for me. I didn't mind the carpentry though, and still enjoy building the odd piece of furniture, but I came home and entered the rodeos around Montana and eventually hit the Montana Pro Rodeo Circuit, working my way up the ranks."

Willow took a bite of her toast. "What made you choose such a dangerous career path?"

"Guess I was chasing thrills, proving something to myself after the carpentry path didn't work out," Eli confessed. "But looking back, out there, on the back of a bull, nothing else mattered. I loved it."

"And now?" she asked softly.

"Now," Eli said with a sigh. "I'm more about finding peace, something steady and real." He locked eyes with her, allowing the truth of his words to sink in. "My home is Jaxon's ranch. I've got a good purpose there."

"It's a beautiful place to spend your days that's for sure," Willow said.

He agreed with a nod, not planning on going any deeper

into his past. Nothing good lived there. "What about your life before moving here?"

Eli watched as Willow played with the rim of her coffee mug, a hint of hesitation in her eyes before she looked up at him. "I grew up in Ann Arbor, which was always exciting, you know? Full of life and fun. Charly, Aubrey and I—we were inseparable. Dreamers, each of us chasing this life we planned all out."

He nodded, taking in the sweet smile that danced across her lips. Eli could picture it—the trio of friends, their laughter spilling, young and brimming with aspirations.

"Got my MBA from the University of California," she continued, as Eli devoured his eggs. "The girls and I lived in this cramped apartment in Berkeley that somehow felt more like home than any place I'd ever been." She paused to shrug. "Until I came here."

"It happens all the time," he said with a smile. "The magic of the mountains makes it hard to leave." According to an old legend in this town, the Absaroka Mountains possessed a unique power that brought soulmates together. With the fresh air, vibrant energy and endless blue skies and water, it was easy to see why some people believed that. Eli wasn't sure about all that, but he did notice that many visitors who came to Timber Falls ended up staying for good.

"I did hear of that legend," she said, before taking a bite of her toast and then continuing on, "After college, Portland called with a promise—a job that would catapult me forward."

"Sounds like you've always been moving forward. Seeking. Striving," he said.

"Maybe," she agreed, shrugging. "But then…"

"You came here," he finished for her, knowing as much as he didn't want to revisit the darkness, he was certain she didn't want too either.

She nodded, picking up her toast again. "I came here."

Eli watched the play of emotions across her face. Her eyes, once clouded with nervousness began to soften.

"And now I'm doing this…with you," she said with a smile.

"Life's funny that way," Eli responded, reaching for his mug. "You end up in places you never expected."

He took a long sip of his coffee as at a nearby table, two women suddenly said, with voices carrying over the noise, "They look good together, don't they?"

"Sure do," the other agreed.

Willow winced, staring down at her plate, obviously hit with the realization that in no time the whole town would know they were dating.

Eli reached out his hand again for permission. She took it as he said, "This isn't real, don't forget that," he said quietly. "We know what we're doing, and why."

Her gaze lifted to his and held. "Right," she said, exhaling softly, her shoulders lowering. "This isn't real."

The heavy door of the Timber Falls Police Station swung open with an authoritative creak, and Willow stepped into its sterile embrace, Eli following her. A knot tightened in her stomach as she inhaled, the harsh scent of antiseptic hanging in the air. With every step toward the reception desk, her heartbeat quickened.

The last time she'd entered a police station…

She swallowed hard.

Eli's fingers brushed against hers, a whisper of contact that shocked her, until she remembered that the affection was for show. She needed as many people to see them together as possible. She began to realize it was impossible for him to ask every time they should do a little PDA, so she took his fingers.

"Hey," Eli's voice cut through the quiet, low and soothing, "just remember why we're here." His words were meant to anchor her, and they did, even as memories surged to engulf her. "You're not alone here."

"Thank you for that," she murmured, forcing herself to lift her chin. This was about taking control, about protecting herself and The Naked Moose, the bar that was more than just a livelihood—it was a dream between three best friends that all started with a pact they'd made to start over if they weren't happy in their lives by the age of twenty-eight.

This was their do-over, and they would succeed.

Her gaze fixed on the badge emblazoned on the front desk, as Eli introduced them and asked to speak with Detective Harris. With the seconds that passed, the flashbacks clawed at her: Niko's sneer, his grip bruising her arms, his voice a venomous roar that left scars deeper than skin.

Before she could sink further into the solace of Eli's grasp, a voice broke through the hush of the corridor.

"Miss Quinn? Eli?" Detective Harris stood before them. There was a gentleness in his eyes that belied the seriousness of their meeting, as if he understood the weight of the pain both she and Eli carried.

"Detective Harris," Willow acknowledged, her grip instinctively tightening around Eli's hand as they turned to face him. "Please call me Willow."

"Willow," he said, accompanied by a soft smile. "Please, come with me." He led them past the bustling hum of the precinct and into a private room with comfortable chairs and a coffee table. The door shut behind them with a click.

"Thank you for coming in," Detective Harris said.

Willow sank into the chair, and Eli took the seat next to her. The detective sat across from them with documents on his lap.

The detective's gaze locked with Willow's. "Before we get to signing the consent forms, I want you to know that I have confirmed that Niko is still incarcerated," he said.

"Thank you," she breathed out. Yet if not Niko, then who would do this?

"Furthermore," Detective Harris continued, "my preliminary investigation traced the online comment to an IP address here in town. My gut is my telling me this has nothing to do with your ex-boyfriend."

"I'm very relieved to hear that," she said, glancing at Eli.

He gave a firm nod. "One worry off the list."

"Indeed," Detective Harris said. "However, this leads me to ask—have you had any recent conflicts or issues with anyone in town? Anything at all that might shed light on who could be behind this?"

Willow searched the depths of her memory, each encounter at The Naked Moose playing out in her mind. But no face stood out, no altercation came to mind. She shook her head slowly. "No, nothing. Maybe at first people's feathers were a little ruffled that big-city girls came in and changed their beloved country bar, but not now—our customers are very happy."

"All right." He scribbled a note, his pen moving in decisive strokes. "We'll keep digging, but if anything comes to mind, even the smallest detail, please let me know immediately."

"Of course," she said with a quick nod.

Detective Harris locked eyes with her, his brow furrowed in a blend of compassion and unyielding resolve. "I promise you, we will not let this go. Whoever is trying to intimidate you, we'll find them. Your safety is our top priority."

"Thank you so much," she whispered, the words wrapping around her like a shield. "I really just don't understand any of this."

Eli added, "No one understands any of this."

Detective Harris agreed with a nod, reaching for a stack of papers on his lap, "I'll need your full cooperation to move forward effectively." He slid the forms across the coffee table toward her. "These are consent forms authorizing me to access your cell phone records. It's crucial for tracing back any communication linked to the text."

"Okay, of course," she said, and quickly signed her name.

"I'll get started right away," Detective Harris said as he collected the signed forms, "and will let you know about any developments."

Willow nodded. "Thank you." As she rose from her chair, Eli joined her.

With final goodbyes to the detective, Willow followed Eli back out into the hallway.

Stepping out of the police station, she felt the weight that had been pressing on her chest begin to lift. The freezing Montana air was a stark contrast to the stifling heat inside, and she lifted her head, letting the snowflakes fall on her skin.

"You did good in there," he said softly.

Willow glanced up at him, and the sun caught the edges of his rugged profile. "Thank you for coming with me. I don't think I could've walked through those doors alone."

His gentle smile was his only response. "I have a hard time with police stations too, but we got through, didn't we?"

"Yeah," she said. "We did it."

Eli smiled big, offered his hand again. "Shall we continue with our show?"

Willow laughed and nodded, sliding her hand into his.

The walk along Main Street was too fast. Willow felt like she could have walked just like this for an hour, in comfortable silence, and still would want to walk longer. Eli had a calmness about him that felt good.

As they approached the bar, Eli glanced around, and she realized he was noting all the pedestrians on the road. Clearly, he recognized some as gossipers since he turned to face her. "Another kiss?" he asked.

She nodded approval. "Seems like the right thing to do."

He cupped her face gently with his roughened hands. His penetrating eyes searched hers, and for a moment, time seemed to slow. Then he leaned down, pressing his lips to hers in a kiss that whispered of protection, promise and something deeper that Willow didn't even want to think about right now. Because she was not ready. And this was not real.

"Call me if you need me," he murmured against her lips.

"I will," she replied, stepping away from his hold. "Thanks for everything today."

With one last lingering look as Eli headed toward his truck parked further down near the diner, Willow turned and pushed open the door to The Naked Moose.

Laughter spilled out, enveloping her as Charly and Aubrey used their hands to make a heart symbol.

"Stop it." Willow rolled her eyes but couldn't help the blush that warmed her cheeks. She slid behind the bar, knowing after her morning, only one thing mattered. And it was five o'clock somewhere. "Can we focus on what matters?" she said.

Charly grinned. "What's that?"

"My killer margarita skills," Willow deflected, grabbing margarita glasses to pour herself a much-needed drink.

Aubrey gave a mischievous smirk, playfully raising her eyebrows. "Feeling hot and bothered?"

Willow looked at her two closest friends. "Not even a little."

Charly just chuckled. Aubrey grinned. Thankfully, neither of them outed her for the liar that she was.

Seven

The following afternoon, Willow's fingertips danced over the laptop keyboard while she sat on the bar stool at the bar. Her gaze never wavered from the screen, where festive fonts bloomed against a backdrop of deep reds and greens, like holly berries nestled in their leaves. She adjusted the layout with painstaking precision, aligning each element of the Christmas cocktail flyer.

The lunchtime rush had dwindled to a gentle hum, leaving behind a few patrons who lingered over their drinks, their murmurs weaving around her. Charly was out at the bank. Aubrey was in the kitchen, coming up with another cocktail to add to their Christmas menu. Willow let out a slow breath, still not happy with the design, no matter how many changes she'd made. Maybe she just needed a break away from the project.

"Willow," came a voice, rich with genuine excitement, behind her.

She turned, her concentration shattering at the sight of Amie approaching. The corners of Amie's lips curled into a radiant smile, one that reached her eyes and made them sparkle. A far different look than Willow had seen when she'd first met her.

"Hi, Amie," Willow smiled in return.

Amie took the stool next to Willow, her gaze glued to the monitor. "Damn, did you make that? Looks good."

"Thanks," Willow said. Maybe someone not in marketing might approve, but Willow knew it wasn't quite right. "We're featuring new holiday cocktails every week over the holidays. This will come out next week."

"Ooh, tell me about it," Amie said, rubbing her hands together.

"I've named it 'Winter's Embrace,'" Willow explained. "It's a white chocolate cocktail Aubrey came up with. It's got rum, white chocolate, nutmeg and vanilla. She said she wanted to create something that felt like a Christmas hug in a glass."

"Sounds delicious! I will be the first one to gobble it right up," Amie said with a laugh. She shifted on her stool. "So." She paused, an impish glint in her eye. "I heard from a little birdie that you are dating Eli Cole." She leaned forward. "Is it true?"

A hesitation snagged at Willow's heartbeat, a quick stutter before it resumed its rhythm. She did not want to lie to Amie. Especially after Amie's past, but in this case, she knew she had to think of herself right now. "We're taking things slow," she said finally, hoping that was not too much of a lie.

"Slow is good," Amie agreed with a nod. "He's a good guy from what my friend has told me. She went to high school with him. Kinda a lone wolf, is what I've heard, but if anyone is going to be good for a guy like that, it's you."

"Thanks," Willow said with a smile. Wanting off this subject, and onto matters that had nothing to do with her, she asked, "How are things with you? Any word from Buck?"

Amie shook her head, her smile fading. "Thankfully, no. He's respecting the restraining order."

"Good," Willow said with relief. "That's good."

"Extremely," Amie said with a long sigh and a slow nod. "It's been nice having the quiet in the house. I don't jump at every little thing now. It just feels...calm."

Willow understood that wholeheartedly. "Peace is a wonderful thing."

Amie agreed with a nod. "All right, enough about all that, there is a reason I came here," Amie said, her voice upbeat again. "What do you think about gingerbread houses?"

"Building them, eating them...?" Willow asked with a laugh.

"Decorating them, actually. Tonight there is a gingerbread decorating event that I'm going to with a friend. Starts at seven o'clock at the Summit Sweets Bakery. It's twenty-five bucks each. Could be fun, don't you think?"

Willow was momentarily touched that Amie wanted to spend more time with her, and she was glad for it. She liked Amie too. Guilt began to set in that she was taking time off work to play this charade, but both Charly and Aubrey new it was necessary for the sake of their plan. She promised herself that she would make it up to them later, as she planned on heading back to the bar after the event was over. "Sounds like a blast." An idea sparked. Eli had done his part to play into the fake relationship. She needed to do her part too. "Do you mind if I invite Eli?"

"Not at all," Amie said, waggling her eyebrows. "The more the merrier."

"Great." Willow grabbed her cell from the bar and fired off a text to Eli.

Interested in coming with me tonight to a gingerbread house decorating event at Summit Sweets Bakery at 7?

The reply came quicker than expected, a ding from her phone slicing through the air.

I'll be there.

"Looks like we're all set, then," Willow said to Amie, a little surprised that Eli would want to take part in such an event, but figured he'd do so for the show. To protect her.

"Fantastic! It's going to be so much fun." Amie grinned, sliding off the stool. "Maybe after we're all done, you could display the gingerbread house here at the bar. It'd be such a cute decoration."

Willow snorted. "I don't know about Eli's gingerbread-making skills, but I'm not exactly confident it'll be worthy of showing it off."

"Oh, hush," Amie said, heading for the door, waving her off. "You're going to kill it."

Willow wasn't fully convinced by Amie's words. "Amie," she called out.

Amie opened the front door and turned, glancing back at Willow. "What's up?" she asked.

"Just wanted to say thank you for inviting us out tonight," Willow said, forcing a smile. "I really do appreciate it."

Amie returned her smile. "You know you're always welcome, Willow. I appreciate you too."

Willow kept her smile in place until Amie left, then let it fade as she looked back at the flyer. She still couldn't stand it. Damn.

Minutes before seven o'clock, Eli approached Summit Sweets Bakery, the familiar scent of sugar and spice wafting into the brisk Montana air. His heart, a wild drum in his chest, hammered with an intensity that matched the quickening pace of his steps. Willow was already there, her silhouette framed by the quaint shop front, looking every bit as beautiful as always.

"Willow," he called out.

She turned toward him, and the sight of her eyes brightening upon seeing him sent a jolt through his veins. It was supposed to be a fake date, a ruse, but something about the way she looked at him right now felt disarmingly real.

He took in her soft smile, the subtle shift of her gaze over him and her cheeks pinkened. He'd made an effort today—shower, clean shave and a new pair of jeans paired with a simple T-shirt under his winter jacket that hopefully said casual but cared enough to try. Her eyes lingered just a moment too long, betraying the lines of their pretense.

"Shall we?" She gestured toward the bakery door.

"Lead the way," he said, opening the door for her.

Inside Summit Sweets, the air hummed with energy— a hive of women and men sharing laughter. The scent of gingerbread and frosting mingled in the air.

Eli's gaze caught on a familiar face who he knew from around town, and Amie waved them forward. "Hi, guys!"

"Hey," Eli said.

Beside Amie, a woman with light blue eyes and long dark hair stepped forward. "This is Jillian," Amie introduced.

"Jillian Summers, right?" Eli asked.

"Guilty," Jillian admitted, a mischievous glint playing in her eyes. "Eli Cole, lab partner for twelfth grade chemistry."

"That's right," he said. "It's good to see you."

"You too," Jillian smiled.

"Good evening," a woman suddenly called, silencing the crowd. "Please find yourself a spot at one of the tables and we'll get started."

"We've got this in the bag," Amie said to Jillian, who laughed following her toward the one free table that had two gingerbread stations set up.

"Ready?" Eli asked Willow.

"Let's do this," Willow said with a grin, moving toward the table.

The timer was set, an hour and a half, to create a ginger-bread house. Eli's hands, more accustomed to the roughness of ropes and reins, fumbled with the delicate pieces of gingerbread. The walls of the miniature house leaned precariously, threatening to collapse at any moment. He let out a chuckle, shaking his head at how terrible he was at this.

"Here, let me help." Willow's voice was soft against the backdrop of festive chatter. Her fingers brushed against his as she steadied a wall, her touch light but electric.

"Guess I'm better with horses than baked goods," he admitted, his voice low and tinged with laughter.

The corner of her mouth twitched upward, that hint of a smile like sunlight breaking through clouds. "Everyone has their strengths," she countered, guiding his hand to pipe a line of frosting along the edge. "But you're doing just fine."

From the corner of his eye, Eli caught Amie and Jillian watching them. The two women exchanged knowing looks, their smiles soft.

"Looks like you've got quite the team here," Jillian commented, her voice carrying over the bakery.

"Teamwork makes the dream work," Amie chimed in, her gaze still fixed on Eli and Willow.

"Or at least a gingerbread house that stands up straight," Willow added, her laughter mingling with Eli's as the final piece slotted into place, the house finally structurally sound.

Minutes turned into an hour, and soon the plain house morphed into gingerbread perfection, as Eli watched Willow add a decorative touch to their gingerbread house—a tiny icing-covered hoof print above the door.

"Perfect," he said.

"It'll do," Willow said with a nod.

Eli kept on adding the circular candies that looked like

pearls to the top of the gingerbread house like Willow had instructed him. He liked this, being with her in public, regardless of if it was real or not. He'd thought on Sally's suggestion about the rodeo more and knew he couldn't pass up the chance at winning that money. A large donation for the shelter. Willow was doing her part, and he wanted to do his. "So, I'm doing a thing tomorrow and wondered if you'd want to come."

Willow's brow lifted, her hands covered in icing as she froze with the piping bag in her hand. "What is it?"

"I'm going back to the rodeo tomorrow night," he said, watching her expression closely.

He liked the worry he found there. "Rodeo? You mean bull riding?"

"Yeah, but not for the reasons I used to go in the ring." Eli took a deep breath, placed another candy on the roof of the gingerbread house. "When I talked with Sally, she told me about the local rodeo where you could win five grand. Figured I could add to the donation to Haley's Place if I claim the prize." He smirked. "Which, of course, is not guaranteed. I could hit the dirt and fast."

Willow's eyes softened. "As long as you won't get hurt, that's an amazing thing for you to do."

"Then you'll come and cheer me on?"

He watched the emotions play across Willow's face, the earnest concern in her eyes giving way to something warmer. The bakery, with its sugary scents and cozy warmth, seemed to shrink around them.

"Rodeo isn't exactly my scene," Willow began, her voice

carrying a lilt of amusement. "But I wouldn't miss it for the world."

"Even if it means trading bar stools for bleachers and cocktails for dust?" Eli teased playfully.

"It's nice to get a little dirty every now and then," she retorted with a smirk. Until she blushed as it dawned on her what she had said. "Er—I didn't mean it like that..."

He raised an eyebrow.

Rolling her eyes, she tried to change the subject. "Let's just focus on building this gingerbread house, okay?"

He chuckled in response, a low rumble. "Whatever you say, ma'am."

Eight

Late the next evening, Willow's heart raced with the distant stomp of hooves and the cheers that erupted from the arena's core. Guilt followed her with every step for again leaving Charly and Aubrey to manage the bar, so she only tagged along for Eli's ride and planned to return to work afterwards.

The indoor rodeo showgrounds were a bustle of activity, with cowboys and cowgirls walking around in their hats, boots and chaps; horses being led to the corrals and the rodeo arena set up with barrels, ropes and bucking chutes. Flags and banners advertised the sponsors of the event.

Willow was settled in next to Jaxon on the bleachers, leather and livestock scenting the air. The clang of metal gates echoed, merging with the announcer's booming voice and the occasional rebel yell from a cowboy psyched for his turn.

"Got us some snacks," Gunner announced, a grin spreading across his face as he handed her a frosty beer and a fry bread taco piled high with seasoned beef and vibrant salsa.

"Thanks," she said, as Gunner sat down on the other side of her. She took a generous sip of the cold beer as she sat beneath large overhead heaters keeping her toasty warm. She then bit into the taco, the flavors exploding into her mouth—spicy, savory and utterly divine.

"God, this is good!" she exclaimed between mouthfuls, a laugh escaping her lips as sauce dripped onto her fingers.

"Nothin' better than rodeo food," Jaxon said with a full mouth. Once he swallowed, he asked, "Coming to the ride tomorrow at the ranch?"

The Sunday late afternoon rides had become a ritual lately, as was dinner after. Willow knew Charly missed living with her and Aubrey, and suspected this was Jaxon's way of ensuring she saw them often outside of work. "Wouldn't miss it."

"Good," Jaxon replied. "It'll be cold, so dress warm."

"Oh, I will, believe me," Willow said, taking another bite of her taco.

The echo of the announcer's voice signaled the start of the Mutton Busting event, and Willow's attention snapped toward the chute where a child, decked out in an oversized helmet and a vest padded for protection, climbed onto the back of a patient sheep.

"Is he riding it—"

She was cut off as the gate swung open and the sheep trotted into the arena, the pint-sized rider clinging on with a determination that mirrored the boldest of cowboys. A collective "aww" rippled through the stands as the little one managed a few bouncy steps before tumbling gently onto the soft dirt, greeted by cheers and encouraging applause.

"How freaking cute!" Willow gasped.

Gunner nodded. "I can't imagine it getting much cuter than that."

They finished the rest of their meal in silence as they watched as another eager child took their turn, laughter and claps filling the air with each ride, no matter how brief.

There was something undeniably pure about the scene, a reminder that strength came in all sizes, and every victory, big or small, deserved its moment of glory.

Willow clapped as the last of the mutton-busting tykes was scooped up in a flurry of dust and cheers. Then the arena shifted before her, the lighthearted energy ebbing away to something more visceral, more raw. Her gaze was pulled inexorably toward the chutes where the bulls were being loaded, their massive bodies casting long shadows that seemed to loom over the festivities.

"Big guys, aren't they?" Gunner's voice, usually so full of mirth, carried a note of respect.

Willow took in the sheer size of the bull. A coil of worry tightened inside her. She thought of Eli. Those bulls, snorting and stomping with pent-up fury, were more than just beasts—they were walking symbols of danger. "Is this…safe?"

"Far from it," Jaxon said, dead serious.

Oh, God! Maybe this was a mistake. Sure, getting more money for the shelter was great, but not at the risk of Eli's life.

"Remember Charger?" Gunner chimed in to Jaxon. "That bull was a legend for throwing riders off before they could even blink. They said he was unrideable."

"Until Eli came along," Jaxon finished with a proud tilt

of his chin. "Eight seconds might as well have been an eter-nity, but Eli held on. He's got this uncanny ability to read the bulls, to move with them like some sort of dance."

As she heard their words, saw the certainty etched into their faces, a sliver of relief pierced through her apprehension. She traced the rim of her beer can with a fingertip, the aluminum cold against her skin. "So, what you're saying is, he's got this?" she asked.

"He's got this," Jaxon agreed, and Gunner gave a firm nod.

The air crackled with anticipation, the charged atmosphere of the rodeo acting as a living pulse beneath Willow's skin. Her gaze roamed the arena hungrily, searching for Eli. "Any sign of him?" she asked.

"Not yet," Gunner replied.

The bleachers vibrated with stomping feet and clapping hands, but all she felt was the thrumming of her own pulse.

As the announcer's voice boomed over the speakers, intro-ducing the gutsy heroes who'd dare to mount the beasts biding their time behind the gates, Willow's attention sharpened. She was perched on the edge of the weathered bench, her breath caught up in her throat as the first bull exploded out of the gate.

Then after a dozen rides, she spotted him—*Eli.*

He was a proud silhouette against the backdrop of restless bulls and bustling handlers, his worn tanned cowboy hat on his head, a black shirt and vest covering his torso with jeans and tanned chaps. His eyes were focused, locked onto the bull he was about to face—a massive bull, who kept ram-ming the gate, as Eli mounted the bull, nestling himself into the groove of the saddle.

"Look, there he is," she said, pointing to him.

"Hell yes," Gunner breathed out. "Let's do this!"

"Eight seconds, that's all he has to do," Jaxon said.

Willow didn't respond; her gaze was fixed on Eli, on the way he rolled his shoulders back, exuding confidence and strength. He wrapped the rope around his palm, securing himself to the beast below.

"Be safe," she whispered under her breath. "Come on, Eli," she murmured again, her fingers gripping the cold beer can.

Then the gate swung open.

Ride for her, Eli thought as the bull beneath him slammed his horn into the gate. It wasn't about proving anything to the crowd or to the ghosts of his rodeo days—it was about helping Willow with her cause, and feeling like he was doing something right by his sister too.

Every muscle was coiled and ready as the gate slowly opened after he gave a nod.

The bull's hooves dug into the dirt. Eli gripped the beast beneath him, as he was molding himself into an extension of the animal's untamed power. The air was thick with dust and expectation.

There was no room for error, no space for second guesses. He was here, in this moment, where skill and spirit met, and nothing else mattered.

With a jolt that threatened to splinter bone, the world became a blur of motion. Muscles long forgotten clenched instinctively, synchronizing with the bull's rhythm in a deadly dance.

Eight seconds, just eight seconds, he chanted inwardly, the time stretching into an eternity, with each and every buck.

The crowd erupted, their cheers slicing through him, a roaring wave of sound that crashed over him. The bull twisted, turned and thrashed, hell-bent on dislodging him, but Eli held on.

For Willow.

For the shelter.

For Miranda.

As the buzzer sounded when his eight seconds were up, he dismounted landing on his back, but the rodeo clowns were there, protecting him as he jumped onto the gate and away from the bull determined to spear him with a horn. He raised his arm in gratitude, absorbing the cheers around him.

But he didn't want their applause. He only craved one person's accolade.

He looked out into the sea of people, instantly finding Willow, like a moth to a flame. She was on her feet, cheering for him, as were Gunner and Jaxon. Her eyes met his, and in the span of a heartbeat, the noise faded, the world receded and he was damn glad she was there. He tipped his cowboy hat at her and her sweet smile stopped him in his tracks. When she looked at him like that, time froze.

When the roaring of the crowd snapped him back to the present, he strode behind the gates, passing by cowboys congratulating him on his ride.

Now it was a waiting game on the last two riders.

Leaning against one of the empty pens, he inhaled deeply, the aromas of sawdust, animal sweat and sizzling meats from

the food stands mingling in a scent that spoke to some primal part of him.

"Never thought we'd see Eli 'The Storm' Cole back here,"
a gruff voice called out, slicing through the buzz of the crowd.

Eli turned to find a burly man with a weathered face and
a wide-brimmed hat, shadows dancing across his features.
"Clay," Eli acknowledged with a nod. "It's good to see you,
man." Clay had been his trainer growing up. His mentor.

Clay slapped Eli on the shoulder. "Likewise. You miss the
bulls or the glory?"

"Neither," Eli said, shaking the man's hand. "Came for a
good cause. Trying to raise money for the women's shelter."

"Good on you, son," Clay said with a warm smile. "What
a way to honor Miranda."

Eli nodded agreement. Clay had been there for Eli through
the best moments of Eli's life and the absolute worst. He'd
been the one to pick Eli off the ground when he'd received
the call about Miranda's murder and had driven him home.

As the cheering continued with the next ride, they talked
briefly, swapping stories about rides gone by and the thrill
of an eight-second victory.

"All right, looks like things are wrapping up here. I'll let
you get to it," Clay finally said, tipping his hat. "Don't be a
stranger, Eli. This rodeo's always got a place for you."

"Thanks, Clay," Eli replied, clapping the older man on the
back before making his way toward the gate.

With every step, more faces from his past emerged. There
was Doc Banks, who once stitched up a gash on Eli's arm

after a particularly nasty fall; and Lila, the barrel racer whose laugh could be heard even above the roaring crowd.

He was Eli "The Storm" Cole, shaped by the very dirt beneath his feet, forged in the adrenaline and the applause. And if he was being honest, he missed this place.

Suddenly the crowd roared even louder this time, and cowboys swarmed Eli pushing him back out into the arena as he was declared the champion.

Cheering came at him from all sides, and he felt instant relief that he wouldn't let Willow down. He waved in gratitude at the crowd, spotting Willow waving her hands in celebration.

Damn, he liked that. Her there, supporting him.

The organizer approached with an envelope. "Hell of a ride, Cole!"

"Thanks, Frank." Eli took the envelope.

With a sudden surge of pride for what this would do for the shelter, and in his sister's honor, Eli yanked off his cowboy hat, the one speckled with dust and memories, and hurled it skyward.

The crowd went wild, the sound ricocheting around him.

When his hat landed in the dirt, he grabbed it from the ground, dusted it off as his chest heaved as the last echoes of applause faded away. His gaze, drawn as by a magnet, found its way to the bleachers again, where Willow stood, a huge smile on her face.

And *that* was worth way more to him than any bull he could outlast.

Nine

The next day, Sunday, the *only* day the bar closed, Eli wrapped his fingers tighter around the leather reins, the horse's breath misting in the chilly air as he, Jaxon, Charly and Gunner gathered outside the barn. The ranch had been coated with snow that had fallen overnight. Although it was cold enough for their breath to fog before them, the sun's rays pierced through the bitterness.

"Ready, girl?" Eli murmured to one of the ranch's trained mares, a sturdy chestnut with a blaze down her nose. She nuzzled into his gloved hand, seeking out a treat that he did not have. Nearby, Charly adjusted the saddle on her gelding, while Jaxon and Gunner shared a lighthearted argument about which trail promised the best views for today's ride.

Getting out of the car parked at the house, Willow and Aubrey approached, Willow's hair escaping the knit cap she wore, her eyes bright. She wore a fluffy black winter coat with a scarf and fleece riding pants, along with tall winter boots, and he knew for certain that beneath all the clothes he could see, there were layers of more. He couldn't take his eyes off her. Lord, she was beautiful.

Aubrey headed toward Gunner who held her horse, as Willow approached him. "Ugh. I feel like I'm forgetting something," she said, patting down the pockets of her thick coat.

"Unless you forgot your gloves, I think you're set," Eli said, the corner of his mouth lifting into a smile.

She reached into her pockets, yanking them out. "Wouldn't forget 'em."

"Everyone ready?" Jaxon called out, mounting his horse with an easy swing of his leg over the saddle.

"Lead the way," Gunner added, before helping Aubrey to mount her horse and following suit.

With a nod to Willow, he helped her up onto her horse, and he fought against his touch lingering longer than necessary. He hoisted himself onto his own mare, Maia, a gorgeous black horse that he'd hand selected for his own personal horse to use for working the ranch. Maia was a solid horse, and he spent more time with her than he spent with anyone. She was a part of him now, their minds seemingly linked through their partnership.

They moved out, the rhythmic crunch of hooves on snow the only sound, leaving a trail of footprints behind them.

As the ranch faded from view, replaced by the sweeping expanse of frosted fields and the distant mountains standing guard, Eli exhaled, falling into the quiet, while Aubrey and Charly rode next to each other, and Gunner and Jaxon led the way. Snowflakes danced in the air as the vast Montana gray sky stretched above them. Eli watched, fascinated, as Willow took in the rolling hills blanketed in snow, her breath fogging out in front of her.

"Beautiful, isn't it?" he eventually asked her.

"I didn't think anything could beat a Montana summer," she said, "but there is something magical about the winter here."

He agreed with a nod, resting his hand on the horn of his saddle. "Never gets old."

Maia blew out a loud breath, relaxing into the walk. The horses' breaths created small clouds in the crisp winter air as they walked across the snowy landscape. Their coats were thick and fluffy, protecting them from the cold.

"I don't think I ever truly knew what the quiet really was until I moved here," she confessed softly, breaking the spell that had fallen between them. "Out here, it's like the world takes a deep breath."

"That's a beautiful way to put it," he said, as his cheeks chilled with the frosty air. "It's the best place to think as far as I'm concerned. Nothing gets in the way out here."

Willow nodded, turning to look at him with an expression that spoke volumes. "And which thoughts to let go?"

"Especially those," he affirmed, the corners of his mouth lifting ever so slightly. His gaze shifted to the mountain range. "After I came back from the rodeo…after what happened with Miranda, this land held me up."

Willow's warm voice brushed across him. "It's good you had that."

Eli felt the old scar in his chest throb, a dull echo of past pain. He looked at her, really looked, and saw not just the strong woman who had faced down her own demons, but someone who might comprehend the shadows that clung to his soul. "It was," he admitted. "It taught me that you always find a way to keep moving, even if it's just one step at a time."

She hit him with that sweet smile. "I can understand."

He knew that she could, and he realized talking to her was easier because it involved less explaining. She just *knew*.

Their horses ambled through the untouched snow, creating a path that would soon be covered again.

The urge to pull back his guards tugged at him—instinct born from years of self-preservation. Yet as he glanced over at Willow, her cheeks flushed from the cold, her smile radiant when her horse playfully tossed its head, something within him stilled. There was a softness to her today, a serenity that draped over her like the snowflakes on her shoulders. It was beautiful.

And so, they continued their journey across the winter-kissed landscape, as he listened to his friends' laughter fill the chilly air. Eli reined in his horse, drawing alongside Willow's mount as they crested the hill.

"What's that?" she suddenly asked, spotting the small log house off in the distance, her gaze tracing the lines of its wraparound porch.

"My house," he replied. "It took me a year and a half to build it."

Willow's eyes widened in surprise. "That's quite a long time."

"It was worth every second," Eli said with a smile, Maia's

gate slow and easy beneath him. "I poured my heart and soul into building that house, every single nail, board and shingle."

Curiosity sparked in Willow's eyes as she tilted her head to the side. "Why didn't you hire someone to build it for you?"

Eli's smile grew wider. "I could have, but there's something special about creating something with your own two hands. This house is more than just a structure, it's a part of me and I'm a part of it."

Willow studied the house before meeting Eli's gaze again. "You must be quite skilled at carpentry to build a whole house by yourself."

He nodded modestly. "I'm not too bad at it."

"Not bad?" Willow laughed. "You must have a real passion for it. Why did you stop working as a carpenter?"

Eli hesitated, considering his answer carefully. "I realized that my work is mine and I didn't want to profit off it, so now I only build for myself and others, without the pressure of a deadline."

Willow watched him closely before saying, "You're a good person, Eli. I hope people tell you that often."

He didn't want other people's validation; he wanted hers. But he simply nodded his gratitude, keeping the thought to himself.

"When I came back from…" *the rodeo*, he almost said, but stopped himself, wanting the truth between them. He cleared his throat. "After Miranda passed away, and I moved back to town, Jaxon's dad gave me a job and that piece of land. He told me to build myself a house. Didn't ask for a dime for the land."

Her gaze swept back to him. "That's amazingly kind of him."

"Very kind," Eli agreed. "He didn't say it then, but I think he knew I needed to keep busy. I needed to rebuild my life. And he gave me the space to do that." His gaze scanned across the land surrounding his house. "He was an incredible man. The best man I ever knew."

She smiled softly. "I wish I could have met him," she said.

"I wish you could have too." His thoughts drifted to his mother and Miranda. He wished they could have been here with him, experiencing this beauty. He could almost feel his mother's arms around him, and hear Miranda's endless chatter in his ear. He had no doubt they would have loved Willow, Charly and Aubrey. The image warmed his heart, and he couldn't help but smile.

"Why are you smiling?" Willow asked, bringing him back to the present.

Eli blinked, realizing he had been lost in his thoughts. He couldn't help but smile even wider. "It's a good day."

Willow looked up at the sky, where snowflakes were fluttering down around them. "It is a good day," she agreed, a smile spreading across her face.

Later that evening, Willow's cheeks glowed with a warmth that had little to do with the crackling fire as the laughter of her friends infused the room with a vibrancy that seeped into her bones. She'd peeled off all the thermal layers beneath her clothes, but sat on the floor next to the fireplace, still warming up from the ride. The space was quaint and cozy, with wooden beams on the ceiling, and the scent of burning wood mingled with a rustic sweetness, and for a moment, she allowed herself to revel in the comfort of Jaxon and Charly's living room.

Her life had been a mess, with so many uncertainties looming over her. But today was different. Talking to Eli felt different too. They had been friends since she moved to town, brought together by Charly and Jaxon. Eli was always there for her as a source of comfort and support. However, he was opening up more than usual and she found herself genuinely liking what she saw.

"Best ride of the season," Eli mused, his voice rough like gravel, yet it carried a lightness that was rare for him. He caught Willow's eye, offering her a smile that was gentler than she'd seen before.

Yet she couldn't tear her eyes off his sculpted lips. A mouth that knew exactly what it was doing. Whether his kiss was sweet and quick, or downright dirty, the passion was all the same—scorching hot.

"I agree," Aubrey chimed in, nodding. "The horses seemed to enjoy the ride as much as we did."

"Nothing beats a snow-covered trail," Gunner said.

Aubrey didn't even acknowledge him. Willow watched the two, noting how Gunner simply shook his head. He caught Willow's gaze and flashed an easy smile, as if everything was fine. But there was underlying tension going on between them. Something that Willow couldn't put her finger on.

"Speaking of beating..." Jaxon said, breaking into Willow's thoughts "this chili would win first place at the Harvest

Festival." He cradled the bowl in his hands, inhaling deeply before taking another hearty spoonful.

The Harvest Festival was like the Christmas market, only more pumpkins, celebration of food and pies instead of Christmas cookies, local vendors and mulled wine.

Charly beamed from her spot next to Jaxon on the plush couch. "I'm glad you all like it. It's my grandmother's recipe. Don't forget the fresh bread too, just out of the oven," she added, pointing toward a basket lined with a red-checkered cloth brimming with steaming loaves.

"Like it?" Aubrey muttered. "Charly, I could marry this chili."

As they devoured the meal, and laughter filled the space, the spice of the chili warmed Willow's belly, its heat a pleasant contrast to the cool kiss of the outdoors still clinging to her skin. She savored each bite of the soft, warm bread, tearing it apart with fingers still thawing from the ride.

When the bowls were empty, Jaxon began gathering up the dishes as Charly suggested with a grin, "What if we take this warmth up a notch? How about a dip in the hot tub?"

"Sounds divine," Aubrey purred.

"Sure, why not?" Gunner said, stretching his arms above his head. "A soak under the stars sounds like a perfect end to the day."

Eli remained silent, but the corner of his mouth quirked upward in approval. Willow caught his gaze again, a tingle running down her spine. The thought of seeing exactly what Eli looked like underneath all those clothes was difficult to resist.

Stacey Kennedy

"All right then, it's settled!" Charly clapped her hands together, the sound sharp and decisive. "Hot tub under the Montana sky, here we come."

Willow's heartbeat quickened, but her excitement cooled when she remembered a crucial detail. "I didn't bring a suit," she murmured to Aubrey.

"Me neither," Aubrey replied, her forehead creasing in disappointment. "Guess we'll have to take a rain check."

Charly waved away their concerns with a warm smile. "Don't you worry about that." She sauntered toward her bedroom and called over her shoulder, "I've got plenty to spare!"

Moments later, Charly returned, an array of colorful fabrics dangling from her hands. She presented bathing suits, a one-piece to Aubrey and a bikini to Willow. "Here, these will fit."

Aubrey's eyes sparkled with mischief as she dashed off to change. Willow, however, hesitated, eyeing the skimpy black bikini Charly had selected for her. It was a sliver of fabric held together by strings, more revealing than anything she'd dared to wear since…well, ever.

"You really have nothing else?" she grumbled.

"Sorry, no," Charly said gently with a scrunch of her nose. "Don't worry about it. You'll look amazing. And besides, it's just us here."

Taking a deep breath, Willow accepted the bikini. The fabric felt light and insubstantial in her hands. Retreat would have been easy, safe, but something in Charly's encouraging gaze nudged her forward.

In the privacy of the guest bathroom, Willow slipped into

the bikini. Her reflection in the mirror was foreign. She turned from side to side... *Dear God!* There was nothing to it.

"Okay," she whispered to her reflection. "You've faced worse than a piece of string and survived."

Steeling herself with thoughts of healing and the desire to reclaim parts of herself long buried, she opened the door and stepped out. The low murmur of conversation in the living room stilled as she walked in.

Eli, shirtless, wearing black board shorts slung low on his hips and leaning against the stone mantel of the fireplace, turned at the sound of her approach. His gaze latched onto her with an intensity that made the air between them sizzle. She was acutely aware of the heat radiating from his eyes, traveling down the expanse of her exposed skin, leaving a trail of fire in its wake.

His body, a sculpted testament to years of physical mastery in the bull riding arena and hard ranch work, was a sight that stole her breath. His muscles rippled beneath taut bronze skin, each curve and angle a silent story of strength and control. The rugged lines of his jaw tightened subtly as he took her in, and Willow felt a surge of desire she hadn't experienced in a long time...if *ever*. It was raw and fierce, clawing through the remnants of her defenses with a hunger that matched the one she saw reflected in Eli's potent stare.

Eli cleared his throat.

Across the room, Charly and Aubrey shared a glance that didn't require words. Their grins were triumphant. They had orchestrated this, and in the moment, Willow didn't care. Even if, she reminded herself, this relationship was not real, she liked that look on him. Heck, she suddenly wanted more of it.

"Looks like we've been outdone, Charly," Aubrey quipped.

"Seems so," Charly agreed with a smirk.

Willow quickly followed Charly and Aubrey out into the backyard, feeling the heat of Eli's gaze behind her. She refused to look back, not sure she'd hold it together if he stared at her with any more heat.

With a breath that was more a gasp than anything, Willow stepped into the swirling warmth of the hot tub. The water enveloped her, a soothing contrast to the biting chill of the mountain air, but it did nothing to cool the heat that Eli's gaze had ignited within her. She settled onto one of the molded seats, the bubbles caressing her skin as she stole another fleeting glance at Eli.

He joined her in the steaming water, his body moving with a grace that belied the power she'd glimpsed moments before. The space between them was filled with nothing more tangible than steam and the scents of winter and chlorine, yet it felt charged, electric. Each time their eyes met, a current jolted through her, setting every nerve ending on fire.

"All right," Jaxon's voice sliced through the tension, his tone playful and teasing. "Who's game for a little dare?"

Charly let out a small laugh. "What kind of dare are we talking about here, cowboy?"

"Simple," Jaxon said, rubbing his hands together with an impish grin. "You get out, take a snow angel break, and then jump back in."

"Absolutely not," Charly retorted without missing a beat,

splashing him lightly on the chest. "After that ride earlier, I'm only just thawing out. I'm staying right here, thank you very much."

"Ah, come on," Jaxon coaxed, nudging her shoulder with his. "It'll be exhilarating."

"Exhilarating is one word for it." Charly snorted. "Hypothermia is another."

Laughter bubbled around them, but amidst it all, Willow's awareness of Eli was a constant thrum in her veins. His eyes, a green so deep she felt she could fall into their depths, were locked onto hers again. And though no words passed between them, he didn't need to say a word. Her nipples puckered, regardless of the hot water surrounding her.

"Aubrey?" Jaxon asked.

She snorted. "I think I'll save the rolling in the snow for when hell freezes over."

"Fair enough," Jaxon conceded with a laugh. "Gunner, show the ladies how it's done."

Willow watched the easy banter between Charly and Jaxon and how he'd taken her so tight in his arms. She'd never seen Charly look so happy. She questioned whether the intense chemistry between herself and Eli could ever transition into a steady, comforting flame or if it was meant to always burn wild and unrestrained. Yet, despite her uncertainties, she couldn't ignore the magnetic attraction that continuously brought her back to him.

Which was all the more confusing since none of this was supposed to be real.

The chill of the winter air brushed against her cheeks, a

stark contrast to the steam rising from the hot tub's surface. She could feel Eli's gaze upon her like a tangible force, and something within her stirred—a wildness she'd kept caged for far too long—and she needed to cool off...and *fast*.

"I'll take that dare," Willow declared, right as Gunner rose.

Before doubt could claw its way back into her thoughts, she propelled herself over the edge of the hot tub. She squealed in laughter as the crisp snow embraced her in a cold kiss as she landed with a soft thud. Her skin prickled with goose bumps as she raced forward.

"Willow!" Aubrey's voice rang out, equal parts shock and amusement.

She sank into the snow and began to wave her arms and legs in and out. She didn't care about the icy sting or the way the snow clung to her barely-there bikini. She was free in this moment—free from the shadows of her past, free from all her own damn worries, and she was trusting in the feeling as the seconds slipped by.

Rising to her feet, a shiver danced up her spine and her breath came out in giggles. She glanced back toward the group, where everyone's faces were illuminated by the multi-colored lights from the hot tub. And there he was—Eli, his eyes alight not with hunger now, but something so much sweeter.

Their gazes locked, and time seemed to hesitate at the way his smile reached his eyes, crinkling the corners and revealing a rare warmth. One that a woman could find herself lost in.

"Get back in here," Charly called out, her voice laced with laughter. "Before you turn into an ice sculpture."

With a final chuckle, Willow bolted back toward the hot tub. Her breath misted in the crisp night air as she plunged back in, her skin tingling and burning.

"Atta girl," Eli commented, pride swirling in his eyes.

"Braver than I am." Jaxon chuckled from across the tub.

"Or crazier," Aubrey added with a playful wink.

"Maybe a bit of both," Gunner replied with a laugh.

She kept on laughing and met Eli's gaze. The smile he gave her was filled with warmth and served as a reminder that the life she had been struggling to regain was finally coming back to her.

Ten

After putting in his training rides in the morning, Eli stood in the arena, the wind howling outside. For most of the night, he had struggled to erase the image of Willow in a bikini from his mind. He finally gave in at around three in the morning and took matters into his own hands. Literally. The pleasure helped temporarily, but when he woke up, her smooth and alluring skin was still imprinted in his thoughts. He took a shower and sought pleasure again, and as he finished, he allowed himself to imagine her while releasing his built-up tension. But even now, if he let his mind drift, his cock twitched.

He was only too glad for a good distraction that came later in the day. Beside him, a woman with a sharp gaze, undoubtedly a riding coach, gave nothing away as she scrutinized the colt being ridden by a teenage girl, probably no older than sixteen, who looked tiny in his saddle. Ranger had been an easy colt to train, with Eli only putting thirty days of training on him, while some took sixty days or longer.

The cold nipped at his ears as he explained, "Ranger's sire and dam were both champions in the western pleasure circuit. He's got the bloodline and the brains. Could take your daughter all the way to the ribbons."

The father nodded, clearly impressed by the elegant lines of the young colt, whose coat shone like burnished copper. "He certainly looks the part," he replied, smiling at his daughter, who guided Ranger through a series of maneuvers, each one executed with increasing confidence.

"Looks and moves like a dream," the coach added, her critical tone softening just a fraction as she took in the colt's fluid movements. "Good conformation, responsive...show him right, and he'll shine."

As if sensing the weight of their expectations, Ranger turned his head slightly and nudged the girl's foot in the stirrup. Her eyes lit up as she laughed, and Eli couldn't help but feel a spark of satisfaction knowing the colt was already weaving his magic.

The father and coach approached the daughter in the center of the arena, and Eli hung back, knowing they needed privacy to talk.

A moment later, the father returned to Eli. "That colt is everything you said he would be and more. We'll need to get our vet out here for a pre-purchase exam, but if all checks out, consider him sold."

Eli offered his hand. As the father shook it, Eli said, "Glad to hear it. He won't disappoint."

The coach smiled, offering her hand. "You've done an incredible job starting him."

"Thank you, ma'am," he said, returning her handshake.

As they continued to discuss logistics, a shadow fell across the barn entrance, and Aubrey stepped into view. Jaxon was hauling a horse today, and Charly was at the bar, so Eli became curious. He turned back to the family, taking the reins from the teenager after she dismounted. "Just shoot me a text when you have that vet appointment scheduled," Eli said, wrapping up the conversation as he caught sight of Aubrey's furrowed brow.

"Will do," the father replied, tipping his own cowboy hat to Aubrey before guiding his daughter and her coach away from the arena.

With the potential buyers gone, Eli brought Ranger back into the barn. Aubrey stood by the crossties, nibbling her lip.

"Everything all right?" he asked her. His voice was even, but his gut tightened as she approached, her eyes sharp with concern.

"Can we talk about Willow?" she asked, her voice cutting straight to the heart of matters, as was her way.

"Of course," he replied, pausing with a halter in hand. "Is she okay?"

"Look, Eli," she started. "We're going to talk straight about this. I've never been one to beat around the bush. This fake relationship thing you're doing is stupid."

Ranger lowered his head as Eli began removing the bridle. "I'm not sure what you—"

"Willow needs stability, honesty," she interjected, her tone firm yet laced with a pleading undercurrent.

Eli slipped on the halter and then tied up Ranger to the

crossties, feeling the weight of her words settle in the pit of his stomach. Charly loved Willow deeply, but Aubrey's protective instinct was fierce, and he respected her for it. But it was the unspoken understanding between them, a shared knowledge of what Willow had survived, that made him take a hard look at his own intentions.

"I won't hurt her," Eli said quietly, as he placed the bridle on the hook on the stall. "I'm trying to help her."

Aubrey's gaze softened slightly. She ran her hand over Ranger's face. "You are, but just make sure you're not giving her mixed signals, okay? I know, Willow, truly know her, and she likes you."

"Well, I like her too," he said, undoing the cinch.

"Like her?" Aubrey said with a snort. "*Is* that all? Because the way you were looking at her last night did not pass the friend vibes."

He couldn't refute that. "Listen, I'm not the one that sent me flying on my ass when I kissed her."

"I know that," Aubrey said. "But that was also three months ago. I know no one has said this to you," she said firmly, and then pointed at him, "so I'm saying it now. Be careful here. If at any moment, this fake thing starts to look like it will hurt Willow, it stops. Promise me."

The truth of Aubrey's words hung heavy in the air as his jaw clenched. "I won't hurt her. That's an easy promise, Aubrey."

She gave a curt nod, her expression softening as she turned to leave Eli with his thoughts, the scent of hay and leather.

With his hands stilled on the saddle, he watched Aubrey's retreating figure, her words still echoing in the barn.

"Aubrey," he called out, his voice firmer than he felt.

She paused, halfway through the door. "Yeah?" she asked.

"This isn't some game that I'm playing. I'm not that guy." He struggled to find the words, his usual composure broken. "I'm truly doing this to help her."

"Are you truly helping her though?" Aubrey asked. "Or was this just a really good reason for you both to play pretend because it's easier to do that than actually go all in?"

He swallowed hard, tasting the dust and the remnants of fear that clung to his throat. Memories of Willow's laughter, the way her eyes sparkled with life, flooded his mind. But so did the shadows that lingered there, cast by a past that had nearly broken her and him.

"Like I said, I'm doing this to protect her." His voice cracked, sharp and raw. "The rules for this have been set out. Determined. We end at New Year's."

"I see," Aubrey said slowly. "Well, I guess all I can say is that's a real shame because Willow…her warm, sunny soul… it fixes everything, Eli. Trust me."

The raw honesty in her voice struck a chord deep within him. His heart was a drumbeat, loud in the quiet of the stable, echoing the truth of Aubrey's words. He couldn't deny the feelings that surged through him whenever he thought of Willow, but he'd taken a step back when she turned him down.

Maybe that was the wrong decision. Maybe he should have pushed more.

He looked away, finding solace in the simple sight of Ranger, standing patiently next to him.

As she walked away, he pulled the saddle off, her words echoing around him: *her warm, sunny soul…it fixes everything, Eli…*

Willow felt lit up all day after the ride, the hot tub, just all of it. She woke up with a grin that stayed plastered on her face all day long. It lingered through her weekly FaceTime call with her parents, where they caught up and chatted for a while. Despite texting or talking on the phone daily, they still made it a point to see each other's faces at least once a week. The smile continued through the busy lunch rush as well. She kept thinking about Eli, and she began to wonder why she'd been so eager to shut him down all those months ago. What would have happened if she hadn't?

Maybe she shouldn't have been so scared and had given him a shot…

Nearing three o'clock in the afternoon, Willow moved around the long table with chairs, setting out the craft supplies, as all the ladies sat around the table, sipping their wine, save for Amie, who hadn't arrived yet. The air hummed with the promise of the approaching Christmas market, and Charly and Aubrey were both beginning to decorate the bar for the festive season. She felt its excitement thrumming through her veins. She spread out spools of crimson ribbon and clusters of pine cones, envisioning the wreaths that would soon adorn the town's doors.

"Willow, where do you want these?" Aubrey called out,

her voice bright like the twinkling lights she dangled from her fingertips.

A couple of hours had passed since she left the bar, looking tense and on edge. But as she returned, Willow noticed that Aubrey seemed to be back to her normal self. Willow decided not to bring it up and give her some space. Aubrey had been acting strange lately, but Willow knew that when she was ready, she would open up and talk about whatever was going on with her.

"Along the windows," Willow responded, pointing toward the pane that framed the wintry world outside.

As the final preparations for another craft group neared completion, the front door creaked open and Betty entered. Widowed yet undeterred by life's trials, Betty brought with her an aura of sweet resilience. Willow would never forget her kindness when she'd first moved to town. Betty wrapped Willow in her love from day one.

"Good afternoon, my dear," Betty greeted.

"Betty, I'm so glad you're here." Willow met her with an embrace.

"Wouldn't miss it for the world," Betty replied, her eyes twinkling beneath the soft creases of her lids. "Now, let me help you get ready." She gestured toward the table and began placing out the fake berries and sprigs of holly in the center of the table for the wreath making.

Willow took in the moment. The Naked Moose had never looked more inviting, bathed in the golden glow of twinkling lights, but it was the thought of Eli's arrival that had her barely able to stand still. Every time the door swung open on its hinges, she couldn't help but glance up, hoping it would be him.

Maybe that was a problem. Maybe it wasn't. She was trying to not overthink things and simply enjoy the ease of life lately.

"Need these?" Charly asked from behind her.

Willow spun around, saw the bundle of cinnamon sticks and nodded. "Thanks," she murmured, accepting them. "These will be perfect."

"Anytime," Charly replied, before returning to behind the bar.

She wasn't only waiting on Eli for his company. He was bringing in a box of donated craft items from Wolf Springs, but she had enough to get the group started this afternoon.

The door swung wide again, though this time, it crashed open. Amie staggered through, her face a canvas of anguish, tears carving rivers through her makeup.

"Willow," she choked out, the name half drowned in her sobs.

Willow rushed forward, swiftly closing the distance between them, taking Amie by the arms. "What's happened?"

"His sister." Amie gasped between breaths, the words laced with betrayal. "Buck's sister…she's the one. The comment… the text." She clung to Willow. "I'm so sorry. It was all because of me." A sob broke from her throat.

A cold fury ignited within Willow. But she quelled it, as she fought against the fear rising up, drawing instead on a reservoir of strength she'd built brick by painstaking brick since the night Niko had shattered her world.

"How do you know it was her?" Willow asked gently, helping guide Amie into a seat.

"Because the detective that worked my case came to tell me, so I could put a restraining order on her," Amie said, her voice hiccupping. "He wanted to make sure I was safe."

"That's good," Willow said, kneeling, taking Amie's hands. "None of this is on you. You are not to blame for someone else being horrible."

Amie's shoulders shook as she clung to Willow, her breaths coming in short bursts. "They're awful people. I should have connected it. They've written so many bad things about me, but I never thought they'd stoop this low."

"Of course you wouldn't," Willow said. "You're a good person. Such an idea wouldn't even come to you." She squeezed Amie's hands. "Please don't feel bad about this. I'm just glad we know who's behind this, and the police can stop them. Okay?"

There was a nod, a subtle acknowledgment that the words were seeping through the cracks of Amie's guilt.

"Willow's right, honey," came Betty's seasoned voice, warm as a woolen blanket freshly pulled from the dryer. Her wrinkled hands, so skilled in knitting comfort from mere strands of yarn, reached out to touch Amie's arm with a grandmotherly kindness.

"Come now, let's try something to take your mind off things." Betty guided Amie toward the table where bundles of evergreen boughs awaited transformation. "Making something beautiful—it helps, doesn't it? Takes a bit of the edge off."

The other women in the room nodded, their faces etched

with lines of empathy. They moved closer, not crowding, but offering silent solidarity. Some picked up the fake berries and began to weave them into the beginnings of wreaths.

"See these?" Betty held up a sprig of holly to Amie, distracting her. "They're tough, like us. Survive the harshest winters and still manage to look beautiful."

A small, quivering smile tugged at the corner of Amie's mouth, and she reached out a tentative hand to accept the holly.

"Exactly," Willow said. "We're all a little like these holly leaves—sharp when we need to be, but full of life. Capable of growing in places no one thought possible."

Her cell phone's sudden ring in her apron cut through the conversation, jolting Willow. She excused herself and strode to the back, her hand steady as she answered. "Hello."

"Hello, Willow. Detective Harris here," came the crisp voice on the other end. "We've made some headway regarding those messages you reported."

"I just heard from Amie that it was Buck's sister," Willow said.

"Indeed. We've identified Buck's sister, Samantha, as the source. She seems convinced Amie is fabricating stories about Buck, and wants to dismantle your support group since word of Buck's abuse is spreading through town. We had a talk, outlined the legal repercussions of her actions. I suspect she won't bother you again."

Relief washed over Willow in an almost physical wave. "Thank you, Detective. This means more than I can say."

"Keeping this community safe is my job, Willow. Take

care now." With that, the line went dead, leaving Willow exhaling a breath of relief.

She tucked her phone back into her apron and returned to the bar where the fragrant pine and cheerful chatter softened the edges of her anxiety. Good. It was…*over*. Now they could continue forward, and the group would be a huge success.

And yet, did that mean the fake relationship had to end? The thought sank heavy into her gut and churned her belly.

Amie sat apart, a wreath barely started in her lap, her hands shaking too much to tie the delicate ribbon.

"You okay?" Willow asked gently, taking the seat next to her.

Amie's gray eyes, usually so strong, now brimmed with unshed tears. "I just hate this—hate that my problems became your problems."

"Listen to me, Amie," Willow began, steeling herself for the vulnerability she was about to expose. "You're not the cause of any of this, okay? The only person responsible is Buck's sister."

Amie sniffled, nodding slowly, but the guilt clearly lingered.

Willow hadn't shared her story. Not with anyone. She never told anyone but the police what happened that night with Niko. Even Charly and Aubrey didn't know all the details, because they'd been too hard to share, too raw. But as she stared at Amie, so broken, she knew she had to share—to show her she understood. "I do understand having to deal with other people's rage and issues," she said to Amie. "I remember the night that Niko changed my life forever." She glanced down at her wreath, beginning to add some cinnamon sticks. "A night he lost himself to rage. I ended up in the ER, ten stitches holding my cheek together."

The words hung heavy, a raw admission that felt like re-opening a wound long scabbed over. The surrounding noise dimmed, the world seemingly narrowing down to just her.

Willow reached for the spool of ribbon, her fingers brushing against the soft fabric, and she forced her hand not to shake. It would never shake for Niko again. "Before that night," she began, "Niko had been rough, sure—pushing, yelling, all sorts of emotional games—and all that was harmful in and of itself, but that night…" She swallowed hard, feeling the memories claw at her throat. "That night, he became someone I didn't recognize. A monster."

The glint of twinkling Christmas lights did little to warm the chill that settled over her skin as she recounted every moment of that night. "He raged for hours, his anger a living thing. I thought he was going to kill me." She swallowed hard, her hands trembling slightly as she wrapped the ribbon around the wreath. "I thought he was going to kill me."

"How did you get away?" Amie asked, her voice barely above a murmur.

"By feeding his ego," Willow replied, adding some holly sprigs into the wreath, tucking them in tight. "I told him I was sorry for what I'd done for making him so mad—even if I had no idea why he was so angry—that it was all my fault for making him mad. God, it was the hardest thing I've ever done. But I needed to survive, to live." She drew in a long, deep breath and then glanced at Amie. "I got him to believe that I wasn't upset and I was hungry. It was like he couldn't even see the blood on me—like his brain had completely forgotten what he'd just done. I've never seen anything like that before." She added more berries, tucking them in. "When he left to get food, I ran. I was just soaked…covered in blood, everywhere. I remember how afraid my neighbor had been when I arrived at her door, but she was brave enough to let me in and call the cops…to help me."

That night she saw the difference between good and evil—it had been so clear. "For a long time after that, I blamed myself for putting myself in that situation," she continued, "but eventually, I realized all I did was love someone. And Niko turned that love ugly." She glanced at Amie and smiled, tears in her eyes. "I wasn't to blame for what Niko did, and you aren't to blame for what Buck or his sister have done. That's all on them."

Tears dried; Amie threw her arms around Willow. "I'm so sorry you went through what you did, Willow, and you're right, we're not the bad people here."

The silence in The Naked Moose was palpable as she held Amie tight. Her heart felt softer in her chest. She had peeled back the layers of her darkest night, exposing the wounds for the very first time, and with those words, came…*peace*.

It wasn't until she leaned away from Amie that she noticed tears spilling over Charly's cheeks. Aubrey stood beside her, hand clamped over her mouth, her eyes glistening with unshed tears.

She was engulfed in their arms a second later.

"Willow," Charly breathed out, her voice quivering with emotion. "I never knew—"

"None of us did," Aubrey chimed in. "You're so strong, Willow. You're so fucking brave."

Willow blinked away the moisture in her own eyes, her gaze lifting to meet theirs. "It's not just my strength that got me through," she said. "It's knowing I have all of you. It's friendships. It's love. It's all the good. That's how we win." As Charly and Aubrey stepped away, a new presence brushed against her senses.

Eli stood just inside the doorway, his towering frame holding a stillness that belied the storm of emotions playing across his face. He seemed to have forgotten the box of craft supplies he was delivering.

Willow's breath caught in her throat. His piercing gaze was fixated on her, and his emotions bled on his face. She saw for a moment how he saw her—not as a victim but as a survivor. She rose and moved toward him.

"Willow," Eli's voice finally broke the silence as she reached him. "You're one hell of a woman."

"Thank you," she said with a smile. "I hadn't meant for you to hear that."

"I'm glad I did," Eli replied, his eyes never leaving hers. He took a step closer, bringing a world of heat with him. "Detective Harris called earlier. I missed the call, but he left a message about Samantha."

"So you heard too," Willow said, glancing back at Amie before saying to Eli, "Amie feels terrible, but I'm just glad the police have it all handled now."

"Couldn't agree more," Eli said, sliding his hands into his pockets.

She nibbled her lip. "I guess we don't have to—" She leaned in and said softly, "pretend anymore."

His eyes searched hers for a long moment, before he dropped his voice, keeping the conversation private. "We did say this ends at New Year's. I think it's best to stick to that. I'd rather be safe than sorry."

She nodded, the tension in her belly easing in an instant. She wasn't ready for the dates to stop with Eli, but she wasn't ready for anything more either. She liked things exactly as they were. "I totally agree."

Relief washed over Eli's face, and his smile was...*sweet*. Again, he said quietly, "But what about doing something tonight just for us, as friends, not pretending nothing?"

She froze a little. This most certainly felt like a step past friends, but it also suddenly felt like the right step. "I think that sounds fun."

"Great," he said, his smile widening. This time he said louder, "Can you get off tonight?"

"Yes," Charly and Aubrey called behind them.

Willow laughed. "Apparently, yes."

He gave a firm nod. "I'll pick you up at your place at seven. Dress warm," he added, before dropping a quick kiss on her cheek and walking away.

She watched him exit the bar, and swiftly turned around to find Charly and Aubrey nearly right behind her. He'd gone from being all in for the fake relationship to suddenly wanting to hang out as friends. She set her stare on Aubrey, folding her arms. "Did your vanishing earlier have some-thing to do with that."

Aubrey scoffed, flicking her hair over her shoulder as she walked away. "A black bikini had something to do with that."

Eleven

Right at seven o'clock, Eli pulled up to Willow's place, the growl of the truck's engine cutting through the frigid Montana air. Snowflakes danced around the headlights, casting a soft glow on her figure as she stepped outside of the house. She was a mix of cozy and gorgeous, with her wavy hair cascading over her shoulders, her usual subtle makeup and glossy lips, but she was bundled up in a warm coat, plaid scarf and black beanie.

He hurried to exit the truck and met her at the passenger side. "You look beautiful." He swung open the door, taking in the sight of her—a vision strong enough to make him forget the chill biting at his skin.

"Thank you." She smiled, climbing into the passenger seat.

He quickly shut the door behind her and then joined her in the truck. A scent of vanilla and sugar filled the cab, and he was certain he'd never smelled anything quite that wonderful before.

As they began driving, Eli stole glances at her while the road stretched ahead, the hum of the tires over the asphalt a steady rhythm beneath the music playing through the speakers. He'd changed the station from his country music favorite to pop music knowing it was her favorite, and she was singing along. Damn, she was cute.

He stayed quiet, listening to her sweet, soft voice, until his truck rolled into Wolf Springs, the larger city north of Timber Falls. The park unfolded before them like a snow-kissed paradise, with thousands of strings of lights draped between trees.

"Wow," Willow breathed out. "It's like stepping into a fairy tale."

"Wait until you see it all up close," Eli promised, glad he got the date idea right. He parked the truck in one of the available spots. "Stay put," he told her, before rounding the vehicle to her side.

As he opened the door for Willow, she said, "It's sweet you open the door for me, but you really don't need to do that."

"How about you leave that decision up to me, hmm?" he countered, offering his glove-covered hand to her.

She laughed softly, shaking her head. "Okay."

He smiled when she took it, and he led her into the heart of Wolf Springs's Winter Wonderland.

"Look at this place," she murmured.

"Every year it gets better," Eli said. "Like I said, I'm not much of a city person, but this is something they definitely get right."

Christmas music drifted from hidden speakers, filling the space between the laughter and chatter of families and couples. Ahead, people skated on an ice rink with a large decorated Christmas tree in the center.

As they strolled past the food trucks decked out in festive decorations, the tempting smell of sizzling meat filled the chilly night air. "Feeling hungry for a bratwurst?" he asked with a grin.

She nodded eagerly. "I haven't had street meat in forever."

"Trust me, you haven't lived until you've tried one from here." He winked at her, enjoying the flush of excitement on her cheeks as they approached the stand.

"Three bratwursts, please," Eli ordered, handing over a couple of bills to the vendor who accepted the order with a nod. The flames licked the brats, and Eli's mouth watered.

"Thank you," Willow said as she accepted the sausage wrapped in a paper napkin, her breath forming tiny clouds in the chilly night air. He couldn't take his eyes off her at the way her nose scrunched up slightly as she took her first cautious bite, then her eyes lighting up with approval.

"Good, huh?" he asked.

"Delicious," she confirmed, her voice muffled by another eager bite.

"Wait right here," he said with a finger raised. "I've got one more thing."

A few paces away, under the soft glow of a string of lights, a hot chocolate stand beckoned. He returned quickly with two steaming cups, the rich chocolatey scent mingling with the crispness of the winter air.

"Here, this will warm you up," he said, handing her one of the cups.

"Perfect."

Her smile hit him like a physical blow, but in the best possible way. He couldn't help feeling a bit foolish that it took Aubrey's straight talk to finally make this night happen, where being together wasn't pretend, but real. Although he would never be happy about Buck's sister's text and comment, he had to admit that pretending to be Willow's boyfriend was what brought them together for this moment.

And *this moment* felt damn good.

He didn't want to make any mistakes. But he didn't want to pretend anymore that he wanted to do things with her. He liked spending time with Willow, as friends, or anything she damn wanted.

They wandered further into the park, finding a secluded bench beneath a canopy of twinkling lights that was covered with thick cushions, heaters installed above providing a comforting warmth. Settling down, he ate his two sausages in the same time she finished her one, as they watched the ice skaters, wonderful memories filling his mind.

"Used to come here every year, my mom and sister and I," Eli shared breaking the comfortable silence between them. "It was our thing, you know? No matter how busy we got, we made time for this. My mom loved Christmas."

"Sounds like a nice tradition," Willow said softly, her gaze meeting his. "My mom makes Christmas a really big thing too. They're coming to town for this Christmas. It'll be nice to have them here."

"I bet it will be." His heart thumped heavily, a mixture of sweet memories and lingering pain.

"Did your sister like Christmastime too?" Willow asked, after a sip from her cup.

"She loved it all, especially baking cookies," he explained, stretching his arm across the back of the bench. "She would've liked you."

"Can you tell me about her?" Willow asked gently.

It almost felt like Miranda was there next to him, urging him to let Willow in. "She was...vibrant. Always laughing." His gut tightened, but he pushed through the emotion, wanting Willow to know his life. "She would always wake me up at the crack of dawn for Christmas morning, no matter how old she got. I always tried to ignore her, but she'd jump on me until I got up so we could open presents." He laughed, warmth filling him at the memory.

"Sounds like she was a special person," Willow murmured.

"Beyond special." Eli cleared his throat, focusing on the skaters twirling below them. "It's tragic what happened to her."

"Very tragic," Willow said.

He took a deep breath, sliding his arm behind Willow on the bench. "Her death was violent," Eli confessed, the admission feeling like shards of glass scraping his throat. "Senseless. And none of us knew, not really knew, how bad things were for her with her boyfriend."

Willow's voice trembled with empathy. "I'm so sorry, Eli." She placed her mitt-covered hand on his leg.

He managed a half smile that felt more like a grimace. "I found out when I was miles away at a rodeo. A call from my mom in the middle of the night. I'd never heard a cry so gut-wrenching. I don't think I'll ever forget that sound."

The memory surged through him, vivid and relentless, the helplessness he'd felt then mirrored now in the tightness of his chest.

"I won't ever understand why Miranda didn't come to me," he continued, his gaze fixed on the skaters. "She always put on such a strong front. It blindsided us all when we learned the truth—the horrifying texts he'd sent, the damage to their house, the fear she masked with smiles."

"Abuse thrives in silence," Willow whispered, her voice carrying a depth of understanding that warmed him.

Eli gave a bitter laugh. "Silence can kill." He lifted his cup for another sip and continued, "I thought rodeo was the life. Going from town to town, always chasing that next win." His eyes briefly met Willow's, filled with understanding. "But while I was out there, chasing fame, my baby sister... was fighting for her life, and I didn't even notice."

"You couldn't have known," Willow countered. "Believe me, I've been Miranda, and the shame in the abuse, it's all so easy to hide."

"Doesn't stop the guilt," Eli confessed, the words easily tumbling out now. "I should've been there, should've seen the signs."

Willow paused for a moment, then said softly, "Your sister probably didn't want to burden you, especially since you were living out your dream."

"I imagine that you're right," he muttered. "My mother took it very hard. After Miranda passed...she just faded away.

The doctors said it was a heart attack, but I could see the grief draining her from the inside out."

"That's just so sad," Willow whispered.

He nodded in agreement.

Time slowed as Willow removed her mitt and lifted her hand to his cheek. In her touch, Eli found something he hadn't felt in a very long time—warm affection.

"Thank you for sharing all that with me," she said, her gaze never leaving his.

"Only seemed right," he admitted, the raw truth of his own words surprising him. "You've been brave enough to share your story. I want you to know mine—all of it."

He had met many individuals throughout his lifetime, but none quite like her. She possessed a unique combination of sweetness and strength that drew him in inexplicably. It felt as though the universe itself was guiding him toward her, perhaps even his own sister and mother were nudging him in her direction. With her, he felt at ease and protected, as if she were his safe place to land and he was her shield against the world.

He exhaled a low, slow breath. "Would you like to go skating?" he asked.

She nodded eagerly in response, but it was the sweetness shining in her eyes that truly captured his attention as they made their way to the rental booth together.

A smile that he knew he would never forget.

The frosty air nipped at Willow's cheeks as she stepped off the ice, her skates dangling from her fingers. Eli was beside her, his breath visible in the cold night. Together, they left the laughter and music of the skating rink behind, their boots crunching on the snow-covered path that wound through the quiet park.

"Thanks for tonight," she said, smiling up at him. "I haven't been skating in years."

"I enjoyed myself too." His voice was a low rumble. He glanced at her with a look that sent a shiver down her spine—not from the cold, but from the heat that always seemed to simmer between them. "Up for a drink at my place?" he asked.

"Definitely," she said.

They reached his truck, and the ride back to his house was as comfortable as the drive there.

Pulling up to the log house, Willow felt a sense of warmth bubble inside her as she exited the truck. It wasn't grand or modern, but it was inviting, with its cozy wraparound porch and the faint glow of light seeping through the curtains.

"Sorry, I don't have much in terms of fancy cocktails or drinks," Eli said as he unlocked the front door.

"Actually," Willow began, following him inside, "do you have any whiskey? My dad and I always share one on ice. It's kind of our thing." She shed her jacket, revealing the soft sweater that hugged her curves beneath.

"Whiskey, I can do." A grin tugged at the corner of Eli's mouth.

As he moved to pour her a glass, Willow let her gaze travel over the interior of his home. It was sparsely decorated, with hints of Eli's life—an old bronc riding trophy perched on a shelf and photographs of Eli bull riding. Yet, there was a tenderness here, a vulnerability in the way he cared for this space, and that he'd built it all with his own hands—that made her heart swell.

"Here you go," Eli said, handing her a glass with a single cube of ice clinking softly against the sides.

"Perfect, thank you." She took a sip, the whiskey warming her from the inside out, spreading a slow, delicious burn through her veins.

While Eli fixed them a fire in the fireplace, Willow moved to his worn-in couch and nestled deeper into the soft cushions as she savored the whiskey's lingering heat. The dim lighting of the room cast a golden hue on their surroundings, and with every breath, she inhaled the faint scent of leather and pine that seemed to emanate from the very walls of his home. And *him*.

When the fire caught, Eli sank down beside her, an easy silence stretching between them before he turned to her with a gentle curiosity in his eyes. "You talk about your family a lot," he observed. "They mean a lot to you?"

"More than anything," Willow admitted. "When I told my parents I was moving to Timber Falls, my mom thought I'd lost my mind—like I was having some kind of breakdown." She laughed softly at the memory. "But then they saw how much I needed the change. They know how important it is for me to stand on my own, especially after...*everything*."

Eli inclined his head in understanding.

"But I think it's more of the story behind how we found

Timber Falls and the pact and everything that they had trouble following," she said.

"What was the pact that you made again?" he asked, before taking a sip of his whiskey.

"Right after college, Charly, Aubrey and I came to Timber Falls on a girls' trip to celebrate graduating. We made this silly pact that if any of us weren't happy with where we were in life by the time we hit twenty-eight, we'd pack up and move here."

"Sounds like destiny to me," he commented, but there was something powerful in his statement.

"Maybe it was," she mused. "Maybe it was even the legend. It brought us here, and then it saved me." He stared at her intently, and she liked the way he watched her, always so focused. The familiar heat rose between them, like it always did. Unyielding and overwhelming. She leaned forward slightly getting closer to his warmth as she shared her truth. "I think there's something magical about this place. It drew me here… for a reason…like I needed to be here."

He stared deeply into her eyes, as if suddenly everything made sense to him, a clear awareness on his face. "Maybe it brought you to me too…to *this* moment…"

She couldn't help it. Her gaze fell to his lips, and with just them there, nothing stopping them from embracing the heat sizzling between them, it didn't seem like it was a question anymore.

She wanted those lips on hers.

She wanted them *everywhere*.

And she could no longer find a reason to not let that happen.

Their eyes locked, their breaths mingling, and in that moment, she knew. There was no shoving him away this time. His eyes, usually so guarded, now burned with a hunger that mirrored her own.

The air between them crackled, charged with an electricity that Willow could almost reach out and touch. She felt the warmth radiating from Eli's body against her side, igniting a flame within her that she thought had been long extinguished. Her breath hitched in her throat as she realized how close they were—so near she could count every shade of green in his eyes.

With a shaky exhale, she leaned in, closing the space between them, and her reward was immediate. Eli's arm enveloped her, their bodies pressed impossibly close as their lips met in a fiery kiss. Heat exploded through her veins as his mouth moved against hers, each caress, each nibble, igniting a fire she only wanted to burn hotter. His hands roamed her back, leaving a trail of shivers in their wake, and she instinctively arched into him, craving more of him.

He plucked her glass from her hand and set it next to his on the table, as Willow's hands found their way into his hair as she pulled him closer, her need growing with each passing second.

His kisses trailed down her jawline, his stubble leaving a delicious trail of goose bumps on her sensitive skin. "Eli," she breathed, hearing the desire in her voice.

"Shh," he whispered against her ear, sending a shiver down

her spine. "I'll take care of you," he murmured, trailing his lips along her collarbone.

She couldn't get enough as his hands moved to her waist, pulling her impossibly closer. Her breath caught in her throat as she felt his hard cock against her sex, her core throbbing in response.

"Eli," she breathed again.

He deepened the kiss, his tongue delving into her mouth, exploring every corner, teasing and tasting.

She whimpered, tangling her fingers in his hair, holding him close. He grunted, and in one fluid motion, he rose, laying her out on the couch before him, his hips grinding against her core. "You have no idea how much I've wanted this," he growled, his voice raw with need. His hand slid up her thigh, lifting her leg to wrap around his, pressing himself even closer.

The contact sent shivers down her spine, and she ground against him. "I want this," she told him. "I want you."

With a groan, Eli's lips skated down her jawline, kissing a trail of fire along her neck, each touch causing her to rub herself harder against his hardened length. Her breath caught as Eli's hands now moved with tender precision to lift her sweater, pulling it over her head. Then he reached back and started on her bra. Each flick sent another blast of heat overwhelming her, until the fabric peeled away.

His gaze never wavered from hers, hungry eyes blazing a trail of silent promises, and in their depths, Willow saw not just desire but safety.

As her bra fell away, a shiver ran down her spine—not

from the chill, but from the heat of Eli's gaze examining her. His lips found the column of her throat, warm and insistent, mapping a path of desire that set every nerve alight. His tongue flicked out, a brief taste that promised more, and fire curled within her belly, sending ripples of pleasure coursing through her veins.

Then his mouth descended. Each brush of his lips against the swell of her breasts left her moaning in urgency.

She'd never wanted anyone or anything this much. She felt a flood of emotion wash over her. It had been so long since she had felt this safe, this cherished. Slowly, she let her guard down, the walls she'd erected for so long crumbling under his tender touch.

His hands traced the contours of her body, drawing lines of fire across her skin. Her world narrowed as he reached between them, removed her jeans and then her panties. She shivered against the weight of his gaze holding a promise she knew he'd deliver on. She ground against him, a silent plea for *more*.

The side of his mouth curved slightly, and his skilled mouth trailed a path of heat down her abdomen, worshiping every inch of her. When he met slicked, hot flesh, she gasped, arching up. Each kiss was a spark, each brush of his tongue a flame, and she tilted her head back. His mouth, sure and knowing, teased her, coaxing forgotten pleasure. The sensation of being devoured by such careful attention sent her soaring.

"Please," she whispered, trembling. Her fingers weaved through his hair, anchoring him to her as she spun wildly out of control. His mouth was warm, insistent, worshipping with intensity.

Overwhelmed by pleasure, Willow felt her body respond with a primal urgency, her hips arching instinctively toward his mouth.

"Please," she repeated. She was so...*close.*

The earnestness in her plea, raw and unguarded, seemed to ignite something within him. His movements became more purposeful.

And when his fingers slid inside her, pumping hard and fast, Willow spiraled upward. She clung to him as wave upon magnificent wave crashed over her, until at last she shattered, crying out her pleasure.

In the stillness that followed her release, Willow's chest heaved against Eli's as she fought to steady her breath. "You," she gasped. "I want you."

He kissed his way back up her body. "Are you sure?" he asked, his voice hoarse, his eyes dark, filled with desire. "I don't want to rush you."

"I'm sure," she said, her voice firm. "I've never been surer."

He cupped her face in his strong hands and claimed her lips in a searing kiss that left no doubt of his desire or his feelings. His tongue danced with hers, tasting and exploring, as if he couldn't get enough of her. Willow's fingers tangled in the short hair at the nape of his neck, her other hand resting on his chest, feeling the muscles contract underneath her touch.

"Condom," he managed to grunt out. He rose and stripped, and she happily took her fill. Eli was all man, thick and hard, in every place that counted. He grabbed his wallet from his jeans, took out a condom and sheathed himself.

Returning to her, he lifted her hips, positioning himself at her entrance. "Tell me you want this," he said, his eyes boring into hers.

"I want this—"

With a growl, he slid into her in one deep, slow thrust, filling her completely. His eyes never left hers. She gasped, her nails digging into his shoulders, her body arching to meet his. Heat coiled low in her belly, pleasure like she'd never known before coursing through her veins.

His response was not in words but in the shift of his body, the way he owned the pleasure. His hands, those strong, calloused hands, steadied her hips as he looked into her eyes. His gaze darkened, heavy with want and soaking in emotion.

He moved slowly at first, their gazes locked, matching each other's rhythm as the pleasure built. "Fuck," he groaned, his voice rough.

"Faster," she begged, lifting her chin, his hips picking up speed.

With each measured thrust, she clung to him, her fingers digging into the muscles of his back. The strength in his arms, the tenderness in his touch, they were all answers to questions she hadn't known how to ask.

"Willow," Eli groaned, his voice strained with passion, his hands gripping her hips, guiding her up to meet him.

"More," she begged. Her body arched instinctively, wanting him deeper, her movements becoming more urgent as something wild rose within.

His pace quickened and became frantic. Every slide, every retreat, every slam of his body against hers, brought her higher and higher.

Until she shattered, obliterating all thought, all restraint, and he followed her over the edge.

Twelve

Eli slowly woke the following morning to the soft light filtering through the curtains in his bedroom. He felt an unfamiliar warmth next to him, and glanced sideways finding Willow, nestled against him, tangled in the sheets of his bed.

Damn, he could get used to this.

She was there, in his space, and he didn't want her to leave. It felt unfamiliar to have someone next to him. Although he had been with other women since returning from the rodeo, it had always been in their homes, never his. He half expected to feel uneasy about letting someone into his personal space, but the feeling never came.

He lay there a moment longer, allowing himself to enjoy her sweet presence, before he kissed her shoulder. With reluctance, he peeled himself out of the bed, muscles stretching in protest. As he made his way downstairs to the kitchen, thoughts of the day ahead swirled in his mind.

Reaching the kitchen, he headed for the coffeepot and

got that brewing. Last night, he had texted Jaxon to let him know that he would be arriving late to work today. Eli rarely took time off, so he wasn't surprised by the lack of fuss. He pressed the button to start the brew, the machine gurgling to life, when his cell phone rang. He retrieved it from where it was being charged on the countertop, noting Harris was calling him back.

"Hey, Harris," Eli spoke into the receiver.

"Morning," Harris replied. "Sorry, I'm only calling you back now."

They'd been playing phone tag yesterday. "It's all right," Eli said. "I wondered if there were any updates on Samantha. I need to know Willow's safe." His gaze drifted out the kitchen window to the mountains off in the distance. The sky was overcast, and even from his spot in the warmth of his house, the air looked freezing.

"She's safe," Harris confirmed. "I personally talked with Samantha yesterday. She's scared of being arrested and she doesn't want any more trouble. She had a warped understanding of thinking she was protecting her brother, but she understands we'll charge her if she reaches out again."

A sigh escaped Eli, the tension in his shoulders easing. "Thanks, man. That's good to hear."

"Keep your eyes open, of course, but I don't think she'll cause you two any further problems."

"Appreciate it, Harris. I know this case wasn't in your department, but I'm grateful for you looking into it."

"It's not a problem. Anything else comes up, I'm just a

call away." The line went dead, leaving Eli alone with his thoughts once again.

Relief washed over him as he grabbed two mugs from the cupboard when a whisper of movement caught his attention. Willow glided into his kitchen, wearing nothing but his faded T-shirt, its hem playfully skirting her thighs. Her tousled hair cascaded over her shoulders, and a grin broke across his face. He moved toward her, instinctively drawn by this magnetic thing between them. "Morning, beautiful," he murmured.

"Morning," she responded, a sleepy smile tugging at her lips. The distance between them evaporated as he wrapped his arms around her, pulling her into an embrace. He dropped his mouth to hers. She tasted of sun and sweetness, and he couldn't get enough.

When he pulled back, she watched him closely. "Last night…"

He frowned. "If you shove me on my ass again, we're going to have a problem."

She laughed softly, shaking her head. "I don't regret it, but I want to make sure we're clear. I'm not ready for a relationship. I can do friends-with-benefits, but I can't offer anything beyond that. I'm not capable."

He cupped her face. "I'm not asking for anything you can't give. As long as I get to keep kissing you, I'm good."

Her eyes warmed in their beautiful way. "Better kiss me again so I can see."

He did as she asked, placing his mouth against hers and putting in everything he had to leave her breathless.

It worked. Her cheeks were pink, and she was breathing heavily when he broke away.

He lifted his brows. "Your decision?"

"You can kiss me any damn time you want when we're alone," she said.

He accepted her decision with a nod. "Detective Harris just called," he told her, turning back to the counter and fixing their coffees.

Willow slid onto the stool at the breakfast bar. "Anything we should worry about?"

"Nah, Harris thinks Buck's sister won't be stirring up any trouble," he explained. He handed her a steaming cup, their fingers brushing—a jolt of heat spiraling straight to his groin.

"Thanks, and that's good." She smiled, wrapping her hands around the mug. "Do you know them—Buck and Samantha?"

"Not well," Eli said, before leaning against the counter and taking a sip of his coffee. "They both went to my high school, but we were all in different grades." He set his mug down and took the cast iron pan from the bottom drawer on the stove. "I consider myself lucky that they weren't in my circle of friends."

"No kidding," Willow quipped, a wry edge to her voice. "Did Amie go to your school too?"

Eli shook his head. "She didn't grow up here. She probably ended up here like everyone else, came for a visit and never left."

Willow laughed. "That seems to happen a lot around here."

"More than you can even imagine." He focused on fixing breakfast, glad he had eggs and bread.

"Need any help?" Willow asked.

He glanced over his shoulder, flashing her a grin. The kitchen was bathed in the soft morning light, casting a warm glow on Willow's face.

"Just keep looking that cute, it's all the help I need." The sizzle of butter melting in the pan filled the room.

"Flatterer," she teased.

"Always." He winked, pouring the eggs into the pan, as they hissed hitting the hot surface.

In no time, he had the bread toasted and buttered and added fluffy scrambled eggs onto two plates. He set them down on the small kitchen table by the window, and she quickly headed his way.

"How are things shaping up for the Christmas market?" he asked, as they sat down.

"Good, actually." She reached for her toast, taking a nibble, her tousled hair falling over her shoulder. "We're in full Christmas mode at the bar. And the Christmas crafts are coming together. I think we'll make a decent amount of money for the shelter."

"That's incredible." He scooped up some eggs on his fork. "Gotta be proud of how far you've all come with the bar since you first moved to town."

"That's probably an understatement," she said with a laugh, "considering no one wanted us here when we first moved here."

"It's not so much as not wanted you here," he countered.

"It's that people around here aren't used to change. Your cocktail lounge was change. Looks like everyone has come around now."

"They have," she agreed with a soft nod. "Everything is starting to feel like it's coming together." She ate some eggs and then asked, "I hope you're coming to the market."

"Wouldn't miss it for the world," he assured her with a smile. "What's your plan for today?"

"I better get to the bar at some point," Willow said. "We've got a big party coming in today. What about you? Will Jaxon be upset you're coming in late?"

Eli snorted. "Jaxon isn't my keeper. I'm sure he'll understand. After I drop you off at home, I'll head to the ranch to get my rides in today. As long as training happens, that's all Jaxon is worried about."

Willow flashed her sweet smile. "Charly and Aubrey have been blowing up my phone with texts, even though they know exactly where I am because I texted them last night." She chuckled. "They're like my personal bodyguards. Always have been, but it's even worse now."

"They care about you deeply," Eli interjected.

"And I feel the same way about them." She paused for a moment, cocking her head. "You understand that, right? You, Jaxon and Gunner are really tight?"

"We are," he confirmed, "but they wouldn't murder anyone for me. Charly and Aubrey, on the other hand…"

She let out a bark of laughter. "They probably would, especially Aubrey."

He'd seen that side of her himself. "She's tough, huh?"

"She's like a bull in the form of a woman," Willow replied, her mouth twitching. "Charly is like a mother hen, but Aubrey is my own personal ninja, ready to take down anyone who hurts me."

"I've come to realize that." Eli chuckled.

Willow held his gaze for a long moment before she focused on her plate and the half-eaten food there. "She came to see you about me yesterday, didn't she?"

"Yeah," he said, not intending to ever withhold anything from her. "Just to set me straight and make sure I had my head on right."

"That's just how she is," Willow replied softly, and didn't look bothered by that fact. "She also went to talk to Niko in jail. I never asked what she said to him, but I can only imagine."

"She's a very good friend to you," Eli pointed out.

Willow nodded in agreement.

Each bite, each sip of coffee, all brought more conversation that Eli couldn't get enough of. He didn't think he'd talked this much to anyone since his mother passed. He swore he could listen to Willow talk about nothing, and he'd still find her riveting.

When their plates were empty, he lingered over the last dregs of coffee, reluctant to have this morning end. He reached for Willow's hand across the table, his fingers grazing hers.

"I like this," he told her. "Just being here, talking. It's nice."

Her smile warmed all the cold cracks in his heart. "I like this too." She gave his hand a firm squeeze and then rose to clear away the plates, and she gave him a spectacular view from his spot of her bare thighs in his T-shirt.

She had to get to the bar. He had to get to the ranch. But with the heat filling him, and his cock twitching, he said, "You know what else I like?"

"What's that?" she asked, not looking back.

"You in my T-shirt." He had her in his arms a second later, and her laughter filling his kitchen was the best sound he'd ever heard.

The Naked Moose buzzed with excitement as Willow entered the bar after Eli dropped her off at home and she'd showered and gotten ready for the day. She couldn't get the smile off her face. Not only the skating, but their hot night, and even this morning after breakfast, had been magical.

Being with Eli was *magical*. Her body felt more than alive this morning. It felt...*reborn*.

When she pushed through the door, the music was already pulsating through the lively bar. Aubrey and Charly were putting the finishing touches on the photo booth, a colorful backdrop flashing "Born This Way" in bold, proud letters.

"Hey, you made it!" Aubrey's voice cut through the music.

"I wouldn't miss this party," Willow replied, heading toward them.

Aubrey grinned. "With *that* smile on your face, I'm surprised you even managed to get out of bed."

Charly came out of the back, stopped dead and said, "I want to hear every single detail, but we need to finish up, so talk while we work."

Willow agreed with a nod. "What can I do to help?"

"Those balloons need to be blown up," Charly said, pointing to the pack of balloons on the bar.

"I can do that." Willow put her winter jacket and scarf behind the bar and then grabbed the package. Her fingers tied each balloon after blowing them up, infusing the room with splashes of color.

Aubrey, perched on a ladder, unfurled the last of the rainbow flags above the bar.

Below her, Charly steadied the ladder. "Perfect, just a little to the left."

Aubrey affixed the flag in place with a tack and then she descended the ladder and turned to Willow. "Now spill it, girl."

Willow laughed, tying up a balloon. "Last night was magical…" She told them about the park, how he opened up about his past, and the skating.

"That certainly sounds incredible," Aubrey said.

Willow agreed with a nod. "And then—" her grin grew wider "—we went back to his house. Those cowboys. They're so damn charming."

"Willow Quinn, look at you!" Charly exclaimed, beginning to tape the balloons onto the walls beneath the twinkling Christmas lights. "And yeah, I get it. I have no control where it comes to Jaxon."

Willow laughed and felt a surge of gratitude for her friends, who had seen her at her lowest of lows and highest of highs. "Thank you," she murmured to Charly. Then she set her gaze on Aubrey. "For everything."

Charly smiled, coming over to hug Willow. "We just want to see you happy."

"We sure do," Aubrey agreed, throwing her arms around Willow too. "I'm glad you're enjoying yourself. It's about time you had some fun."

Just so happened, Willow agreed too. She kept waiting for the fear to rise that she was letting Eli in, but it never came. She wasn't sure if it was because Eli was who he was, or they had a good friendship before, but she felt...*safe*.

She wasn't certain where this would lead, but she felt okay with this next step with Eli. Maybe it'd only ever be fun between them. Or maybe not. But right now, she didn't need to know that answer, and there was freedom in that.

Minutes ticked by quickly, which eventually turned into hours. As the night wore on, the bar began to fill up with people, all there to celebrate James and his coming out to the world. The pop music from the speakers above the bar were loud and pulsing, and the drinks flowed freely. In the midst of it all, James stood tall and proud, dancing in the middle of a circle surrounded by his friends and family.

Willow watched from the sidelines, her heart bursting with love and admiration for a man finally living authentically.

Then, as if on cue, the music cut off and a figure emerged from the back—a vision in sequins and feathers, the spitting image of Cher in all her glory. The crowd cheered, turning to the stage, as the drag queen took to the microphone.

"Darlings! Tonight, we celebrate love in its purest form!" the performer declared, their voice sending the crowd screaming in joy. They launched into a rendition of "Believe," their movements a blend of grace and power.

Willow watched, mesmerized, as the Cher doppelgän-ger killed it. Her message rang clear: *Be unapologetically you.*

In that moment, Willow felt the gravity of all the good that they were doing with the bar. In The Naked Moose, people could be themselves, free from judgement and fear.

With tears welling in her eyes, Willow twisted off the cap of a bottle of beer. She caught Aubrey's eye at the end of the bar, and she smiled, obviously understanding Willow's line of thought.

"Need a hand with those drinks?" Charly called, sliding up to Willow behind the bar.

"Please, thank you," Willow replied.

As Charly garnished the margaritas with tiny paper pride flags, Willow moved to the next customer approaching the bar, a wide grin on her face as they eagerly awaited their drink.

"Beer please," the woman called over the music.

Willow cracked open another beer and slid it across the counter. "Here you go," she said with a friendly smile.

The brunette accepted the drink with a nod of thanks. "You guys always throw the best parties," she remarked.

Willow's heart nearly exploded. "We try our best," she re-plied, before taking the woman's payment and returning to Charly's side to assist with the flurry of drink orders.

As Charly balanced the tray full of drinks, she made her way through the dance floor, and delivered them to a group of people who eagerly reached out to grab their drinks.

Charly's eyes were filled with pride as she returned to Willow's side. "Just look at them," she said, her voice soft and full of emotion, gesturing to the crowd.

Willow followed Charly's gaze and felt her heart swell with joy as she took in the scene of celebration. "Look at us," she whispered, turning to Aubrey and Charly. "We did this together."

Aubrey wrapped an arm around Willow's shoulders and pulled her into a tight hug. "And we'll keep doing it," she declared firmly. "Because this is what truly matters." She gestured to the happiness surrounding them.

Willow nodded in agreement, a smile spreading across her face. The bar's success was a result of their combined efforts. Charly's experience in owning a bar, Aubrey's culinary creativity in crafting drinks and appetizers and Willow's skills in marketing all contributed to its success. They had poured their hearts into this venture, and it was thriving. "Isn't this a wonderful feeling?"

Charly glanced sideways. "What feeling?"

"Being happy." Willow smiled. "Not being scared all the time."

"Yeah, Wills, it's pretty damn good," Aubrey said.

Charly nodded in agreement, glancing between them. "Now is it a good time to point out that doing a backpacking trip to Yellowstone after college was so much better than going to Rome?"

Willow's laughter filled the air. It was hard to believe that a drawing they had made as tweens, depicting their perfect future town where all their dreams would come true, closely resembled Timber Falls. And even harder to believe that Charly had stumbled upon both the picture and the town itself. But Willow was a firm believer in fate and its unpredictable ways. And that camping trip had ended with the town and the pact that changed their lives forever. "I'm going to say, yes," she said with a laugh.

"Hmmm, I'm not quite there," Aubrey called over the loud music before hurrying off to assist a customer.

Charly grinned mischievously. "The Timber Falls magic hasn't reached her yet, but it will."

"How can you be so sure?" Willow asked.

Charly's smile widened, and she motioned toward the crowd. "Because Timber Falls is brimming with magic. It hit me. It hit you. Aubrey is certainly next."

Willow wholeheartedly agreed. For all that had gone wrong in her life, she now felt the blissful flow of magic that had gone through it, and she just knew…that it had brought her to this new reality where life was…*good*.

Thirteen

Eli returned home after completing his training rides and a quick dinner and stepped out of the steamy shower. The warmth had relaxed his muscles, but his mind was still filled with thoughts of Willow and the way her body felt pressed against his. He reached for a towel and dried off, his mind replaying every touch, every sweet moan, every kiss.

As he wrapped the towel around his waist, his hand brushed his hard cock, but he was saving himself for her. Right then, his phone buzzed on the counter. He scooped it up when he saw Willow's name illuminate the screen.

Meet me outside in 10. I've got a surprise for you.—W

A smile crept across his face. Surprise? He moved back to the bedroom, and quickly dressed. He pulled on a pair of dark jeans and a soft gray sweater. He barely glanced at his reflection, running a hand through his damp hair. On his way out the door, he grabbed his worn leather winter coat and slid on his nicer black cowboy hat.

As he opened his door, he spotted her car parked outside—a small black vehicle that he assumed had significantly better gas mileage than his truck. He couldn't help but smile as he squeezed himself into the compact passenger seat. It was a snug fit but being in close proximity with Willow was fine by him.

"Thank goodness you're not any taller," she joked, a playful smirk forming on her face. "Otherwise, we'd have to tie you to the roof."

"Wouldn't be the first time I've ridden out under the stars," he shot back.

"Let's stick to the car for tonight though. Safer for everyone involved." She laughed, and he laughed along with her.

Damn that felt good. Just laughing.

He fastened his seatbelt. "Going to tell me where you're taking me?"

"Nope," she replied.

The road unfurled before them as Willow drove right at the speed limit. He smiled at that, not expecting any different. His gaze shifted from the passing scenery to her, trying to read clues in the set of her jaw or the occasional glint of her eyes when they caught the flash of a streetlight. But only her smile was telling that she had something up her sleeve.

"Are we going line dancing?" he ventured, watching for any telltale sign in her expression.

"Keep guessing," she said with a playful lilt to her voice that made him chuckle despite himself.

"Karaoke?"

A smiled danced on her lips. "No, not karaoke."

He leaned forward slightly, watching as she took the turn that headed west. "I'm running out of guesses here."

"Good," she said. "You'll see soon enough."

As they drove on, he spotted the Deer Point sign. The buildings rose higher, the streets became busier.

"Deer Point, huh?" he asked.

"Look at you, playing detective." She glanced over, the corners of her eyes crinkling. "Yes, Deer Point. But where in Deer Point, that's the question."

"Can't blame a guy for being curious." He settled back, allowing the city's energy to wash over him. It was a stark contrast to the quiet comfort of Timber Falls, yet it held a familiar allure.

"Curiosity is good," she agreed. "Keeps things interesting."

As they neared the heart of the city, his anticipation sharpened. The buildings towered above them, their windows reflecting the stars peeking through the evening sky. People bustled about, and the air was charged with the electric hum of city nightlife.

Willow soon parked in the public parking lot.

Eli stepped from the warmth of Willow's car into the crisp night air, his breath forming a ghostly mist before him. The chill in the air faded away at the warmth radiating from her hand as it enveloped his. They moved in silence, each step taking them further into the secluded pockets of Deer Point's quaint town square.

The city's energy enveloped him like a living thing as he

followed Willow's lead toward the town hall, its grand facade glowing with the golden light of countless bulbs that spilled onto the cobblestone square.

"Surprise," Willow said.

A massive, majestic Christmas tree loomed before them, commanding the space with its towering presence. Its branches were heavy with ornaments, each one glinting under the soft radiance of strung white lights. These were not mere decorations; they were symbols of hope, lovingly crafted to honor others. Eli's gaze traced the silvery garlands, the ribbons that fluttered in the wind.

"Tree of Hope," he murmured, reading the sign set next to the tree.

"Yeah," Willow said softly beside him. "Every ornament tells a story."

"It's beautiful," he said.

"It is, but I think this one is even more so," Willow said, pointing to one ornament. "I hope you don't mind, but I made a donation to the Tree of Hope," she began, her gaze unwavering. "In your mother's and sister's names."

The words landed heavily, reverberating through Eli's chest. He swallowed hard, the impact of her gesture reaching deep into places he rarely let see the light. The ornament was a photograph of his mother and Miranda hugging. "How did you get the photograph?" he managed.

"Jaxon gave it to me," she said.

He could barely breathe, move...anything. "Willow, I..." His voice trailed off, lost amidst the swirl of emotions that threatened to overwhelm him.

Her smile was tender, laced with an understanding that went beyond words. "They're part of you, Eli. And seeing how much they mean to you... I wanted to honor that."

The gravity of her kindness anchored him in the moment, rooting him to the spot beside her. A swell of something he couldn't quite name—gratitude, affection, reverence—washed over him. It was as if she'd woven a thread between their two souls, stitching together something he thought irrevocably broken.

"Thank you," he managed to say, the simplicity of the words inadequate for the weight of his gratitude.

Their eyes locked, and in that instant, Eli felt the walls he had meticulously built around himself begin to crumble. The need to be close to her—to share in the solace she offered so freely—pulled at him with an urgency he hadn't realized he was capable of feeling.

"Come with me," he murmured, his voice rough with emotion, as he scooped up her hand, leading her away.

They wove through the throngs of people. The city hall loomed ahead, its stately columns promising the privacy they needed. He pushed open the heavy door, and they slipped inside, the echo of their footsteps mingling with the hallowed silence of the grand hallway.

His pulse quickened as he searched for an unlocked door. A janitor's closet, perhaps, or an unused office—it didn't matter. All that mattered was the space behind it.

When he finally found one unlocked, he opened it, and tugged her inside.

Willow's breath hitched. Her eyes widened. "We can't just

go into a room here," she gasped, the words barely above a whisper.

"Can't we?" he challenged.

Before she could protest further, he shut the door behind them. The room was steeped in shadows, the faint glimmer of streetlights filtering through a crack in the blinds.

"Trust me," he breathed against her ear. He gathered her in his arms, hot and hard now. As he pressed against her, his restraint shattered, and with a growl that rumbled from deep within, he pushed Willow against the closed door. He crashed his mouth against hers in a fiery kiss that spoke more to any words he could say. His lips moved against hers with a fervency that left no room for doubt of his gratitude toward her, his tongue tangling with hers in a dance that was both primal and achingly intimate.

The world outside the walls seemed to fall away, leaving only the two of them. Here, in this moment, he allowed himself to feel everything—every minute of his wanting her—as their lips crashed together.

The urgency of his kiss gave way to a frenzied undressing, hands grappling with the stubborn denim that encased her legs. With a swift tug, her pants were discarded and so were his. Without pause, he sheathed himself in a condom.

She panted against the door, and he stepped forward, hooking her leg onto his arm, pressing the tip of his cock against her entrance. The air was thick with desire as he gripped her hip. Her breath hitched, and it was the only invitation he needed, he surged forward in one swift stroke.

She moaned loudly, and he ate the sound with his hungry kiss.

His world narrowed to the rhythm of their breaths, the squeeze of her sweet, slick heat against him, clenching tighter. Every moan that escaped her lips was a call he answered with a deeper thrust.

She clung to him, nails digging into his shoulders, urging him closer, deeper. He grabbed her other leg, and she wrapped both around his waist, heels digging into his lower back. There was no space for thoughts—only the electric slide of skin on skin, the sweet friction that built a wicked fire.

As the pleasure rose, time seemed to warp. Seconds stretched into eternity; each moment filled with sensation that burned hotter with every touch. And when the heat spiraled down his spine moving toward completion, he thrust forward hard, bucking against her, as her cry of release soared over him.

When his mind returned to him, Willow shifted, lowering her legs, her movement drawing Eli's gaze to hers.

Her eyes sparkled, her lips curling into a smile that reached deep into his core.

"Your gentle side has its charm," Willow teased, breathless. "But whatever side that was of you—I really, *really* like it."

He chuckled. "Good, because apparently, I have no control around you." He took her chin, sealing that truth with a kiss.

Fourteen

Two weeks had flown by in a whirlwind of sweet and sizzling late nights with Eli and endless Christmas crafts. The Christmas market was only five nights away, and Willow felt Christmas magic sweep over all of Timber Falls. She threaded her way through the clusters of laughter and chatter in the bar, her heart swelling as she took in the scene before her. The whole crafting group was there, working hard to finish as many crafts as they could before the market.

"Look at this one, Wills!" Aubrey called out, holding up an ornament shaped like a moose, its tiny antlers wrapped in shimmering twine.

"I absolutely love that one," Willow said. "Keep it for me. I want to buy it for the bar."

Aubrey grinned. "Can't. I already bought it."

Willow smiled, but then focused back on all the crafts spread out on the four tables pushed together. They had pulled out all the crafts they'd done so far to get an overall look at them, determine pricing and form a plan for the market.

"Did I ever tell you about the first tree I decorated after leaving him?" Joanne asked the group, a hint of nostalgia in her laugh. "My kids and I hung up spoons and forks because it was all I had. But it was mine, you know?"

Amie said, "I bet that is one of the best memories for your kids too."

"It was," Joanne said, agreeing with a nod. "It truly was a wonderful Christmas."

Charly grumbled something incoherent, drawing Willow's attention. She was adding price tags to the wreaths. "Legit you're all very good at crafting. I can't even tie on these price tags properly."

Laughter rippled through the circle, and even Willow chuckled, the sound mingling with the clink of glasses and the soft rustle of paper.

"Who did this one?" Amie asked out, holding up a crocheted snowman.

Betty raised her hand. "That'd be mine, dear."

"It's so cute," Amie said, spinning the ornament in her fingers.

Betty grinned from ear to ear. "I'll make you one."

"Really?" Amie said. "Thanks, Betty."

Willow just smiled at the room bursting with love. She glanced to Charly and Aubrey, who smiled too. The first Christmas craft group had been quiet...*sad*. But no longer was the pain shared, or hearts bleeding—laughter filled the bar now. Friendships had formed over the passing weeks.

And Willow knew that was the best thing that could have come from Empowerment Elves, regardless of the money they made for the shelter.

"I'm really going to miss these crafting days," Amie said.

"They don't have to stop," Willow said. "Seems around here there is a festival or market for everything. We'll just change what we make."

Betty laughed. "We do love our markets in Timber Falls. I think that's a wonderful idea, Willow. I have so many knitted items we could sell too."

Before Willow could answer, the bar's door crashed open.

Willow's gaze snapped toward the entrance, spotting a thirtysomething man with tousled black hair. He had a long, dark unkempt beard and his jeans and black T-shirt were covered in dirt. His nearly black eyes, predatory and unforgiving, scanned the room until they fixed on Amie, who sat frozen, a half-finished angel clutched in her trembling hands.

"Buck," she breathed.

The temperature seemed to plummet, and Willow felt a chill snake its way down her spine.

"Hi, Buck," Charly called in a light voice, taking a step forward. "This is a closed event. You should—"

"Shut it," Buck spat. His boots thudded heavily against the wooden floor as he entered further.

Silence descended. Willow glanced at the ladies around the table. They all froze in their seats, their eyes wide with alarm, silent signals passing between them—a sisterhood united in fear that understood this moment meant *danger*.

Buck's rage was a palpable force that seemed to suck the

air from the room. "You think you can hide her from me?" he roared, his voice slicing through the silence.

Willow forced her voice not to betray the fear raging in her. "Amie doesn't want to see you. You need to leave, or we'll call the police."

"Who the hell do you think you are?" he bellowed, stepping into her space, his breath hot with the stench of whiskey and anger. "I'll wreck this whole damn place if I have to!"

That scent had Willow spiraling to another man...another time...*pain*...

"Please, Buck," Amie's voice was a frail whisper. "Don't do this."

"Don't you say a fucking word, you stupid bitch." Buck turned on her, his heavy hand flying up and crashing down across her face. The impact sent Amie sprawling to the ground, her chair clattering beside her.

Gasps filled the room, and Aubrey yelled, "Leave. Now."

Buck sneered, his gaze flickering over the roomful of Christmas crafts and the women who had painstakingly created them. "This fucking place. You fucking women. All out to ruin a man's good reputation. I was fired because of the lies spread here." With an animalistic growl, he swept his arm across a nearby table, sending delicate glass ornaments crashing to the ground.

"Look at this crap! You think this junk is going to change anything?" Buck's voice dripped with hatred as he stomped on a hand-painted ornament, grinding it beneath his boot. He began ripping up the Christmas cards, one by one.

Willow couldn't move...couldn't breathe...could only

watch as each stomp felt like an assault on the happiness they'd discovered these past weeks.

The room, once filled with laughter, now echoed with the sharp breaths of fright. Women huddled together, their eyes round with terror as they watched Buck's rampage.

"Call the police," Amie begged.

Buck snarled, turning back to Amie.

Willow wasn't thinking, but only knew she couldn't let him hit Amie again. She raced in front of Amie, trying to form a human barrier between them and Buck's wrath. "No," she barely managed. But even as she spoke, she knew it was a futile gesture; he was a tornado of rage, and she was in his way.

"What are you going to do, huh? Protect her?" he sneered, his voice slicing through the air, sharp and malicious.

With a grunt of rage, he lunged forward, shoving Willow hard in the chest. She stumbled backward, her legs tangling with a chair that toppled over, sending her soaring toward the ground. A gasp escaped her lips as fear gripped her, the coldness of the floor a stark reminder of how quickly things could turn from bad to worse.

"Willow!" The cry came from multiple directions.

But as she struggled to right herself, her palms pressed against shards of glass, causing her to cry out. Buck towered above her. She could feel the heat of his anger, a palpable force that threatened to consume everything in its path. And with his looming presence over her, she was right back there with Niko that night...the pain...the fear...it all blanketed over her. She curled into herself, placing her hands over her head, protecting herself from the fury she knew was coming her way.

Suddenly, the front door of The Naked Moose burst open with a force that shook its hinges, and through it stormed a figure with eyes glinting with a dangerous fire as he held a box. Eli's broad shoulders heaving, his gaze locked onto the scene before him. Until those blazing eyes landed on Buck towering over Willow, from her spot on the floor.

"Move. Now," Eli said calmly—too calmly, setting the box down.

Buck's face contorted into a mask of rage. "Stay out of this, Cole! This is between me and—" Buck's sentence was sliced short as Eli charged forward, the very air seeming to ripple with the power of his movement.

The world seemed to tilt on its axis as Willow watched Eli bulldoze over Buck, his body a battering ram against Buck's looming threat, as Eli tackled Buck into the table with the wreaths.

Willow forced herself up onto her feet to get out of the way, wincing against her bleeding palms. Aubrey gripped Willow's arm a second later, yanking her away.

"Stop, please!" Amie's voice rang out, as Buck managed to get back to his feet.

"Back off, Cole, or I swear—" Buck roared, his threats cut short as Eli landed a punch that sent him staggering back, his footing unsure.

Just as Buck regained his balance, Eli lunged with a blind ferocity.

The door suddenly crashed open again, and yet Willow

couldn't even find it in herself to feel relieved that the police had arrived, racing toward Eli and Buck. She stood frozen, unable to even process what had just happened. She should feel *something*, but she felt…*quiet*. Too quiet. Too silent. Too… disconnected.

But one thing she knew for certain, every wreath, ornament, Christmas card, all the items they made for the Christmas market were now destroyed…

"Timber Falls PD! Calm down!" A commanding voice shouted out as Eli was pulled off Buck and restrained with handcuffs. Finally, the adrenaline began to wear off and he struggled to recall what had occurred. He had dropped off Ranger at his new home with a very happy teenage girl and then picked up a craft box full of donations for Willow on the way back. But upon seeing her on the ground with Buck hovering over her, clearly having been pushed down by him, something inside Eli…broke.

"Stand down, Buck," came another shout, followed by the scuffle of a brief struggle.

Eli turned his head, trying to see Willow, but only saw the damage then. All the Christmas crafts were destroyed, and the remainder of the adrenaline engulfing him left in a rush as he saw broken wreaths, smashed glass ornaments.

"It wasn't Eli," Charly said from somewhere behind him. "He was protecting us."

The officers paid no attention to her as they forcefully pulled him up and led him out. He looked over his shoulder, hoping to catch a glimpse of Willow, but she was nowhere to be seen. "Willow?" he called but was met with silence.

Eventually, he found himself being shoved into the back of a police car and then driven to a jail cell. He heard that Buck had been taken to the hospital; Eli had apparently broken his nose during the scuffle.

Nothing about any of this felt good. All those crafts were gone. Every minute of hard work the Empowerment Elves had made was now erased. Buck might have been the reason, but Eli had been a part of that destruction. His gut twisted.

In the jail cell, Eli sat on the metal bench, the back of his head resting against cold steel bars. He shut his eyes, breathed past the tension in his chest.

"Eli," came a familiar voice.

He opened his eyes to Detective Harris, who stood outside the cell. "Interesting day?" Harris asked with a frown.

"You could say that." Eli's voice was gritty, raw.

"Listen, you know this is just protocol, right?" Harris leaned in closer, his voice dropping to ensure confidentiality. "Just gotta give your report, go through the motions. It's all part of the process."

Eli's jaw clenched and he nodded, as he grappled with the reality of his situation.

"You protected people today," Harris said, his eyes locking onto Eli's with a steadying force. "So, whatever you're feeling, stop. That's nothing to be ashamed of."

Eli couldn't even find it in himself to respond. He needed to think. He needed to get his head back on straight. His thoughts were muddled, cloudy.

"Come on," Harris said after a long moment. "I'll take you to give your report." He unlocked the jail door.

The cell door swung open, and Eli stepped out, squaring his shoulders. He didn't regret punching Buck. His fingers twitched to do it again, but all he could see were those broken crafts, and he knew there were broken hearts back at the bar. Including Willow's.

The tension twisted inside him like barbed wire as they approached the door marked Interrogation Room. Each step felt heavier than the last, grounding him in a reality he couldn't escape.

Before Harris opened the door, Eli said, "Before we go in there, can I make a quick call?"

Harris eyed him for a moment, then nodded with understanding. He gestured toward a phone mounted on the wall a few steps away. Eli's fingers trembled as he dialed Willow's number.

"Hello?" Charly's voice filled the line.

Disappointment washed over Eli. "Charly, it's Eli. I need to speak to Willow. Is she—"

"Willow can't talk right now," Charly interrupted, her tone gentle yet firm. "She's giving her report."

Eli closed his eyes briefly, imagining Willow's tears. "Tell her I—" Eli started, but the words tangled up in his throat.

"I'll tell her you called for her," Charly promised. "Just focus on what you have to do there, okay?"

"Okay," he whispered, the receiver cold against his ear. "Please have her call me when she can."

"I'll mention it to her."

With a click, the line went dead, leaving Eli turning to Harris.

"Ready?" Harris asked, his hand resting on the door handle.

"Let's do this." Eli took a deep breath and tried to steady himself. He entered the cold, sterile room and heard the door shut behind him with a loud thud. The walls were bare, except for a one-way mirror that he knew concealed others watching in. In the center of the room sat a single table, flanked by two hard metal chairs; one was already taken by a stoic police officer whose emotions were impossible to read.

"Mr. Cole?" The officer beckoned, gesturing to the chair across from him.

Eli took the seat.

"Whenever you're ready," the officer prompted, pen poised above a piece of paper. "Tell me what happened today."

"All right," Eli replied, his voice steady. He leaned forward slightly, resting his arms on the table. "Let's start at the beginning..." he began.

By the time he was finished, he couldn't stop thinking about the million things he should have done differently. He should have kept his cool. He shouldn't have punched Buck. He should have held him down until the police came. He shouldn't have ever let Buck get up. He shouldn't have crushed all the hard work the group had done.

The police officer's pen stilled above the paper; he leaned in slightly, his gaze never leaving Eli. "Did you feel Buck posed a direct threat to Ms. Quinn and the other women there at the bar?" the officer inquired.

"Yeah," Eli replied without hesitation, the muscle in his jaw clenching. "Willow was on the ground, cowering away from him. It was clear Buck had shoved her, and Amie's cheek was red as she sat on the floor, an indicator he'd hit her. Everyone there looked terrified."

The officer nodded, his hand moving across the notepad, capturing every word. The rhythm of the pen scratching against paper resonated in the quiet room, a testament to the seriousness at play.

"I have your report written out here," the officer informed Eli. "Take a few moments to read it over and if everything looks accurate, sign and date it."

Eli took the paper and reviewed the contents, making sure they were correct. He then signed and dated it before returning it to the officer.

"We're all good here for now," the officer said. "I'll reach out if there is anything further. You're free to go."

Eli nodded his thanks and walked out of the interrogation room. Harris met him out in the hallway and then showed Eli the way out. He was talking, but Eli couldn't hear anything past the thoughts battering his mind.

Once outside, with Harris not following Eli out, the cool evening air brushed against his skin, a stark contrast to the stifling confines he'd just left. Jaxon and Gunner were there waiting, leaning against Jaxon's pickup, expressions somber.

"All right?" Jaxon inquired, his voice calm and steady.

"No," Eli answered.

Gunner pushed off the truck and approached, placing a comforting hand on Eli's shoulder. "Want to talk about it?"

He swallowed hard. "No."

"Eli," Jaxon started, reaching out to place a hand on his other shoulder.

"Don't." Eli shrugged them off. He turned away from his friends and started walking toward his truck. He didn't look back. He didn't want to see the emotion in their eyes. He just needed to get to his truck, parked up ahead, and drive away from this goddamn mess.

The air in The Naked Moose was thick with tension, and Willow couldn't make sense out of anything that happened. The police asked the rest of the women in the group to leave the bar after they got their statements. Charly and Aubrey began throwing out the crafts, keeping the ones that were salvageable. From Willow's spot at a table, she watched as Amie gave her report on the other side of the bar to a female detective, while the paramedic administered first aid to Willow's cut hands.

"I'm not seeing any glass in here," the paramedic said, drawing Willow's attention. "It's up to you if you'd like to go to the hospital."

"I'm fine," Willow said, wincing as he wiped the small cuts with an antiseptic wipe.

The paramedic gave her a firm nod. "All right, let me just bandage your hands up for you."

When the paramedic finished with ointment followed up by bandages, the female police officer came over to Willow, taking a seat next to her at the table.

"Ms. Quinn, right?" the woman with the tight brown bun and sharp blue eyes asked.

"Yes, that's me," Willow replied.

"I'm Detective Nelson," she said, pen poised over a piece of paper. "I've got Amie's report, but I'd like to get yours too, if that's all right." Her tone was professional yet tinged with empathy. "Can you tell me what happened?"

Willow nodded again and drew in a shaky breath, her chest tight. "Buck—he arrived," she began, sure not to leave a detail out. Her words came out in a rush, laced with the sickness that swirled in her stomach at Buck's rage.

The officer nodded solemnly, writing down her account. "I'm sorry this happened," she said when Willow finished. "Buck is currently at the hospital under police watch but he'll be taken back to the station and arrested on a slew of charges."

Willow glanced over at Amie who was now helping clean up, her gray eyes meeting Willow's with a silent strength. At least she'd be safe now. And possibly would be for a while if Buck ended up in jail.

"Thank you," Willow said, looking to Detective Nelson again. "And Eli?" Her breath hitched.

"Mr. Cole? What about him?"

"He… He was defending me. I know how it looks, but Eli isn't violent. He saw Buck standing over me being violent, he just…reacted. His sister was murdered by her abusive ex. He's not like Buck. Please, he was only trying to help. He shouldn't suffer for protecting someone. For protecting me."

Detective Nelson gave a small nod, the lines around her

eyes softening. "We'll take his statement too. Self-defense is taken seriously, Miss Quinn."

"Thank you," she whispered in relief. The last thing she wanted was Eli arrested. She turned her gaze toward the bar, where all the crafts lay strewn across the floor, and her heart shattered.

All their hard work. Just gone.

"Is there anything else you can tell me that might help with the investigation?" Detective Nelson asked.

Willow shook her head, glancing back to her. "No, there's nothing else."

"All right then. We'll be at the station if you remember anything else. And we'll make sure both you and Amie are safe tonight," she assured her, closing her notepad with a soft snap.

"Thank you," Willow said, grateful.

As Detective Nelson walked away, Willow closed her eyes briefly, searching for strength in the very depths of her soul.

A hand suddenly slid over Willow's arm, bringing much needed warmth. She opened her eyes to find Charly and then Aubrey there. They both wrapped their arms around her tight. With each inhale, Willow drew in a little more strength; with each exhale, she released a fraction of her fear.

When she backed away, her vision blurred as tears spilled over. The crafts had been more than mere decorations; they were symbols of the sanctuary she had striven to build within these walls. Each piece represented a promise of happiness, a whisper of hope in the darkness, now broken and scattered.

Stacey Kennedy

"I wanted this place to be safe for everyone," Willow choked out. "I wanted…"

"Shh, it's still safe because of you," Aubrey soothed, squeezing her shoulder. "This…this is just stuff. We can clean it up, and we can fix this."

"How?" Willow asked. "We don't have time to make all new crafts before the market. We don't have the supplies."

"Not everything is gone," Charly said. "There's a few items and we can make more with what's left."

Willow glanced at all the garbage bags and knew the truth. There wouldn't be enough for a substantial donation to the shelter. She felt the air grow thick, cloying, as if the very essence of the bar were tainted now.

"What do you need?" Charly asked gently.

"I just want to go home," Willow admitted.

"Then let's close up and go," Aubrey said decisively. "Nothing's keeping us here tonight. This place will still stand tomorrow, and we'll put it right again."

Willow rose, just as Amie said, obviously having watched their exchange, "I'll go home too."

"No, you'll come with us," Willow said firmly. She gingerly wrapped an arm around Amie's shoulders, pulling her close. "You need friends right now. Not an empty home."

"Willow, I—" Amie began.

"No arguing," Willow said firmly, leaving no room for argument. "Friends look out for each other."

"Okay." Amie smiled, teary-eyed.

It took no time to lock up the bar. The air outside felt cool against Willow's skin as they stepped outside. Though the moment she looked right, she froze, spotting Eli walking down the street.

"Willow?" his voice was rough, tinged with concern and something darker, something that made her heart constrict.

"Just give me a minute," she said to the others.

They nodded, heading for the car at the curb when she approached him. None of the rage she'd seen glimpsed in his stormy eyes remained. It was gone now, replaced by a clear regret.

"They didn't press charges?" she asked. She saw the cuts on his knuckles, the mark on his cheekbone.

He shook his head, shoving his hands into the pockets of his jeans. "Not yet, no. I'm free to go home."

She didn't know the words—didn't *have* the words but forced her voice not to fail her. "Thank you, for...for what you did for me," she managed, her words halting. "But Eli, I..."

"Don't," he interjected, his gaze dropping. "Don't say anything yet."

Silence stretched between them, a chasm filled with questions and fears too large to voice. In the quiet, Willow could hear her own heart, confused and tired of something always going wrong...*so very tired.*

"Go home, Willow," Eli said softly, lifting his gaze to hers. "I'll give you space, as much as you need. Come talk to me when you're ready."

Her lips parted but shut again, as Eli turned, heading for his truck, and Willow's resolve wavered. She wanted to reach out, to bridge the distance, yet confusion, and her bleeding heart, held her rooted to the spot.

"Come on, let's get you home," Charly urged gently, guiding her toward the waiting car.

As Aubrey drove away, Willow's gaze remained fixed on Eli, until his truck faded away, and all she felt was...*tired*.

Fifteen

Perched on the weathered Adirondack chair on his porch, Eli's hand tightened around the neck of the whiskey bottle as he downed another long sip. The sky, black but with twinkling stars, offered him no peace tonight. An icy breeze whispered through the towering pines that bordered his property, carrying with it the faintest scent of pine and earth. He squinted into the darkness of the night. The sharp bite of winter couldn't numb the frustration deep in his gut.

Suddenly, the darkness was interrupted by a pair of headlights, carving a path toward him. Eli knew those headlights—Jaxon, and he assumed probably Gunner too.

The truck stopped next to the house. Jaxon emerged, and then Gunner, with his guitar case strapped over his shoulder onto his back.

"Man, it's colder than a witch's tit out here," Gunner quipped, rubbing his hands together for warmth as he walked up the porch steps.

"Needed some air," Eli muttered.

"Air's one thing," Jaxon said, eyes scanning Eli's face, "drowning in whiskey is another."

Gunner nodded solemnly, taking a seat next to Eli, while Jaxon leaned against the railing. "Heard from a friend on the force that Buck's in jail. A handful of charges, and probably more by the end of it, should get him put away for a while."

"Good riddance," Eli growled, the words tasting like bile. The mere mention of Buck's name stoked the embers of anger still smoldering within him. "Too bad it won't be for the rest of his fucking life."

Jaxon agreed with a nod. "Ready to talk about any charges you're facing?"

Eli shifted in his seat, the worn wood of the porch creaking under his weight. He took a deep swig from the bottle, letting the burn slide down his throat, desperate to wash away this fucking day. "I'm not facing any charges."

"Then why do you look so damn miserable?" Gunner asked, taking the bottle from Eli to have a sip.

"I can't shake all the fucking things I should have done different," Eli admitted to the two men who had gotten him through the hardest parts of his life.

The porch light cast half of Jaxon's face in shadow, the other half illuminated by the soft glow from the window next to him. "What else could you have truly done, Eli?" he said softly. "You stood up for what's right."

"Did I?" Eli scoffed, the taste of the word more bitter than the whiskey. "I let my anger dictate my actions. That ain't right, Jax. That's losing control."

"You're being too damn hard on yourself." Jaxon's voice carried a commanding yet gentle edge. "If Buck had laid hands on Charly like he did Willow, I would've come un-glued. Hell, I'd have done worse. You were protecting some-one you care about. That's not losing control—that's being human."

Eli dropped his head back against the house, staring off into the darkness. The reassurance from Jaxon should have brought comfort, yet it did not. Eli was drowning in a thou-sand should-haves. He accepted the bottle back from Gunner, and the weight was familiar, almost comforting, but tonight it was a mocking reminder of weakness.

His hand trembled slightly as he brought the bottle to his lips again, the burn rushing down his throat. "When I saw Buck standing over her, I didn't even think. It was like my head just shut off." He choked a humorless laugh, raking a hand through his hair. "If the cops hadn't shown up when they did, I don't want to imagine what I might've done. What I was capable of in that blind rage."

"Nobody would've blamed you," Gunner said softly, his voice laced with compassion.

"Maybe not," Eli admitted, his eyes cast downward. "But what if next time, there's no one there to stop me?"

"You would have come back to yourself," Jaxon inter-jected, his voice firm and unwavering. "I know it."

Eli lifted his head to meet Jaxon's reassuring gaze. The three of them had been friends since childhood, bonded by a shared love of adventure and a fierce loyalty to each other. Even now, as they sat on his porch, the wind howling around them, Jaxon and Gunner's steady presence gave Eli a sense of peace. He knew he was lucky to have friends who had stuck by him through thick and thin.

But Eli couldn't shake the feeling of fear and doubt that gnawed at him. He had been so close to the edge with Buck, and he wasn't sure if he could trust himself that his rage wouldn't take over if anyone ever threatened any women—especially Willow—in front of him again.

He closed his eyes and took a deep breath for a long moment before glancing to his friends again and admitting truths he never spoke of. "Every time I close my eyes, I see Miranda's face. I see *him* standing over her, and it's like—I'm right there all over again. Powerless."

Gunner leaned in, elbows on knees, his gaze steady. "But you're not powerless now, Eli. You have choices."

"Choices?" Eli scoffed bitterly. "Yeah, I made a choice all right. I chose to fight Buck." He scrubbed a hand over the scruff on his face. "What happened tonight..." he muttered, "I became a man who can't keep his demons leashed."

Jaxon shifted, his boots thudding softly against the snow-covered wooden planks. "You've been through a lot, Eli. It's understandable."

"Is it?" Eli countered. "Or is it just an excuse?"

Gunner began, "Eli—"

"It's an excuse," Eli said, cutting him off, a bitter laugh scratching its way out of his throat. "Today I was all fists and fury, ready to take out my anger over Miranda's murder on some other asshole."

Jaxon stayed silent.

"I hear what you're saying," Gunner chimed in. "But I honestly don't think you should beat yourself up about this."

Eli's hand clenched around the bottle. "This isn't just about tonight. It's about Miranda. About how her murder hollowed me out and filled the empty space with rage." He spoke the words and they felt like glass in his throat. "Sometimes, I'm afraid I'll never get free from it. That it's just biding its time, waiting to consume me. And if it does…" His voice broke. "I don't want that anywhere near anyone I care for."

Jaxon stepped forward, placing a steady hand on Eli's shoulder. "You won't let it consume you. Because you're stronger than that."

Gunner nodded, his presence a solid reassurance in the uncertain dark. "And you're not alone in this fight."

Eli looked up into the starry sky and told them a truth they all couldn't ignore. "I'm a bomb ready to explode, and I can't avoid that. Not anymore."

A long pause followed.

Until Jaxon snagged the bottle of whiskey and took the other seat beside Eli. "Well, it seems we won't be able to solve this tonight. We might as well warm ourselves up."

"Damn straight," Gunner chimed in, reaching for his guitar and leaning back in his chair. He began strumming a tune.

Eli accepted the bottle from Jaxon and took a long swig before passing it on to Gunner, who paused his song to take a shot.

Then Eli did what he'd done many nights after Miranda's murder. He let Gunner's soothing voice and music take it far away from there.

★ ★ ★

Sunlight crept through the slits of the blinds as Willow's eyelids fluttered open the next morning, a groan escaping her lips as consciousness forced her to acknowledge the day. Her head throbbed in sync with her heartbeat, each pulse echoing the confusion that had kept her tossing and turning throughout the night. She lay still for a moment, allowing the heaviness in her limbs to anchor her to the bed, hoping it might pull her back into the depths of sleep where she didn't have to think about yesterday.

But reality wouldn't leave her alone, and with a deep breath, she pushed herself upright and swung her legs over the mattress, settling her nightie back into place. Steeling herself, she made her way down the stairs to the living room. As she entered, the scent of freshly brewed coffee wafted toward her, a small comfort this morning.

When her last foot left the bottom stair, she found Amie, Charly and Aubrey were gathered around the coffee table and on the comfy living room couch full of mismatched throw pillows. Their faces, etched with concern and support, turned toward her as she approached. Amie's eyes were soft with empathy. Charly's nurturing warmth radiated from her. And Aubrey, with a reassuring smile that could break through the darkest days, sipped her coffee.

"Hey," Willow managed, moving to the kitchen and fixing herself a coffee.

"Didn't sleep great?" Charly called, as Willow headed back into the living room.

"Terrible," Willow confessed, sinking into the plush embrace of the couch in the middle of Aubrey and Charly. She took a long sip from her mug, warmed by the familiar comfort. "How about all of you?"

Charly shrugged, gave a lopsided grin. "Jaxon called drunk in the middle of the night so that was fun."

Aubrey rubbed her obvious tired eyes. "And I had to listen to him blab on about love and words that didn't even belong together."

"You shouldn't have given up your room to me." Amie laughed softly, sitting in the chair in the corner of the room, then said without the amusement, "I slept terrible too."

Willow was aware that Jaxon and Gunner were most likely with Eli, which could explain why he was drunk. It was probably the same for all of them. She felt reassured knowing that Eli wasn't alone last night; that was the last thing she wanted for him.

"I'm leaving for San Francisco," Amie announced.

Willow finished her sip and lowered her mug. "Really?"

Amie nodded. "I booked a flight last night after talking to my mom. I need to be with family and…" She paused, as if the next words were lodged in her throat. "And away from Buck. From everything here."

"I totally get that," Willow breathed out, her voice thick with emotion. "You'll be safe there with your family. It was the best thing for me after Niko to go somewhere familiar surrounded by love. You'll finally be free."

"Free," Amie repeated, like testing what the word truly meant to her.

"San Francisco will give you the fresh start you deserve,"

Willow continued, hugging the mug with her hands, embracing the warmth. "Away from him. You can heal, really heal."

Amie nodded, a small smile tugging at the corner of her mouth. "I hope so. I'm a little scared, but...it feels right."

Willow held Amie's gaze, her own smile radiating the pride that swelled in her chest. "Being scared doesn't mean you're not brave, you know? It means you're human. And making this choice—that's the bravest thing to do."

"Thanks," Amie said with a soft smile. Then she paused, her gaze holding Willow's intently. "It may be none of my business, so just tell me to stuff it if you don't want to talk about it, but why didn't you talk with Eli last night?"

Willow felt the weight of her friends' gazes. "I..." she started, her voice barely above a whisper as she searched for words that seemed to dissolve before they reached her tongue. "I just needed some space, you know? To breathe...to think."

Charly reached out, her hand gently brushing against Willow's arm. "We're here for you, no matter what you need," she said.

"Thanks, I know that." Willow smiled.

From her spot next to Willow, Aubrey spoke with a gentle firmness. "I'm sure Eli is feeling horrible this morning, and not from the obvious hangover he likely has."

"I'm sure he does, and I'm sad about it." Her voice was steady, but the churning feelings beneath were anything but. "I'm just... I can't explain what it's like to not trust your thoughts or your feelings, but that's how I feel right now. I need to sort through these emotions on my own...and I just... I feel...*uncomfortable*. It's not that I'm not grateful he was there, because I am. But there was violence, and I don't know how to explain it more than saying I need to think how I feel about what happened yesterday. I need to feel steady, and I don't feel that right now."

Aubrey and Charly exchanged a look, before Charly replied, "Take all the time you need."

"We're right here," Aubrey chimed in with a smile.

Willow smiled, but doubted it reached her eyes. "I know that too." She sighed heavily. The warmth from the coffee seeping into her skin as she looked across to Amie. "I can take you home to pack. And I'll drive you to the airport later."

Gratitude shimmered within Amie's eyes. "Thank you, Willow. That means a lot."

"Of course. I need to keep busy," Willow confessed, her gaze flitting between Aubrey and Charly. "Busy has always just been good for me. It helps me process."

Charly reached out, touching Willow's arm again. "We've got the bar. We'll clean up, get everything ready for opening later. Take the day off."

Aubrey nodded. "Yeah, leave that to us."

"Are you sure?" Willow asked.

"Positive," Charly confirmed, her gaze unwavering, and Aubrey simply nodded.

"Thank you." She couldn't understand the quiet in her mind, and that was the confusing part in all this. She couldn't tell if she felt mad, happy that he protected her, sad about the Christmas crafts, scared of the violence. She just felt...*nothing*. And that brought a discomfort she couldn't run from. "I'm going to take some time, sort through everything that's happened. But I won't shut myself away—I promise."

Aubrey reached out, squeezing Willow's hand. "That's all we ask. Take care of yourself, Wills. We're here if you need to talk."

Willow gave a little nod of thanks. "While I'm off today, I'm going to reach out to some of the craft stores and see if they'll make some more donations. Maybe do a social media post or something. We've got a few days, so hopefully we can make some of the crafts again."

"That's a great idea," Aubrey declared.

Amie interjected, "I'm sorry I won't be here to help."

"Don't be," Willow said, shifting against the cushions on the couch. "You need to take care of yourself right now. That's all that matters. Nothing else."

"She's right," Charly agreed, her nod decisive. "Although, I might not be much help. You know me and crafts don't get along."

Willow looked to Amie, who burst out laughing, and that, for a second, made Willow's heart warm.

Sixteen

Midafternoon, Eli followed the Timber Falls Ranch cowboys back to the ranch, their movements practiced and efficient despite the biting cold. Maia was feeling fresh with the wind running up behind her, her mane blowing wildly. With a roar that shattered the tranquil silence, one cowboy maneuvered a snowmobile, pulling a trailer that held the round bale of hay across the frosted landscape that they'd brought to the herd. A necessity during the winter's harsh months.

The frost-tinged air bit at Eli's cheeks, but he welcomed the sting, his thumping head not letting him forget he drank too much last night. The sun, high in the sky, created shadows and patterns on the snow that seemed to dance before his eyes. He took a deep breath, tasting the crispness of the air as he approached the edge of the ranch, his breath forming silver clouds that dissipated into the clear air. He'd gone out on the ride for peace and to clear his head, which he got neither of.

The coldness sank into his bones, but it was Willow's approaching figure that sent a shiver down his spine—a mix of anticipation and uncertainty. Her long hair cascaded down her back, catching sunbeams that seemed to thread gold through the strands. She was glowing warmth against the snowy pasture, and for a moment, Eli forgot the chaos in his head. The sight of her, stunning and vibrant, pierced through his gloom, offering a sliver of light in his darkness.

"Hey," she called out as he drew closer, a tentative smile gracing her lips.

"Hey." He dismounted and led Maia up to Decker, who waited by the stables. Maia huffed, her breath mingling with Eli's in the chilled air as he stroked her neck. "Mind taking her in for me?" he asked Decker.

"Nah, no problem," Decker said, giving Willow a quick smile before striding into the barn.

Eli turned to join Willow by the pasture, feeling the weight of his burdens ease fractionally with each step toward her. When he reached her, the sun bore down, enough to give some warmth and the barn blocked out the brutal, unforgiving wind.

He leaned against the fence, silence stretching out between them.

"I'm sorry I didn't call you last night," Willow said, staring out at the pasture. "I just… It was a lot to process, you know?"

He nodded. "Don't worry about it. I understood."

She turned to face him. Her gaze soft but distant. "I need you to know—I'm grateful for what you did. For protecting me against Buck."

That distance ate him up. "Willow, I—"

She shook her head, cutting him off. "And I know you, Eli. You're not violent. You were just… It had to remind you of what your sister went through. I understand that."

Words lodged in Eli's throat, a tangled mess of gratitude and regret. He wanted to tell her everything, lay bare his soul, but now was not the time. Instead, he let her words wash over him. "Thank you for seeing that," he said, his voice barely above a whisper.

She glanced to the horses off in the distance and sighed. "I've been trying to sort through my thoughts. After what happened with Buck… I'm a mess, if I'm being honest, and I don't even know why. My head is just jumbled, and I don't trust myself."

"It's hard, I'm sure," he admitted, "to see violence again. It must take you back too."

"It does." She wrapped her arms around herself, as if holding together the pieces of her composure. "I don't know if it's from the trauma, or what, but it's like my mind has gone silent. I don't feel anything, and I just feel like that can't be a good thing. I can't trust my judgement and sometimes not even my thoughts. So, I have to be really careful when this happens."

He nodded, a heavy sigh escaping him. "I understand I've got my own messes too. My sister…her murder… I have so much anger about that. When I saw Buck over you… I had no control, no thoughts."

"I'm sure you didn't—that's understandable," she whispered, her expression softening.

He met her gaze. "We're both a little broken, aren't we?"

"Seems like it," she said with a small, sad smile. "Maybe... maybe that's okay too. Maybe we just need to give ourselves permission to be a mess for a while."

"Maybe," he agreed.

She watched a few of the horses run from the barn back to the herd—Maia with them—before addressing him again, "I just hate how I'm feeling right now. I feel...weak."

"You're not weak, Willow," he said firmly. "You're anything but that."

She held his stare. "You're not either, no matter what you think that anger does to you."

Of course she understood him. He understood her too. "I'm sorry if my actions made you feel this way," he told her.

"It's not you," she said. "It's my trauma, and it's a battle that I will always have to face."

"I get that," Eli said. "I face a very similar battle."

She turned to him, wiped a tear off her cheek. "I know you do."

It took all his strength not to wipe those tears away. Not to take her into his arms and make them both feel better. But this was her battle to fight. And while, he felt relieved he hadn't hurt her by his anger, he didn't trust himself either. Not anymore. He needed to trust he could *think* when faced with a situation like that again, not see red and lose all control. And Willow couldn't help him do that. He needed to do that alone.

They fell into a silence as heavy as the snow that blanketed the ground around them; even the air seemed to hold its breath.

Willow finally broke the silence, and when she spoke again, her words were deliberate. "I've enjoyed spending time with you. I've *really* enjoyed the passion we share. I know we said our agreement was to New Year's Eve, but I just can't pretend anymore." She paused, met his gaze. "I can't pretend that I'm not ready for a relationship, no matter how much fun pretending was."

The suggestion struck him hard in the chest, but he couldn't deny the wisdom in her words. There was no going forward as it was. To deserve her, and be right with himself, he needed to fix his anger. "I care about you, Willow," he said, the statement laced with reluctance at letting her go. "That was never pretend for me."

She gave him a gentle smile. "I care about you too." Her chin quivered before she controlled it. "But we owe it to ourselves to heal completely. I'm not there, and I don't think you are either. To continue on like we are, or make anything official, will only become messy."

He bowed his head, breathing deep. He hated it, but knew she was right. "It's not a *never*, it's just a *no for right now*?" Lifting his gaze, he met her soft stare.

"Exactly."

His jaw clenched. Once. Twice. "All right," Eli conceded, the agreement bitter on his tongue. "Back to just friends?" His question hung in the air.

"Friends," she affirmed, a small yet genuine smile gracing her lips.

He felt the twinge in his chest. He didn't want this, not truly, but he knew this was best. Perhaps he'd hoped he could have controlled everything to make this work and thought she'd see how great they were together, but the reality was glaring him in the face. He couldn't.

Too much history. Too much pain.

"Remember, this isn't goodbye," she said, tears welling in her eyes. "It's just...see you around."

"See you around," Eli echoed, forcing a smile offering comfort despite the heaviness of his heart.

Seventeen

Willow paused at the threshold of her therapist's office located in the lower floor of a charming light blue one-story house on Meadowood Lane, a five-minute walk from the bar. Therapy sessions had once been etched into her calendar every four days, but now they were sporadic—only when she felt she needed them.

Outside on the porch with the bright yellow front door, she inhaled deeply, drawing in the crisp mountain air as if it could steady the unease in her chest. With a breath that was more determination than calm, Willow pushed open the door and stepped inside.

"Willow," greeted Dr. Thorne, her voice a warm blanket wrapping around Willow. Her smile was kind. Her colorful glasses as unique as her pale blue eyes. Dr. Thorne was around her mother's age, and Willow had felt immediately safe with her.

"Morning," Willow replied, her voice steadier than she

felt. She shed her jacket and scarf, placing them on the hook by the door.

"Come in—make yourself comfortable," Dr. Thorne offered, gesturing toward the plush couch, while she sat in a wing-backed light pink chair.

As Willow sank into the cushions, she said, "Thank you for seeing me."

"Anytime, Willow," Dr. Thorne said, her eyes reflecting a depth of empathy. "Why don't you start with what's been going on lately?"

So, she did.

Willow explained about Eli and his past, the kiss all those months ago and everything that had followed. Her fingers traced the edge of the plush throw pillow as she spilled her heart out in that room.

Across from her, Dr. Thorne did what she did best, she listened.

"Being with Eli," Willow said, "it was like discovering a part of myself I'd forgotten—or maybe never knew existed. With him, laughter came effortlessly, and moments felt… full, alive."

Dr. Thorne nodded. "It sounds like he brought a great deal of joy into your life."

"He did," Willow said, allowing herself a small smile at the memory. "I know it was all for pretend, but then it wasn't, and I was happy."

"Was there a specific moment that stands out to you as the best?" Dr. Thorne asked.

"I guess it being Christmas right now has helped," Willow answered. "The bar's all decorated, so full of life, and festive cheer."

"Sounds magical," Dr. Thorne murmured.

"It was," Willow affirmed, before that day came back to her mind. "Until Buck stormed into the bar, drunk and belligerent."

She paused, her heart hitching as she relived the terror that had gripped her when Buck's hands shoved against her, the force of his anger palpable.

"Go on," Dr. Thorne urged softly.

"His eyes were wild, unfocused," Willow recounted, as she wrapped her arms around herself. "He went after Amie, and I tried to intervene. That's when he pushed me, hard, and I fell to the floor."

In the silence that followed, Willow could almost hear the echo of the impact.

"Then Eli…" She trailed off, the protective fury in his intense eyes filling her mind. "Eli didn't hesitate. He lunged at Buck, fists flying. It was chaos. Our Christmas decorations— the ones we had all worked on together to raise money for the shelter—were ruined. Ornaments shattered, wreaths broken— everything we created was destroyed."

"Must have been devastating to see something you cherished so deeply come apart like that," Dr. Thorne observed.

"Very devastating," Willow admitted, a single tear breaking free to trace a path down her cheek. "But I also saw Eli defend us without a second thought, even if I know it came from his own personal demons."

"You liked seeing him protect?" Dr. Thorne said, leaning in slightly.

Willow nodded. "I've always felt safe with him." She drew in a long, deep breath before she continued, "But right after, when the chaos was over, it felt like my brain just…shut off. Everything went blank. And now it's like I'm frozen, standing outside of myself, watching everything happen around me. It's like I'm proud of Eli, and totally understand where his anger came from, but I just feel…empty. And I don't think it's fair to bring someone into that, you know?"

Dr. Thorne folded her hands in her lap. "That sounds incredibly difficult, Willow. Shutting down is a response to stress that many people experience. When you feel overwhelmed or threatened, your mind is trying to protect you. It's a survival mechanism that you had to use to endure what happened with Niko."

"Is it really?" Willow asked.

"Yes, it's a very common response," Dr. Thorne affirmed. "In those moments, your body decides that the best course of action is to conserve energy and minimize potential harm. It's an instinctive, automatic reaction that you've developed over time."

"So, I'm not broken?" Her voice hitched.

"Far from it," Dr. Thorne said warmly with a gentle smile. "Your reactions have been a form of self-protection. Now we work toward understanding them better, so you can start to feel more in control when they happen."

Tears began to pool in Willow's eyes, the realization washing over her. The walls she had built, brick by emotional brick, weren't necessary shields any longer. They were remnants of a past self who had to put them up to protect herself.

"Though it is okay to start working on letting those walls down again," Dr. Thorne said gently. "You're safe here." Her voice was a soft hum, comforting and familiar. "Let yourself feel whatever it is that's trying to surface."

The tears flowed over, and a sob caught in her throat.

"Embrace what you feel," Dr. Thorne encouraged, handing her a box of tissues. "It's the path to healing."

Willow dabbed at her eyes. She hesitated, her thoughts snagging on Eli—Eli with his piercing eyes that seemed to see right through her defenses. Eli, who always seemed intent on protecting her. His touch that made her feel so safe and alive again.

"I don't know what to do about Eli," Willow confessed. "We have this...connection. It's sweet and wonderful and— if I'm honest, it scares me." She dabbed at her cheeks with the tissue. "It's like when this happened with Buck, I just felt weak all over again, and told him we need space."

"Because you're afraid of getting hurt?" Dr. Thorne prompted.

"Partly," Willow admitted, playing with the tissue in her hand. "But also, because I do care for him. I realize now how pretending was just a way to experience him with all the safety nets. I want that closeness, that realness he offers. It's just—" She paused, her sob breaking, "I'm scared of losing myself again. Of disappearing into someone else's shadow."

"Your fears are valid, of course they are, Willow. But remember," Dr. Thorne said with gentle firmness, "you've emerged from that shadow. You're standing in your own light now, even if it doesn't always feel that way."

Willow absorbed the words, letting them seep into all the broken parts of her heart.

"None of this is easy," Dr. Thorne began. "Healing isn't linear. It weaves through our lives at its own pace. You've taken incredible strides, but it's okay to take your time to understand what you're feeling. And if Eli truly cares about you, he will understand this."

"Okay," Willow said with a sniff.

Dr. Thorne smiled gently. "It's okay to be unsure, to have days where you feel like you're moving backward. It feels uncomfortable in this state that you're in because of what happened with Niko. It's all part of the process. What's important is that you prioritize yourself, your well-being."

"Can I...just let things unfold?" she asked.

"Absolutely," Dr. Thorne assured her. "You don't have to rush or force answers. They will come to you in time, and you'll know what to do when they do. Just let yourself breathe, Willow."

Inhaling deeply, she let the air fill her lungs, let it reach the deepest parts of her where fear and hope danced. There was a release in the exhale, letting it all go, feeling lighter, freer.

"Let things be," she said aloud, tasting those words. It was so easy to forget she didn't have to have all the answers to her trauma and how to move forward.

"Let things be," Dr. Thorne repeated with a kind smile. "And don't forget, you are doing the work and strengthening your soul because of it. You have the power to shape your own future. It's in your hands, not anyone else's. You've already taken back so much of what was wrongfully claimed from you."

The air around Willow seemed to shimmer as she took in the truth of those words. *I have the power to shape my own future.*

Eli's grip tightened on the reins as he led the new colt he was training back to the paddock, the horse's hooves crunching against the snow. The sun hung low, casting a golden glow over the ranch, but the beauty of the afternoon couldn't ease the turmoil churning inside him. Thoughts of Willow spiraled through his mind, fierce and unbidden, threatening to break wide open.

He could feel her in every part of him—her laughter echoing in his ears, her warm eyes haunting his dreams. But with those thoughts came the reality, sharp and relentless. He was a man who had ridden bulls, faced down danger without a second thought, yet the idea of hurting Willow left him feeling unsure in his steps forward.

"Eli," Jaxon called out as he and Gunner approached, his eyes narrowing with concern. "You look like you've just gone ten rounds with a grizzly."

"Feels like it too," Eli muttered, releasing the horse into the paddock. He watched the colt trot away before turning to face his friends. Jaxon leaned against the fence, while Gunner stood beside him.

"Talk to us, man," Gunner urged, his voice laced with a seriousness that belied his usual easy grin. "We heard Willow came by."

"She did," Eli countered, his jaw set. "We're taking a step back. We both know neither of us was ready for anything beyond a fake relationship. Just can't avoid that anymore."

Jaxon frowned. "It's pretty clear to everyone you two are the real deal."

"Maybe we are. Maybe we're not," Eli said, "But there's a reason I've been single, and that reason is glaringly obvious now. The last thing I want to do is hurt Willow because I don't have my shit together. She *deserves* to be with someone solid."

Neither of them could argue with that.

Though Gunner just said, "I know you're going through it, but don't let your fears rob you both of something real."

Eli looked between his two friends, their faces earnest and supportive. They were right, of course—he knew it deep down. Willow had somehow breached the walls around his heart, and now the thought of losing what they had was unbearable.

But what did that change?

Not a damn thing.

"I need to head to the hardware store," he said, avoiding the topic altogether.

They both shook their heads at him but stayed silent.

Eli made his way to his truck, the sound a steady reminder that he was walking away from more than just the ranch. His friends' words echoed in his mind, but it was the memory of Willow's smile, the one that shined with her incredible heart, that clenched his heart with an iron grip.

He climbed into the truck, determined to get his mind on something else. The hardware store had always been his refuge. He had some projects he needed to work on at the house—and working with his hands always quieted his mind.

The drive was short, too short for Eli's liking, and before he knew it, he was pulling up to an open parking spot in front of The Book Bean. It wasn't part of the original plan, but the thought of warm coffee sliding down his throat, bitter and strong, was too tempting to ignore.

Stepping inside, the café enveloped him in its cozy embrace. The scent of freshly ground coffee beans hit him first. Soft murmurs of conversation played background to the gentle clink of porcelain. The warmth of the room, filled with rustic bookshelves and worn leather armchairs, welcomed him.

The owner of the café, Isabella, gave him a wave as she brewed a cappuccino. He knew her from high school, when she dated Jaxon.

He waved back. "Black coffee, please," he ordered, his voice rougher than he intended.

The barista nodded and went about preparing his drink.

When she returned with his coffee, Eli found a secluded corner. He settled into the chair, leaving his coat on. Not planning to stay long, he took his cell from his pocket to respond to the emails he heard dinging in his inbox on the drive. Emails from potential horse buyers awaited his attention.

As he typed responses, he sipped the scalding liquid, welcoming the burn, when the chime above the door sang out. Eli's thumb was still over his phone as a gust of laughter and conversation swept through the room. The Empowerment Elves ladies filtered in with a flutter of excitement, their hands filled with bags of yarn, felt and an array of colorful craft supplies.

"Isabella!" Willow's voice, clear and bright, cut through the hum of the café. "How's the little one?"

"Growing faster than a weed," replied Isabella, her warm brown eyes crinkling at the corners. A child that Jaxon had helped birth on the side of the road when Isabella and her husband couldn't make it to the hospital on time.

"That's so great," Willow said. "Thanks again for your coffee donations for the Christmas market. We've got them all bundled up with ribbon and bells. They look great."

"Wonderful news," Isabella said. "I'm so pleased. I heard there was an incident at the bar. Are you all okay?"

"We're all good now," Willow said. "We're just busy trying to fix some of the crafts that got damaged before the market."

Conversation soon turned into orders, and then the group began leaving the coffee shop.

As Willow turned, her gaze landed on Eli, her eyes widening before her face transformed into her sweet, gentle smile. She raised her hand in a wave, and time slowed, every second feeling like a minute longer.

Eli felt his chest tighten, the sight of her like a punch to his gut—a mixture of elation and dread. He acknowledged her with a nod, the corners of his mouth lifting in a faint smile that he could not truly feel. The warmth that radiated from their connection seared through him, even as he realized the coldness of the distance between them.

And damn it all, he hated that he might be losing the best thing to ever happen to him.

"Come on, Willow," someone called, drawing her attention back to the group, but not before Eli caught the flicker of something unsaid in her eyes—something that made him wish he could cross that distance in one stride and never look back.

But then she was gone.

As the hum of the Christmas craft support group faded as they left the café, Eli tried to refocus on his screen, to lose himself in the mundane task of responding to emails. But the words blurred, his hand shaking.

The chime of the door signaled someone's arrival. Betty, with her gentle demeanor and knowing eyes, stepped back into the café, her hands patting down her jacket pockets. "Oh, fiddlesticks," she muttered under her breath, scanning the area until her gaze landed on the forgotten gloves resting on the counter.

Eli watched as she retrieved them. Then, unexpectedly, her path veered toward him. "Eli, dear, I don't suppose you could do me a favor?" she asked.

"Of course, Betty," he said. "What do you need?"

"Could you give me a ride the day after tomorrow? Around 10:00 in the morning? I'll meet you here." She clasped her gloves to her chest, a hopeful tilt to her head.

"Sure, I can do that. But where to?" Eli asked, his curiosity piqued, not just by her request but also by the twinkle of mischief he thought he saw dancing in her eyes.

"Just a little errand in town. I'll explain everything on the way," she assured him, her smile mischievous.

"All right. I will see you then," Eli said, though he couldn't shake the feeling that Betty's simple request wasn't all what it seemed to be.

Eighteen

Willow was awakened the next day to Charly and Aubrey jumping on her bed with a *plan*. Which led her to exiting the car after a thirty-minute drive, her breath frosted in the crisp air. Charly and Aubrey flanked her, their smiles bright under the farm's twinkling Christmas lights. The trio approached the barn, a rustic haven transformed into a cozy retreat for this morning's unconventional festivity: Christmas goat yoga.

"Isn't this exciting?" Aubrey beamed.

Charly nodded. "It's going to be so much fun, and these goats are supposed to be total stress relievers," she chimed, a soothing lilt to her voice that often calmed Willow's stormiest days.

The scent of pine and a hint of lavender greeted them as they entered, the space alive with the low hum of conversation and the occasional bleat of a goat. Overhead heaters radiated warmth, inviting them deeper into the heart of the barn where mats were laid out in neat rows. Soft Christmas music melded with the sound of laughter, creating an atmosphere that was at once festive and serene.

"This place is legit adorable," Willow said, her gaze sweeping over the space. Twinkling lights adorned the wooden beams above, and the air was subtly infused with essential oils that promised relaxation. Yet, despite the allure, Willow felt an undercurrent of apprehension, a tightness in her chest that had little to do with the playful antics of the goats milling about.

As Charly and Aubrey chatted with a few regulars from The Naked Moose, Willow took a deep breath, trying to let the peaceful ambience seep into her bones. She settled onto a mat, catching sight of a couple laughing softly together as a kid goat nibbled at the edge of their mat. Eli's face flashed in her mind—the curve of his smile, the depth of his eyes— and Willow's heart squeezed painfully—confusingly.

"Hey, you okay?" Aubrey's voice broken through her thoughts, as she dropped down onto the mat next to her.

"Y-yeah, just...taking it all in," Willow managed, forcing a smile that didn't feel honest.

"Remember to breathe," Charly added gently, taking the mat on the other side of Willow. "This is about healing, about being present. Let the rest fade away, even if just for this morning."

Nodding, Willow exhaled slowly, trying to silence her mind.

The yoga instructor's serene voice soon flowed through the space, a soothing balm against the backdrop of twinkling Christmas lights strung around the barn. "Let's transition into

Child's Pose," she coaxed, and the group followed her lead, their movements a harmonious dance of limbs and breath.

"Remember," she continued, her tone infused with warmth, "each pose is a conversation between mind, body and spirit. Listen to what they're telling you."

Willow eased onto her feet, pressing the palms of her hands against the soft mat as she surrendered to the stretch. She felt her heartbeat slow, her muscles relax, and for a fleeting moment, the world outside the gentle stretches ceased to exist.

"Willow, your goat is doing the Downward Dog better than you," Aubrey quipped, breaking the silence with her infectious laughter.

Startled out of the relaxation, Willow lifted her head to see a small goat mimicking her pose with an almost comical seriousness. The sight was so absurd, so unexpected, that Willow couldn't help but join in the laughter.

"Looks like you've got yourself a yoga buddy," Charly chimed in, amusement lighting up her eyes as she smoothly transitioned into the next pose.

Willow chuckled, feeling the tiny hooves as the goat jumped onto her back. "Does that mean I'm done for the day?" she asked with a smirk. The small creature bleated in response, content to remain perched on its newfound human platform.

"Let's move into Warrior II," the instructor directed, her voice rhythmic and soothing like a gentle stream.

Feeling the peace of the stretches, Willow rose, the goat hopping off with graceful agility. She spread her legs wide, arms extended, feeling the strength and resilience of her own body.

Charly and Aubrey mirrored her stance, their breaths synchronized in the collective effort. But the goats, emboldened by the open energy, saw an opportunity for play. One particularly spirited kid bounded toward Charly, nudging her leg with its soft head, causing her to wobble and let out a surprised yelp, which only encouraged the animal further.

"Hey, no fair!" Charly laughed, trying to maintain her pose as the goat enthusiastically headbutted her thigh again, looking for attention.

Aubrey was faring no better; a pair of twin goats had taken an interest in her feet, nibbling on them as if convinced they were hay. "Ouch, okay, that's my toes, not a snack," she scolded them playfully, her laughter mingling with the soft jingles of Christmas music.

"All right, everyone, let's acknowledge our furry little helpers and find our way to a seated position," the instructor suggested, her voice laced with laughter as she observed the chaos unfolding around her.

As they settled onto their mats, cross-legged and still chuckling, the goats meandered between them, seeking out scratches and affection. Willow reached out to stroke one that approached, its coat warm under her fingers. In that moment, surrounded by friends and the innocent antics of the goats, Willow felt a surge of gratitude. Here, in this space of light-heartedness and connection, she could momentarily shed her armor of all the thoughts clogging up her mind.

"Deep inhale," the yoga instructor instructed. "And exhale all that does not serve you."

Willow closed her eyes, breathed out slowly, and allowed

herself to just be—one with her breath, her friends and the playful spirits of the goats.

The class came to a gentle end. The playful goats were back, nuzzling against their hands, looking for treats.

"Anyone up for some hot apple cider?" Aubrey suggested, her voice bubbling with enthusiasm.

"Definitely," Charly agreed, taking the lead toward the small counter where steaming mugs awaited.

Willow followed, the spicy aroma of cinnamon mingling with the earthy scent of hay. They each took a mug.

"To friendship," Aubrey toasted, raising her mug.

"And to Christmas goats," Charly added with a giggle, clinking her mug against the others.

"And to being here, together," Willow concluded, finding truth in her own words. She took a long sip and set her mug down, watching as a mischievous goat, adorned with a tiny Santa hat, nudged Aubrey's side, seeking attention.

"Okay, spill," Charly said, her tone soft but insistent. "You've been miles away all morning. What's going on in that head of yours?"

The question hung in the air, mingling with the soft strums of "Silent Night" playing in the background. Willow hesitated. "I'm still just trying to get my thoughts together."

"That's okay. Take your time. You don't need to rush any of this," Aubrey said gently. "We've got you, okay? No matter what happens."

"Exactly," Charly chimed in, offering a supportive squeeze to Willow's shoulder. "You're not in this alone, and you never will be."

The words seemed to wrap around Willow like a warm blanket, their truth sinking into her skin. "I know I can be...a lot," she whispered, feeling the vulnerability sliding through her veins.

"Everyone's 'a lot' in their own way," Aubrey said with a chuckle that held no judgement, only affection. "And we love every bit of your 'a lot,' Wills."

"Besides," Charly added with a knowing smile, "being 'a lot' means you have that much more to offer. Your heart is huge, which can sometimes be emotional, and that's not something to ever apologize for. It's the most wonderful thing about you."

Willow looked from one friend to the other, their faces alight with earnestness and care. A small laugh bubbled up inside her chest, surprising her with its lightness. "I love you both so much."

"We love you too," Charly said.

"Always will," Aubrey agreed.

Willow leaned into their warm embrace as they threw their arms around her, until a goat began nibbling on her ankle.

She glanced down and told it, "I'm not food."

It kept on nibbling.

Aubrey laughed. "I think it disagrees with you."

Out in front of his house, Eli stood at his table saw. With every deliberate movement, he sent sawdust spiraling into the frosty air, the rhythmic hum of the sander pulsating against the raw wood. It was a desperate attempt to silence the chaos in his mind. His hands knew their task, rough and steady as they glided over the planks, but his thoughts were elsewhere—entangled in a mess in his mind, lost in thoughts of Willow.

He wasn't sure what he was building. A bench? A table? A chair? It didn't matter. He needed to keep his hands moving, to somehow carve out a new purpose from the cedar beneath his fingers because nothing made sense anymore.

A sudden crunch of gravel broke through the monotony of his task, snagging his attention. Eli's hand stilled, the persistent drone of the sander falling silent as he straightened up, eyes narrowing with curiosity.

The old truck that came into view was familiar. It rumbled toward him, kicking up a cloud of dust in its wake, the sound growing louder as it approached. Eli wiped his hands on his jeans, the fabric stained with oil and sawdust.

He watched, rooted to the spot, as the vehicle rolled to a stop and the engine cut off. A brief silence fell, one that seemed to hold its breath, before the door creaked open. Eli's gaze followed the figure emerging from the truck.

Clay's boots crunched over the gravel as he ambled toward the house. "Hey, Eli," Clay called out, his voice raspy like gravel tumbling in a tin can. "Got a minute?"

Eli turned off the sander, its whirring protest ceasing abruptly as sawdust settled onto the snow-covered ground. "Hey," Eli acknowledged, with a nod. "How 'bout we crack open a cold one?" Clay always loved his beer.

"Thought you'd never ask." Clay chuckled.

Clay followed Eli up the porch steps, and Eli retrieved a couple of beers from the fridge, quickly returning outside.

With a flick of his wrist, Eli popped the caps off, the sound crisp and satisfying.

Clay took a long pull from the bottle before he said, "Remember that summer in Stone Creek? The whole circuit thought you were gonna be the next big thing."

"Feels like another lifetime," Eli replied. He took a swig, the bitter tang of hops lingering on his tongue.

"Sure does." Clay took a seat, the wood of the chair creaking under his weight. "But you rode like hellfire."

"I did, didn't I?" Eli mused softly, leaning against the post.

"Every damn time." Clay nodded, his gaze fixed on Eli. After a pause, he asked, "You ever think about getting back in the saddle? Back to the rodeo?"

Eli felt the question like a jolt, his heart thudding against his chest. There was a part of him, wild and untamed, that hungered for the roar of the crowd, the adrenaline surge of eight perilous seconds atop a beast made of muscle and fury. But there was another part, scarred and tender, that wouldn't leave Timber Falls again.

"I'm not interested in anything that takes me out of Timber Falls again," he admitted.

"I get that." Clay's words were simple, but they held a depth of understanding. He took another long gulp of his beer. Then he shifted in his seat, clearing his throat. "Ya know, Eli," he began, "I've been doing some thinking about my own sunset years."

Eli arched an eyebrow, a silent invitation for Clay to continue.

"I reckon I'm ready to hang up my spurs for good. The

wife wants to travel." Clay's gaze was steady, almost piercing, as he studied Eli's reaction.

Eli felt a surge of respect for the man before him, knowing full well the courage it took to step away from the life that had defined you. But it was the next words out of Clay's mouth that truly caught him off guard.

"I've been pondering over who could take the reins of teaching the young bull riders coming up. You ever thought about passing on your knowledge, Eli? Teaching bull riding at my ranch?"

Surprise jolted through Eli, sizzling down his spine and igniting something deep within him—a spark of possibility. He searched Clay's face, seeking any sign he was pulling his leg, but found none.

"Teaching, huh?" The idea rolled around in his mind.

"Yeah," Clay said, nodding slowly. "You've got a gift. And it ain't just staying on a bull. It's understanding them, reading them. Kids could learn a lot from you."

Eli let out a breath he hadn't known he was holding, feeling the weight of the decision already bearing down on him. "Appreciate the offer, Clay," Eli finally said, his voice gruff with emotion. "Means a lot, really. I've never considered myself much of a teacher, but..." He trailed off, unsure of how to articulate the thoughts and feelings swirling inside him.

"Take your time. No pressure." Clay's eyes twinkled with a mix of mischief and wisdom. "Just think it over and get back to me when you've decided."

"Thank you," Eli said, tipping his bottle in a salute. "I will."

Clay polished off his beer in three big gulps and belched, like he always did. He handed Eli the empty bottle and the corners of Clay's mouth twitched upward. "There's honor in shaping the future. Not just in living your own past."

Eli nodded, the truth of Clay's words seeping into him.

"Think on it." Clay waved, heading for his truck, like he hadn't just dropped a bomb on him.

It was a big decision, but then again, so was every ride he'd ever taken. And this one was tempting...

Nineteen

The next morning, Willow pressed a stamp onto a freshly inked Christmas card. They were fitting in crafts every minute they could now, hoping to restore some of what they'd lost. Empowerment Elves had returned to the bar—minus Amie—their hands just as busy, weaving ribbons and cutting paper to create new Christmas cards. The scrape of scissors against construction paper, the soft thump of rubber stamps and the murmurs of concentration soothed that worry in Willow's chest that they wouldn't bring enough to the shelter.

On top of that, her heart felt raw, something she was trying to avoid. She missed Eli. There was no ignoring that. She missed talking to him, laughing with him, experiencing life with him. And she missed his touch.

First, she needed to make the Christmas market successful for what it meant to the Empowerment Elves and Haley's Place. After that, she could let all the emotions that were slowly gnawing at her rise to the surface as the fog in her head began to clear.

"Two days," Willow said, glancing up at the group. "We've got two days to do as many crafts as we possibly can."

"We totally got this," Jenna, the owner of the diner, responded without missing a beat, her fingers deftly tying a bow.

She'd shown up today—apparently Charly and Aubrey had told her what happened with Buck, so she wanted to help where she could.

"I'm just so grateful to the stores who were willing to give more donations," Willow said. "Seriously, there's some really good people in this area."

"That's why I love it here," Lisa chimed in. "People are made of good stuff."

Willow allowed herself a small smile, feeling the pride too. They weren't just rebuilding the inventory for the Christmas market; they were showing Buck he didn't win. And damn, did that feel good.

Charly breezed through the door of The Naked Moose, arms embracing a cardboard box. As she set it down with an audible thud on the wooden table the contents inside clinked together.

"Got some more donations from the folks over at Timber Falls Goods," Charly announced. "Seems everyone's happy to pitch in."

Willow wiped her hands on her apron, flecks of glitter falling away, and moved to help Charly unpack. "You're amazing, you know that? Thank you so much for driving around for me."

"We're in this together," Charly replied. "Besides, it's better me driving around than actually making the crafts."

Willow shook her head at Charly. She almost couldn't believe how many good things had happened today. They needed this win.

"Speaking of being in this together," Betty interjected, her voice tender yet tinged with concern as she added a little bell to her cardstock, "how's Amie doing?"

Willow paused, a card half-finished in her hand, and met Betty's gaze. "She's staying with family for a bit," she explained, keeping the whole truth to herself.

"Smart girl," Betty nodded, her eyes softening with empathy. "Sometimes the strongest thing you can do is allow yourself to be cared for by the people who love you."

"Gosh, do I ever know that," Willow agreed, taking more crafting items from the box. "She needs a safe space—to heal, to breathe."

"Strength comes in many forms," Betty stated. "And sometimes, it's found in the quietest of places."

"Like here," Willow murmured, motioning to the room filled with friends and laughter, with hands busy at work.

"Like here," Betty affirmed, a smile touching the corners of her lips.

Willow finished emptying the box and then returned to her seat and her card. She slid ribbon through the punched hole of the Christmas card, her fingers dancing nimbly over the sparkling paper.

"Willow, dear, I've been meaning to say," Betty began, "how much I admire Eli's protective nature. I can't even imagine what would have happened if he had not arrived just in time."

Willow paused, the ribbon slipping from her grasp as she raised her gaze to meet Betty's. Right, they hadn't told anyone they were *fake* dating. She couldn't mentally handle that load right now. "Yes, he's very protective."

"Reminds me of my Henry," Betty said with a nostalgic sigh. She plucked up a crimson card and ran her thumb over its edge before setting it aside. "He wasn't a man given to violence, mind you. But there was this one time..."

Willow's curiosity piqued at the mischievous glint sparking in Betty's eyes. "Don't stop now. What happened," she urged gently.

"We were at a barn dance, many moons ago," Betty recounted, her hands pausing over her craft. "I was fetching us a couple of sodas when this slick-haired man thought it wise to pinch my bottom."

Willow snorted a laugh. "You are kidding?"

"Oh, it's hard to believe now, but the men did love me back then," Betty said with an easy grin.

"Of course they loved you," Willow countered. "You're a beauty and have got spunk."

Betty laughed softly. "Well, maybe, but didn't Henry see red?" Her gaze grew distant, lost in the memory. "He was like a bull with a matador. He strode right over, calm as you please, tapped the man on the shoulder, and when he turned..." She mimed a swift punch with her fist. "Broke his nose clean."

"Betty!" Willow exclaimed, laughter spilling out around

the table. "From what you've said of him, I'm surprised he'd do such a thing."

"Only when it came to protecting his family, dear. That man loved us fiercely," Betty said, her tone turning tender. "And never raised a hand otherwise. Or his voice for that matter."

Willow watched the love wash across Betty's face. "You must miss him so much," she said.

"I do miss him, dearly," Belly replied. "But I also feel very lucky that I was loved by someone so intently that they'd break another man's nose for not treating me right."

"That's very sweet, Betty," Willow said softly, her heart feeling lighter.

"Oh, yes, our love story was very sweet," Betty replied, reaching across the table to give Willow's hand a reassuring squeeze. "Just remember, my dear, that some men, they deserve a good knock to the teeth to teach them a lesson they need to learn."

"Don't I know that," Willow agreed.

Betty held Willow's stare in that knowing way she always did. "You deserve a love story like I had with Henry," Betty said, drawing Willow's gaze again. "One that fills you up and leaves lasting wonderful memories."

Willow remembered a time where she dreamed of a love like Betty and Henry had. One that included marriage, kids and a happy life like her parents shared. Niko stole that from her. But staring at Betty and her wisdom, she began to realize that Niko was still winning because she wasn't allowing love to grow where it should.

And there was someone she could have that kind of magical love with...

"Dear Lord, I am terrible at this," Charly said, holding up a card adorned with a clumsy, endearing attempt at a reindeer. "I think I should stick to serving drinks rather than crafting."

"It's perfect," Willow said.

Charly stared at her dead serious. "No one will buy this, Willow."

Aubrey called from behind the bar, "One person will."

Charly spun in her seat, glancing over her shoulder. "Yeah, who?"

"Jaxon, because he loves you." Aubrey grinned.

Laughter rippled through the bar, and around the table, and the sound of laughter once again filling the bar brought warmth to Willow, erasing the remaining chill that Buck had caused.

At precisely ten o'clock in the morning, Eli spotted Betty standing next to a snow-covered wrought iron bench outside the coffee shop. He slowed his truck and pulled over next to her, and was out a moment later, joining her on the sidewalk.

"Morning, Eli," she greeted him with a smile that crinkled the corners of her eyes.

"Betty," he nodded, pushing open the door for her. He noticed the subtle determination etched in her movements as she got into his truck. "Where are we off too?" he asked.

"To the old church, across town." Her voice was firm, leaving little room for discussion.

"Sure thing," Eli replied, still not quite sure why he was

even there before joining her in the truck. He'd have expected Betty to ask Willow to take her. They often did things like this together but hadn't been because of the upcoming Christmas market.

The drive was silent, filled only with the hum of the engine and the quiet country music coming through his speakers, only making him more curious. As he neared the corner of the road, the old church emerged, standing tall and majestic against the clear blue sky. Its stone walls bore the marks of time, but the stained glass windows were stunningly flawless.

"Beautiful, isn't it?" Betty's voice broke the silence.

"Gorgeous," Eli agreed, pulling into the gravel lot beside the church.

He killed the engine, as Betty said, "Let's head inside."

Eli glanced sideways at her. "You need help going in there?"

"Gosh, these old bones ain't what they used to be," she declared.

Eli lifted his eyebrows at her. "Betty, you don't have a fragile bone in your body." He knew better than to buy into her charade; Betty was sprightlier than most women half her age.

"Ah, but I do love the gallantry," she quipped.

Obviously not taking no for an answer, he shook his head, but jumped out and then opened her door, offering his arm to her.

She gave him a pat, with a sly smile.

They approached the arched entrance of the church, the heavy wooden door groaning open at Eli's touch. A myriad of colored light spilled through stained glass windows, casting a kaleidoscope across time-worn pews.

"Follow me," Betty said, pulling her arm from his.

He trailed behind her, as they headed down the stairs to the basement. A murmur of voices grew clearer. He hesitated on the final step, his gaze landing on the circle of chairs occupied by men and women of all ages.

Eli stayed at the doorway, but Betty took his hand, tugging him into chairs near the door, but not in the circle.

"John used to say cancer wouldn't beat him," a middle-aged woman recounted, her pain on her expression was raw, unfiltered. "But in the end, it took him away, and all I have left are memories."

Eli frowned, turning to Betty, saying quietly, "Why am I here, Betty?"

"Oh, my dear, this room..." Betty began, just as quiet, her gaze sweeping over the assembly of somber faces, "holds a key to happiness." She paused, glancing back to him, and leaning in to keep the conversation private. "Time," she continued, "is our most precious gift. We're given moments, mere moments to hold, to cherish. Every second is a treasure. And it's up to us, the living, to honor those seconds, to weave them into a beautiful life."

Eli couldn't move, couldn't breathe, couldn't do anything but listen to her.

"See," she began, "people handle grief in so many ways." She motioned toward a man who sat hunched over, his hands clenched tightly around a photograph. "Some folks, they cling to their pain, afraid that letting go means forgetting."

He looked in the same direction she was looking, noticing the rigidity in the man's stance and the way his knuckles turned white as he gripped the picture frame. Eli could feel a similar tension within himself, holding on tightly to memories he never wanted to lose.

"Then there are others," Betty continued softly, "like me, who choose gratitude." Her eyes danced with an inner light. "I'm grateful for every laugh, every moment of love I had with my Henry. It doesn't make the loss any smaller, but it makes the life we shared so much bigger." She looked around the room. "I come here, not to grieve, but to remember this important lesson. That I was lucky to have had true love at all. That I won't tarnish its memory allowing my pain to consume me."

Eli felt the room shrink down to just the two of them.

"Living in the now—that's what's important." She reached out, her hand resting lightly on his forearm. "You can hold on to the anger, the loss, or keep moving forward."

Her conviction, so fierce and yet so tender, stirred something within him. A longing for the kind of peace she described, for the ability to see beyond the pain, the anger, the loss. To only remember the happy times.

"Gratitude," she said, the word hanging between them, "for the time given, for the love shared... That's what keeps us whole."

"Betty," he began, his voice hoarse with emotion, "I've been..." He paused, struggling to find the right words.

"I know," she replied softly. "Sometimes there aren't words to explain how we feel." Her hand squeezed his arm tighter. "But I saw the way you looked at Willow in the coffee shop day before yesterday. I know that love because Henry looked at me like that." She patted his arm. "Don't waste that love."

As the session wound down, the group members rose from their seats, exchanging hugs and quiet words of encouragement.

"Time to go," Betty said, standing up and smoothing the fabric of her pants. She turned to him. "Before you drive me to the bar to do more crafts, there's one more thing." Her eyes twinkled. "My husband was the sweetest, kindest man alive—so long as no one touched his family. You touched someone he loved, and you paid for it. Not from anger. Not from trauma. But because sometimes people need to learn not to touch something that doesn't belong to them." Her gaze scanned over his face, and she smiled sweetly. "You remind me of my Henry, you know. That same fierce loyalty, that protective streak. That's not a fault, Eli. That's simply a man that loves his family."

Eli felt a smile tug at the corner of his mouth, an unfamiliar warmth spreading through his chest. "Thank you, Betty, for the reminder," he said, meaning it more than he could express. Somehow, within her words, he felt like he'd just received some good hard motherly advice that he should listen too.

"You're welcome," she said, patting his arm. "And now, you need to figure out how to make everything all right again and clean this whole mess with Willow up."

Eli couldn't help himself. He chuckled, now realizing he should have expected Betty to firmly plant herself in his business. "Yes, ma'am."

Twenty

"Looks like the North Pole threw up in here—in the best way," Willow muttered to herself late into the afternoon, a chuckle escaping her as she pictured the bustling Christmas market that would soon fill the bar tomorrow. From corner to corner, decorations were everywhere in the bar and Charly was finishing putting the ornaments on the Christmas tree on the stage.

"It's perfect," Aubrey said, glancing around the bar.

"Maybe a bit much," Charly agreed. "But hey, can you really overdue Christmas?"

"I don't think so," Willow said. "Especially considering outside looks even more festive than in here."

"There is that," Charly agreed.

Timber Falls went all out for the Christmas market. There were little wooden huts that were already brought in, and town workers were busy setting up Christmas lights, turning Main Street into a little Christmas Village.

A bang outside the window caught Willow's attention. She glanced through the frosted window, her heart catching in her throat as a familiar person came into view. "They made it," she gasped, dashing to the door.

The cold nipped at her cheeks as she flung the door open, revealing love personified. "Mom! Dad!" she called.

Her parents' eyes sparkled.

"Willow, sweetheart!" Her mother's voice was a soothing melody that always seemed to make the world stand still. An inch shorter than Willow, she had the same hair color as Willow, but cut in a bob, and her bright blue eyes were as sunny and warm as ever. "And wow, look at the place. Christmas has definitely hit Timber Falls."

"What a lovely town this is," her father chimed in. He was a few inches taller than Willow and seemed to be aging backward. Fifty looked good on him. His blond hair, streaked with gray only made him more distinguished-looking.

"I'm so happy you're here." Willow sank into their arms, letting the familiar scent of home—a blend of her father's spicy cologne and the soft lavender her mother always wore—fill her senses.

"Thank you for coming," she said, her words were muffled against their shoulders. "Having you here for our first Christmas in Timber Falls means everything."

As they pulled back, Willow grabbed her mother's suitcase. "Let's head inside," she suggested. "I might even have your Christmas favorite—spiced whiskey, Dad."

"Lead the way, darling," her mother replied, slipping her arm through Willow's as they crossed the threshold.

Aubrey rushed forward, her smile wide. "Diane. Cliff!" She enveloped Willow's parents. "It's so good to see you."

Charly followed, wrapping them both in her arms when Aubrey backed away. "Did you have a good flight?" she asked.

Her father's eyes sparkled as he took in the bar, surveying the improvements. "Girls, this place—it's stunning," he murmured, running a hand over the smooth surface of the bar.

"Thank you," Willow said. "It took a lot of elbow grease, but every moment was worth it."

From the corner of her eye, she caught her mother's gaze lingering on her. The concern in those familiar eyes was unmistakable, and it tugged at Willow's heartstrings. She knew that look all too well—the gentle furrow in her brow, the slight tilt of her head—it was the silent language of maternal intuition.

"Mom?" Willow asked, faltering for a second as she met her mother's searching stare.

"Everything looks so beautiful, Willow," her mother reassured her, her words floating like a soothing melody. "You girls have really outdone yourselves."

"Really, you have," her father agreed, wrapping an arm around Willow's shoulders. "We're proud of you—all of you—and of the Empowerment Elves you've formed."

"Yes, so proud," her mother finished. They wandered past the handmade crafts that the group had managed to remake. It wasn't as much, not even by half, but it was something. "Are these all the crafts you'll sell?"

Willow nodded. "But it was more about the group that made all this so special."

Her parents exchanged a glance, their shared pride radiating.

"Darling, you've always had such a big heart," her mother said, reaching out to cup Willow's cheek tenderly. "And you've poured it all into this Christmas group. It's so wonderful."

"Nothing could make us happier than seeing you follow your dreams, especially after all you've endured," her father added, his voice steady and reassuring.

"Thank you," Willow whispered, allowing herself to lean into their love for a moment longer before she straightened her spine. "Come on, let me show you the rest of the bar."

Her parents followed, and Willow saw the way Charly and Aubrey were gushing over her parent's pride too.

By the time the tour was nearing its end, the Christmas music playing through the bar's speakers had her mother singing along. When they came out of the back into the bar, Willow spotted a most welcomed guest.

"Betty!" she exclaimed. "I'm so glad you're here."

"Couldn't stay away, could I?" Betty replied, her eyes crinkling with genuine affection as they embraced.

"Mom, Dad, this is Betty, who I've told you all about," Willow introduced. "She's been…well, she's been like my grandma away from home."

Her mother's gaze softened, "Betty, we've heard so much about you," she said, stepping forward. She offered Betty a warm embrace. "Thank you for being there for Willow when we couldn't be. Your kindness means the world to us."

"Only doing what any friend would do," Betty responded. "I cherish having Willow in my life."

"We're glad for it," her father said with a genuine smile. "It's much easier for us, with having Willow so far away, that she's here surrounded by wonderful people."

Betty smiled softly, glancing at Willow. "I'm quite certain we are the lucky ones."

Willow felt her heart grow three sizes. Her family was here. Her friends were here. But there was someone missing...and with each hour that had gone by, the more her mind cleared, and the more she missed him.

"Let me grab us some drinks," Willow said, hurrying behind the bar to pour some of her father's favorite spiced whiskey.

As Willow grabbed the whiskey bottle, her mother joined her at the bar. She leaned across the weathered wood of the counter, her eyes locking onto Willow's with intensity.

"Sweetheart," she began, her voice low and laced with concern, "is everything all right?"

Willow hesitated, the weight of unspoken thoughts suddenly heavy on her chest. The festive atmosphere around her faded into the background as she met her mother's gaze. "I'm okay," she said with a smile.

"Is it the market?" her mother prodded gently, reaching out to cover Willow's hand with her own.

"Partly," Willow admitted. "I'll tell you about it later, but there's a guy..."

Her mother's eyes widened. "A guy?"

"A really, really good guy," Willow said. "He's a very close friend of Charly's boyfriend, Jaxon."

"Ah," her mother breathed, nodding as if everything made

sense now. "I should have known that look on your face had something to do with love."

"Love?" Willow gasped, shaking her head. "No, it's not like that."

"Hmm," was her mother's reply.

"What does *hmm* mean?" Willow asked, beginning to pour the drinks.

Her mother gave her a stern look, took one of the half-full glasses and angled it toward Willow. "Sweetie, you know what *hmm* means. It means what it always has."

"That you don't believe me?" Willow offered.

With a knowing grin, her mother clanged her glass against the one Willow was holding and stated, "No, sweetheart, I don't."

Truth was, even Willow didn't believe herself.

Betty's words had stayed on Eli's mind all day. He knew listening to her was the best thing to do, and the only way for Eli to do that was to face something—someone—he had never wanted to face.

Coldness sank into his bones as he stepped into the stillness of the jail in Red Deer. The corridor stretched before him, dimly lit and narrow, walls closing in with each step he took. There was no turning back now, only forward, into the darkest place he'd gone yet. To stare into the eyes of a killer that shattered his family.

He passed by uniformed officers as he followed the correctional officer leading him toward the room.

And then he saw *him*—the bastard who had extinguished

the brightest light Eli had known growing up—seated on the other side of a glass partition, his posture rigid, yet indifferent. Wearing an orange jumpsuit, Johnny watched Eli's approach. His eyes were voids, empty of any semblance of human warmth or regret.

"Sit down," came the gruff instruction from a guard at Eli's side.

Eli took the seat across from Johnny, who had taken everything from him, the hard plastic chair offering no comfort. He'd met Johnny a dozen times over the years, whenever he'd come home, and he looked the same—dark eyes, scruffy beard, but seemed to have put on more muscle behind bars. Probably to survive, Eli wondered.

He picked up the phone receiver as did Johnny. Eli leaned forward, palm flat against the cool surface of the table. "Look at you," Eli said, his voice low. "Sitting there like you don't have a care in the world."

Johnny tilted his head slightly, a gesture so devoid of empathy. "Did you come here for closure, Eli?" Johnny asked, a smirk playing at the corner of his mouth. His tone was casual, as if discussing something as mundane as the weather, not the shattering loss of a life.

"Satisfaction," Eli corrected sharply. "I came here for satisfaction."

"Satisfaction?" Johnny snorted a laugh. "And what does that look like to you?"

"Seeing you sitting in this cage like the animal you are, unable to ever get out," Eli spat out.

"As if anything I do now changes what happened," Johnny said. "She's gone, and she's never coming back."

The callousness dripped from his words, thick and venomous. Eli felt the sting, the implication that his sister's life could be so easily dismissed, her memory reduced to nothingness by this hollow shell of a man.

"Her life mattered," Eli growled, slamming his hand down. "You took someone precious from this world, from me. You don't even have the decency to acknowledge that you did something horrific."

"An apology? Is that what you were looking for when you walked into this place?" Johnny's eyes, cold and dead, met Eli's. "You won't find that here. Regret is a useless emotion, something for the weak."

"Then you are weaker than any man I've ever known," Eli countered with a cool indifference. "Because it takes strength to feel, to understand the weight of your actions. You've got none."

Johnny simply shrugged.

Eli's heart pounded, the rhythm syncing with a pulsing desire for retribution. But vengeance wasn't his to claim—not in the way he wanted. The justice system had seen to that.

"The greatest revenge here is that you are locked away in a cell and this is your pathetic life now," Eli said, his words deliberate. He'd avoided this meeting, but he knew he couldn't put that off any longer. His rage only belonged to one person. His anger directed *here*, and no longer would he direct it at others. "But Miranda is free. Her memory changes lives for the better, gives to others, and her sweet soul is your burden to carry."

Eli leaned forward, a barrier between him and the man who had shattered his world. His gaze was unwavering, locked on Johnny's empty eyes. "You'll rot in here," he added. "Forgotten. And every second you're locked up is a moment you can't hurt anyone else. That's all the satisfaction I need."

Johnny's lips twitched into a semblance of a smirk, but Eli found his heart unclenching with each breath. He'd carried this anger with him for too long. He'd directed it at Buck because he hadn't said his piece to the one man who deserved it.

He'd never spoken a victim impact statement. His mother had. But this was his moment to share his truth.

After this day, he'd do what Miranda would want him to do. He'd forget this evil, and he'd live in the light.

Eli stood, his chair scraping back. "You think you won because she's gone. But you forfeited your life. You have no authority, no choices, no control. And *that* is the ultimate punishment you could receive." He leaned in, chuckling in Johnny's face. "Enjoy wasting away in here with your only power being when you take a shit."

Johnny snarled, the dig hitting the mark.

Eli didn't look back as he walked away, each step deliberate and sure. The heavy metal doors clanged shut behind him, resonating deep within his bones. Every step he'd take forward would follow Betty's advice—live for the now. Create the life he wanted, not the one stolen from him.

Live the life Miranda would want for him. The life his mother would hope he'd have.

Stepping out into the night, the cold air embraced him, a sharp contrast to the stifled atmosphere in the jail. Eli wrapped his jacket tighter around himself. As he walked back toward his truck, thoughts of Willow crept into his mind—sweetness, resilience, passion. She, too, had known darkness, yet she emerged not hardened, but more compassionate, her spirit undimmed, seeking to help others. In her, he saw a reflection of what he aspired to be, of what he could be if he let go the rest of what he was holding on to.

Once back in his truck, he reached into the pocket of his jacket and retrieved his phone. His thumb hovered, then pressed with purpose.

"Jaxon," he said when the call connected, "get Gunner and meet me at my place in an hour."

Jaxon's response crackled through the line, "We'll be there."

Eli ended the call, slipping the phone back into his pocket, and hit the road. As the distance closed between himself and his house, he felt the weight of the past beginning to lift. He'd never forget what happened. He *couldn't* forget. The trauma was there, always, but he had to walk past it. Because as much as Willow deserved peace, so did he.

Forty-five minutes later, he drove up his snowy driveway, finding Jaxon and Gunner were already waiting for him.

"Hey," Jaxon greeted him the moment Eli got out of his truck, welcomed by a frigid breeze.

"Thanks for coming," Eli said, approaching his porch steps.

Gunner asked, "What's going on?"

"Let's get inside," Eli said, trotting up the stairs. "I need a drink."

They followed him, and he poured them all a glass of whiskey, before heading to the living room.

"I went to visit Johnny," he stated, met by a stunned silence.

Jaxon and Eli settled onto the worn-out couch, their combined weight causing the cushions to sink. Gunner took a seat across from them. He recounted his trip to the jail, Betty's intervention the day before, and everything else that had happened. And he also mentioned Clay's offer for him to become a coach.

A tense silence filled the room as unspoken questions hung in the air and decisions loomed over all of them.

Then Jaxon spoke up. "I know I value your help at the ranch, but teaching kids how to ride bulls is an opportunity you can't pass up."

Eli took another sip of whiskey, feeling the burn travel down his throat, and nodded. "It's definitely an interesting offer, but there's something I need to do first."

Gunner tilted his head. "What is it?"

"I have to show Willow that stepping back isn't the right choice," Eli explained to his friends. "Instead, we should be stepping closer together."

Jaxon raised his glass in agreement. "Now that's what I'm talking about."

Gunner flashed a wide grin. "What do you need us to do?"

Eli's smile matched his, feeling like a weight on his mind had been lifted. "Round up all the cowboys and their significant others. We've got some serious work to do."

Twenty-One

Willow had never seen Timber Falls so lit up. Main Street had been closed off since yesterday, and on the street now were little wooden huts. The Christmas market was a feast for the eyes, with vibrant twinkling lights strung across the road and a giant sparkling Christmas tree at the center of the square. The huts were adorned with colorful decorations, from snowmen to reindeer, and filled with an array of gifts and treats. With the snow-covered mountains standing tall behind, the town had never looked so magical, making the legend seem all too real tonight.

"Charly, try not to give away all the mulled wine," Aubrey said with a laugh, "we're trying to make money." They were set up outside The Naked Moose, pouring steaming cups of mulled wine for chilled customers.

"Hey now, a little holiday cheer never hurt anyone," Charly shot back, winking at Willow.

With every transaction throughout the day now leading

into the night, and with every shared smile and laugh, the sense of community thickened, wrapping around Willow like a warm blanket on a cold winter's night. Charly, with her nurturing calm, handed out cups of mulled wine, her laughter mingling with the music. Aubrey's infectious energy was a beacon, drawing more onlookers to taste the mulled wine themselves.

Willow's breath misted in the frosty air as she took in the bustling Christmas market. Further down, a brass band and carolers played Christmas songs, where a crowd gathered and were dancing. Aromas of roasted chestnuts and freshly baked gingerbread wafted through the wintry atmosphere, mingling with the scent of pine from the rows of decorated trees.

After months of planning and hard work, they had finally made it.

"Done," Betty exclaimed, placing the last Christmas card on display. "It looks wonderful!" She looked around at the Empowerment Elves group who had all gathered to help set up. "Just look at what we've created together. It's truly special."

Joanne smiled and yet there was a little sadness in her eyes too. "I wish Amie could see this."

"Me too," Willow agreed, stepping away from the booth. "Let's take a photo together. I'll post it on social media and tag her so she knows we're thinking of her."

They all quickly squeezed in for the photo, with Willow asking a passerby to take it for them.

"It's perfect," Willow said proudly, showing everyone the photo to big smiles all around. She quickly posted it on the bar's social media accounts, tagging everyone in the group who had given their consent, and also including Amie. "Now go enjoy the market," she said, tucking her phone back into her pocket, "I'll take care of the booth."

"I'll come back in an hour or so to give you a break," Lisa said.

"That would be great, thank you," Willow replied gratefully as she hugged each one of them before they went off to explore the market.

Betty leaned in closer, her wise eyes twinkling as bright as the Christmas lights around the booth. "Look at their smiles, dear. It's an amazing thing what the group has given them, isn't it?"

Willow wrapped her arms around Betty. "It truly is."

"Enough hugging for now. Until I get more of that delicious mulled wine." She grinned. "That deserves all the hugs."

"It certainly does," Willow agreed. Aubrey's mulled wine was to die for.

"I have to go help with the pies now," Betty said, waving as she headed into the bustling crowd.

Willow smiled after her and turned back to the task at hand. She placed a delicate, crocheted ornament with silver thread, upon the velvet cloth covering the tabletop. Next to it, a collection of hand-painted wooden reindeer stood guard, their intricate detail begging for admiration. But even as her hands were busy at work, a whisper of disappointment curled in her chest; there simply weren't enough crafts.

The proceeds from these sales were meant to light up the holidays for those who had suffered like she once had—

women striving to rebuild their lives after escaping abusive relationships. And Willow knew the difference every dollar could make.

"Beautiful work," a woman commented, picking up a painted reindeer. "You can see the love that went into it."

"Thank you," Willow replied, her smile genuine. "Each piece sold goes to the women's shelter to help over the holidays."

"Oh, how wonderful," the woman beamed. "I'll take this one."

"Excellent. Thank you." Willow carefully wrapped the reindeer in tissue paper and handed it to the woman, who paid her with a generous tip and a heartfelt thank-you.

As Willow checked her out, her parents emerged through the throngs of marketgoers. Her mother's cheeks were rosy from the brisk air, her father's broad shoulders wrapped in a cozy old scarf that he'd owned for as long as Willow could remember.

"Hey, hon!" her mother called out.

"Hi!" Willow greeted, her heart lifting at the sight of them. They approached her booth with open arms, enveloping her in an embrace that felt like home.

"This market is amazing," her dad said, his eyes twinkling like the Christmas lights strung above their heads. "No wonder you girls wanted to live here."

"It's an absolutely charming town," her mother chimed in, admiring the array of handcrafted ornaments and wreaths adorning the booth. "As is your bar. Look at it, all glowing, and so many people over there."

"Couldn't have done it without Charly and Aubrey," Willow replied, gesturing to her friends.

"Speaking of which, we promised to help them out," her father mentioned. "Got to keep those customers warm and happy!"

"Don't drink all the wine," she called.

Her parents just waved her off. They'd totally drink the wine.

Warmth consumed her, watching as her parents joined forces with Charly and Aubrey, their laughter mingling together. They fit right into the market, her father's booming chuckles drawing in passersby while her mother charmed anyone who walked up.

Her chest expanded with a sense of pride watching them. Yet as the moments passed, her gaze returned to her own booth—modest in comparison to the bustle around her— and the pang of disappointment gnawed at her once more. Each craft sold was a triumph, yet the pile seemed too small, the impact too limited.

She shook off the unsettling thought, forcing her attention back to the present. This was what mattered: the smiles, the shared joy, the collective effort to make a difference. Any money helped, no matter how much.

Right then, something tickled her consciousness. Amidst the sea of merrymakers, a sudden shift caught her attention— a cluster of curious glances and parted waves in the crowd. Then Eli, emerging from the crowd. He was hefting two boxes that looked ready to burst, his stride confident yet unassuming as if he were merely another vendor arriving late to the party. But the rugged lines of his jaw set him apart, as did the intensity in his eyes that found hers across the distance.

His smile caught her breath in her throat, as he closed in, "Hope I'm not too late for the festivities," he said.

"Late?" Willow repeated. This wasn't part of the plan—Eli, here, with boxes. "What's going on?"

"Got a little somethin' for your cause," Eli said, a lopsided grin tugging at his lips as he set down the boxes with a thud. He opened the first box, revealing a flash of metal. "The cowboys and their better halves, Jaxon, Gunner and I, and really anyone we could rope in to help, put these together for you. You know, to help."

Willow gasped as Eli lifted a wreath from the box. The craftsmanship was undeniable; each wreath shaped like a horse's head, the twigs and evergreens meticulously woven in beautifully.

"Wow…" The word fell from Willow's lips.

"We made these too. To add a little piece of the ranch in there," Eli continued, his excitement infectious as he lifted an old horseshoe that was wrapped in ribbons of deep red and forest green, tiny silver bells chiming softly.

"Eli," Willow whispered, finally finding her voice. She glanced up at him, his presence suddenly filling her with a warmth that seemed to right her world. "I don't even know what to say."

"You don't have to say anything," he said. "Let's get them put out and sell them."

She held his gaze, her heart in her throat. "Thank you," she whispered, teary-eyed. "Not just for the crafts, but for being here—for being a part of this...with me." The words fell easily. Because if she looked deep into her heart, she knew, tonight wouldn't be right without Eli there.

He stepped closer, a smile tugging at the corners of his mouth—a smile that told her all she needed to know. "Where else would I be, Willow?"

Eli surveyed the Christmas market with a sense of quiet pride. His plan to help Willow had all come together and worked, and for that he was grateful. The last light bulb around Willow's hut flickered off. Beside him, she stood with an equal measure of satisfaction and sweetness etched into her features. Her eyes reflected the twinkling lights that still adorned the trees lining the market square.

"Looks like it was a success, huh?" Eli said, a grin tugging at the corners of his mouth.

"More than just a success," Willow replied. "We've raised over three thousand dollars for the shelter, and then we've got your five grand from the rodeo." She turned to him, taking a step closer. "Couldn't have done it without you bringing the new crafts today."

The paper cuts, the exhaustion, it was all worth it for that sweet look on her face. "It was a group effort for sure."

She smiled in return and then her gaze drifted to a bunch of drunk marketgoers ambling by, tinsel draped over them and sporting Santa hats askew. They sang carols off-key, arms slung around one another.

Eli chuckled, the sound mingling with Willow's laugh–

ter. "Only in Timber Falls," he remarked, shaking his head at the group.

"It's fun, though," Willow said, nudging him playfully with her elbow. "Come on. Let's join the others and warm up before we freeze to death."

Eli followed her lead, entering The Naked Moose where the bar's amber glow enveloped him. Willow's parents, along with Aubrey, Charly, Jaxon and Gunner, were nestled into the nooks of the bar, drinking up the last of the mulled wine.

"Here's to a successful Christmas market!" Jaxon raised his glass.

"Here, here," Gunner said, echoing the sentiment.

"Couldn't have pulled it off without everyone pitching in," Willow responded, pouring herself and Eli a generous serving of the mulled wine. "Thank you so much everyone." She looked to Jaxon and Gunner. "Especially for making more crafts. You're all the best."

Eli accepted the glass from Willow with a nod of gratitude. He took a sip, its spices dancing on his tongue, as Willow said, "Eli, you haven't met my parents yet. This is Diane and Cliff."

Her father stuck out his hand. "Good to meet you, Eli."

He was a stoic-looking man. White-collar, for sure. "Likewise, sir," Eli said, returning the handshake.

Willow's mother, a petite woman with the same strawberry blond hair as her daughter, only cut above her shoulders and very straight, approached Eli with open arms. Her embrace was surprisingly strong, engulfing Eli in a scent of cinnamon and vanilla.

"It's wonderful to meet you, Eli," she whispered, her voice laced with genuine warmth. "I've said to Jaxon and Gunner, but I'll say it to you too. Thank you for being so wonderful to our Willow."

He felt a lump form in his throat as he returned her hug, a gesture so simple yet loaded with emotions he wasn't used to anymore. It wasn't often that Eli allowed himself to be pulled into the folds of his feelings, but this felt right—like a mother's hug. Something he had deeply missed.

"No thanks required," he managed to say, eyes meeting hers as she leaned away. There was a certain sparkle in her gaze as she looked between Willow and him, and Eli didn't know if Willow had spoken to her mother about their fake relationship, but by that knowing look, he assumed her mother's intuition could sense something between them.

He knew he'd have work to do to earn their trust. But he loved hard work.

Though by the soft way she watched him, he knew Willow had mentioned him and had said only good things. Her warm smile engulfed him as Willow's father turned away to focus on the bar, sliding his hand along the polished wood.

"Before you two came in, I was talking about this bar. I swear things are built better here," he said, admiring the craftsmanship.

"Eli built that," Jaxon said.

Eli gave Jaxon a *look*. Talking about his work wasn't exactly comfortable.

"Really?" Cliff asked, glancing up through his glasses. "You made this?"

Eli nodded, rubbing the back of his neck. "When Jaxon opened the bar, I built it for him."

"It's remarkable work, Eli," Cliff said, peering at the intricate design that swirled at the edge of the counter. "Tell me, what's your secret to getting these curves so smooth?"

Eli slid his hand across the familiar grooves he had sanded down countless times. "Patience and steady hands," he replied, his voice threaded with memories of hours spent laboring over the wood. "Lots of patience."

Charly, Aubrey and Willow had drifted closer. There was surprise etched on their faces.

"Wow, Eli, I had no idea you made this," Aubrey exclaimed, her smile soft.

"Neither did I," Willow added, her eyes dancing over the craftsmanship before resting on Eli. He watched as Willow's gaze lingered on the bar, her eyes tracing the whorls and knots in the wood with tenderness. Her fingers danced lightly over the surface, much like they had explored his body not that long ago.

He clenched his jaw tight, not letting those thoughts fill his mind with her parents there.

"I love that you made this," Willow murmured, finally turning to him with her sweet smile that undid him. "It's beautiful, Eli."

"Thank you." He shifted uncomfortably, unaccustomed to such praise, yet unable to tear his gaze from the emotion flickering across her features—admiration, yes, but something deeper too, something that matched the slow burn in his chest whenever she was near. "I'm glad you think so," he said, his voice low. "I'd really hate to have to get it out of here. It wasn't fun getting it in."

Her laughter, light and unguarded, filled the space between them. "There's no way we'd ever get rid of it."

"Willow, sweetheart," Diane interjected. She gave a yawn so fake it was laughable. "It's been a day. I think we should get some rest."

She nudged her husband, and Cliff chimed in, stretching, not looking tired at all. "Yes, just exhausted."

Diane nodded at her husband, mischief twinkling in her eyes as she turned to Aubrey. "I'm sure Willow and Eli can clean up the rest of this. Would you mind driving us back to the house?"

"Of course, not a problem at all," Aubrey said, obviously reading between the lines. "Come on, I'll call a taxi since we've all been drinking."

"I can drive you all home," Gunner interjected. He pushed back his chair and stood. "I've only had one drink."

Aubrey hesitated. Her lips pursed in a reluctant frown. "Okay, yeah, that'd be great."

Eli wondered what her hesitation was, but he nodded his gratitude at Gunner's offer. He wasn't quite ready to end the night, and he didn't mind Willow's parents were totally setting up for them to be alone. Hell, he appreciated it. They needed to talk.

Turning to Aubrey, Gunner motioned toward the door. "Shall we?"

After goodbye hugs all around, and as they left, Eli felt the space around him shift, the atmosphere subtly changing as if the very walls were conspiring to push him closer to Willow.

It wasn't much longer before Jaxon stood, offering Charly his hand. "We should get going too," he said.

Charly turned to Willow. "You're really all right to clean up?"

Willow nodded, her cheeks turning pink. "There's not that much more to do. We're good."

"All right. Good night, you guys," Charly said, as she wrapped her scarf tighter around her neck. "And thanks again for today. Gosh, the Christmas market was a total blast. Timber Falls really knows how to do Christmas."

"You're not wrong," Jaxon said and then gave Willow and Eli a wave. "Night."

"Drive safe," Eli said.

As the door closed behind them, it was as if the world outside ceased to exist. The bar felt more intimate, the space between him and Willow charged with a new energy.

"Looks like it's just us now," she murmured, a hint of playfulness dancing through her words.

"Yeah, just us," Eli echoed.

They were alone, truly alone, besides all the million things he needed to say.

Twenty-Two

Time seemed to slow down as Willow headed behind the bar, wiping down the bar's polished surface, while Eli's boots scuffed against the wooden floor as he began to collect empty glasses. Her mind felt clear and steady, and she knew the conversation ahead of her was going to change everything. For the better.

She just had no idea where to start.

After he returned from taking the glasses into the back, he headed straight for her. Nervously, she wiped the bar down again, before he stepped forward, gently taking the cloth from her and placing it in the sink.

"Willow," he said tenderly. He moved to stand in front of her, but gave her a little space. "We need to talk."

She leaned back against the icebox, held his emotion-packed gaze. "We do."

He watched her closely a moment and then sighed heavily, removing his cowboy hat to carve a hand through his hair.

"I've spent a lot of time running," he confessed. "Running from pain, from memories, from the parts of me that felt too broken to fix."

The heaviness in his gaze had her instinctively reaching for his hand, urging him on with the silent support she knew he needed.

"Betty—" his voice hitched slightly. "She took me to this group for folks dealing with grief."

Willow felt her eyes widen. "Did she really?"

He nodded. "And you know what?" Softness entered his tone. "She talked my ear off about not letting grief bury me, and to realize the beauty that is the present and to not forget to live, and…her advice struck a chord with me. It made me realize I have two choices. Live in the pain or live in happiness." His thumb brushed across the back of her hand. "I want to live in happiness. I went to the jail. I visited *him*."

Her eyes went even wider now. "You did. You went alone?"

"I needed to," he explained. "I said what I needed to say, and I left what I needed to leave there." He took a step, closing the distance and cupping her face. "From the very start, the fake relationship was never fake for me. It was safe. I could have you without having to face my own shit. But that's over now. No more pretending."

She leaned into his touch. "And Betty helped you see that?" Oh, Betty. Gosh, Willow loved her. She laughed quietly. "You know, Betty's like Santa Claus for the emotionally stubborn. She sneaks into your life, delivers the gift of unsolicited advice, and just like that—you find what you didn't even know you were missing."

Eli chuckled, giving a small nod. He reached out, his fingers gently brushing a lock of hair from Willow's face behind her ear. "Guess I was on her nice list this year," he said, voice low and husky.

"Or maybe she knew who deserved a little Christmas magic this year," Willow said softly.

"I think that's very much true." Eli hesitated, and his expression had never been so revealing. "What Betty did—it made me realize how much I want to be here. With you. Not running, not hiding, but facing everything head-on, together."

Willow's breath caught in her throat. "I want that too," she said, pushing her voice out. "It wasn't fake for me either, and it was safe for me too. But I want us, Eli. Whatever that looks like, whatever we have to face, I want to do it with you because you make me happy." She took a step closer, pressing herself against him. "Betty talked to me too, and so did my therapist. I don't want to shut down with you. I want to feel it all, the good, the bad and everything in between. I want to believe in that happily-ever-after that I once thought possible."

He cupped her face, brushing his thumbs across her cheeks. "We've got this, don't we?"

She nodded slowly. "Yeah, Eli, we got this."

His brows drew together tight before he pressed his mouth to hers in a kiss that was as sweet as it was beautiful. "I should have said it before," he said, pulling back for a moment. "I should have done a lot of things, but I'm not getting this wrong anymore. I'm falling in love with you, Willow. I can see a future together, one that I want."

She placed her hands over his on her face, happy tears welling in her eyes. "I'm falling in love with you too. I'm still dealing with everything, and I know you are too. I know there is no magic fix, but I want to be dealing with it together."

"Together," he offered.

She smiled. "Together." She stared into the weight of Eli's stare, the intensity of his eyes like a physical touch that sent shivers down her spine. His presence was a comforting warmth, a silent promise. She wanted to get closer, as close as she could get.

"Come with me," she whispered, reaching out and capturing his calloused hand in hers. His fingers were strong and sure, yet they yielded to her lead with a surprising gentleness.

She led him out behind the bar, flicking the lights off as she went, and the Christmas lights from the tree cast the bar in a kaleidoscope of colors. She brought him to a stool that couldn't be seen from the window, far from prying eyes, giving the privacy she needed.

She reached for the edge of his sweater, pulling it up and over his head as he helped her. It landed on the floor with a soft thud. She then went for his jeans, but he took out his wallet and placed it on the bar before stripping off the rest of his clothes, his hard cock springing free.

"Stay there," she whispered.

His eyes blazed, burning hot. "Yes, ma'am."

She held his gaze as she knelt before him, her fingers tracing up his thighs. His low groan brushed across her as she took his cock in her hand. And his head fell back with a moan that shivered through her as she took him deep into her mouth.

To taste him…it was *everything*.

The rise and fall of his chest quickened, his breath hitching as her lips slid up and down his rock-hard shaft, and her tongue swirled around the tip, tasting the salty moisture. She stroked him with her hand, following her mouth as she squeezed tight, using her mouth in all the ways she knew how to pleasure him.

Until she began bobbing on the tip, and Eli's resolve crumbled under the onslaught of pleasure. His thighs trembled as he reached down to thread his fingers through her hair. The raw need in his eyes ignited urgency within, a blaze stoked by each caress, each slow swirl of her tongue.

She refused to look away, gliding her tongue over him with every bob of her head and stroke of her hand. Deep grunts filled the air as his jaw clenched and unclenched.

Then, without warning, Eli propelled upward, drawing Willow into his arms with a fierce urgency. Their bodies collided and his lips captured hers in a kiss that tasted of burning desire as he stripped her bare.

With a grunt, he bent her over the bar he'd meticulously built with his own hands. Pressed against the solid wood, Willow felt the heat of his body sear into her, as he squeezed her bottom, then smacked the other cheek.

He reached for his wallet, and she heard him ripping the foil packet open, leaving her shivering in anticipation.

Then he was behind her. His hands roamed over her curves, and she wiggled her bottom, needing him…desperate for him.

"We're in this. Together," he murmured into her ear, his voice rough with desire as his fingers slipped between her thighs. He stroked her, circling her clit, readying her. But it was pointless—she was drenched. Shivers cascaded down her spine and pooled warmth low in her belly as he murmured, "Tell me," he murmured.

"It's you and me—"

Her voice died on a moan as he entered her with one swift stroke, and she bowed against him. Her pulse hammered in her ears as Eli thrust from behind, gripping her hips tightly. The cool surface beneath her was a stark contrast to the feverish heat radiating within, sending shivers along her spine. His body heat seeped into her, and there was no room for thought, only sensation—the fullness of him, the brush of his breath on her neck, the hardness of his cock stretching and filling her, the strength encompassing her.

Their movements became a dance, bodies in sync as she gave in to the smoldering passion. Each touch, each moment brought her higher as their moans mingled. The loss of control rising with each hard thrust.

She met him, stroke for stroke, hard and fast, building and building, wanting *more*…and *more*.

Until the truth of their feelings was laid bare, and in his safety, Willow clung to the edge of the bar, fingers gripping the wood that Eli had built. Her thoughts evaporated, sensation was all she knew as she crashed over the edge, hearing his roar and feeling his frantic thrusts follow as they fell in something better than pleasure. They fell into love.

Twenty-Three

The following morning, Eli's hands gripped the steering wheel as the snow-dusted Montana landscape whisked by. The road ahead was lined with frosted trees, their branches weighed down by the heavy snow. Beside him, Willow clutched the leather-bound checkbook, her fingers tracing the embossed initials—*WQ*—etched into its cover. He'd woken up this morning feeling like for once, in a very long time, he was getting things exactly right. He knew Miranda would be cheering him and his mother would be proud of him.

"I wish the drive was faster," she murmured, bouncing in her seat. "I just want to get the shelter this money."

"We're not far now," Eli said, grinning at her, when the ringtone sliced through the cab's warmth, jolting them both.

Willow fished out her phone from her purse, glancing at the caller ID before answering, "Amie! Merry Christmas."

Eli listened as Willow and Amie chatted, and even if he only heard one side of the story, he could tell by Willow's growing smile that the news was good news. Willow's perfume filled the air of the truck, a light floral scent that mixed with the smell of leather and gasoline, and Eli inhaled it deeply, sure he'd never grow tired of it.

After a dozen minutes, she ended the call and reported, "Amie's doing so well. She was saying that she's thinking about starting college courses next year."

"Good for her," he agreed.

Willow nodded, slipping the phone into her purse. "I'm so glad she's safe now, away from Buck."

"You're not the only one," he confessed. From what he'd heard, Buck would get some good jail time, and he was glad for it. He only hoped the prick moved away from Timber Falls after he got out of jail. But he trusted Detective Harris and knew he'd keep tabs on Buck the moment he got out.

"Almost there," Willow said as they neared the shelter, her excitement palpable, as she bounced again in her seat.

"Ready to make some Christmas magic happen for others?" he asked, though he already knew the answer. Willow didn't just make things happen; she sprinkled magic wherever she went, including into his life.

"Always," she replied, her smile infectious.

And as they pulled into the shelter's driveway, Eli couldn't help but think that this was what healing looked like—not just mending broken pieces but creating something beautiful in the process.

After parking, he stepped out of the truck, and a cool breeze nipped at his skin as he rounded the vehicle to open the door for Willow. The women's shelter was a small weather-worn building with a sign that read Haley's Place. The windows were barred, and the door was reinforced with multiple locks. They walked side by side toward the entrance of the shelter. The heavy door opened after they were approved by security, and they entered the lobby, where one woman was sitting in a chair reading with her children who were playing near the Christmas tree. Beyond them was a metal door that Eli knew he'd never get through, and he was glad for it, as he also was for the security guard with a weapon on his hip watching him like a hawk.

The ambience enveloped him—a delicate blend of hope and determination hung in the air, harmonizing with the laughter of children examining all the ornaments on the tree. While plain outside, the interior walls were lined with motivational posters and bright, cheerful colors to bring warmth to the space.

"Willow!" A woman with lines of kindness etched into her features waved them forward.

"Hi, Sharon," Willow said, stepping into her warm embrace. "Eli, this is Sharon, the director of the shelter. Sharon, this is Eli. He's a big part of our donation today too."

"Oh, Eli," Sharon said, embracing him tight, warmth pouring from her arms. "Your generosity is going to change lives over the holidays. We can't thank you enough."

"You don't have to thank us," he began, his words jagged with emotion as he scanned the faces before him. So many women and children were there, hanging around the living room–type room with the television and Christmas tree. "It's us who should be thanking you. For your dedication, for every night you spend making sure these folks have a safe place to rest their heads."

Sharon's smile beamed. "Thank you also, but your generosity will help to keep lights on, and the pantry stocked, but it goes beyond that. We're setting up a program for financial literacy, job training and education. It's about giving these women the tools they need to build independent lives, free from fear."

Eli's gaze lingered on Sharon, then shifted to Willow, whose smile filled his chest with more warmth than he'd ever felt in his life. He knew the importance of what Sharon described; it wasn't just about survival; it was about reclaiming life itself. "Independence is priceless," he murmured.

"Exactly," Sharon replied, her smile deepening. "Every dollar you've raised is a step toward that independence." She looked out to the children, before addressing them again, "You should know, the funds you've raised have already changed lives. Like Sandra." She pointed to a picture on the wall of a woman with a bright, hopeful smile holding a set of keys. "She's in her own apartment now, going back to university to become a nurse. She's building a future she never thought possible for herself."

"Financial independence—it's one of the first steps to freedom," Willow added.

"Yes," Sharon said with a soft nod. "It's more than just a roof over their heads. It's about reclaiming their lives, their dignity. You've given them that chance, Willow, Eli, and that's a wonderful thing that we're all grateful for."

Eli felt something within him shift, stirring just below the surface. He had entered the ring countless times, faced down beasts made of muscle and fury, but nothing compared to the courage he saw in this room. This was a different kind of strength, one that didn't roar but quietly persevered.

Obviously reading the emotion on his expression, Willow reached out, her hand finding Eli's, and in that touch, he felt the weave of their shared purpose—a way to truly honor Miranda's life.

Just then, the sound of small footsteps drew Eli's attention downward. A group of children had gathered around them.

"Are you the ones bringing Christmas?" a little girl asked, tugging on the hem of Willow's sweater.

"Santa is coming tomorrow, yes," Willow confirmed, kneeling down so she was eye level with her.

"Will Santa find us here?" another child piped up, his question laced with concern.

"Santa always knows where to find good boys and girls," Eli assured him.

"Really?" the little girl asked, her voice tinged with excitement.

"Really," Willow echoed, smiling softly.

A chorus of giggles erupted from the children, and Eli fought back his emotion. He watched another little girl, no more than six, twirl near the Christmas tree, her laughter a bright chime cutting through the weight of the world. Her mother, with lines of hardship etched into her face, looked on, a tentative smile blossoming as she observed her child's carefree spirit.

"Look at them," Willow murmured, her voice barely above a whisper. "It's just so sweet."

He wrapped an arm around her, pressing his lips to the top of her head. "I wish Miranda had known about this place."

Willow wrapped her arms around him tight. "In her honor, we help. Always."

Gratitude filled him as he watched the children playing. He imagined his sister as one of them, her laughter mingling with theirs, safe and sound in a haven much like this one. "Thank you," he said, his voice thick, glancing down at her. "For everything you've done here. For bringing me into this. For showing me another way."

Willow stared softly up at him. "We did this together, Eli. And it's only the beginning." She gestured around the room, to the smiling faces, where hope seemed to hang in the air with Christmas magic.

Twenty-Four

"Strange way to head to the ranch," Willow murmured, more to herself than to Eli, as they drove home. She was still reeling from his having told her he was quitting the ranch to become a coach for young bull riders, but she saw the sparkle in his eyes. The choice was the right one.

"Thought we'd take the scenic route today," Eli replied. He flashed a quick, enigmatic smile.

Willow shifted her attention back outside, her curiosity gnawing at her. Before they had left the shelter, she'd caught Eli in a hushed conversation over the phone.

"Does this have something to do with the phone call before we left?" she asked casually, though the question felt anything but casual in her chest.

"You'll see," Eli said with a laugh.

"Okay," she conceded.

Silence settled once more, but it was a living thing, pulsing with the heartbeat of questions left unanswered. Willow searched the passing scenery, looking for clues, for signs, for anything that might reveal where he was going.

Until the truck slowed. Her breath hitched as they approached the wrought iron gates of the Timber Falls Cemetery.

The truck's engine hushed to a low purr as Eli shifted into Park, the silence of the cemetery wrapping around her. Willow's gaze was drawn to the lone figure of the woman. "Betty?"

"I asked her to meet us here." Eli's door creaked open and shut with a soft thud.

She followed him out of the truck, her heart catching as he circled to the truck's bed and withdrew something large and obscured by a tarp. With careful hands, he unveiled the object—a bench of rich cedar, its surface sanded to a satiny finish.

Willow put two and two together. "Did you make that for Betty?" she managed, emotions lodged in her throat.

A nod. "When I didn't have you," he said softly.

"Betty doesn't know…" Willow asked.

Eli shook his head. "Not yet."

"Oh, Eli," Willow said, dropping a kiss on his lips. "You're a good man."

As expected, he dodged the compliment with a small smile. Together, they lifted the bench and approached Betty, the silence of the cemetery wrapping around them like a thick winter shawl.

Eli cleared his throat as they neared. "Betty," he called gently.

She turned, her eyes widening at the sight of the bench cradled between them. "Hi, dears."

"Got something for you," Eli said, and there was a tenderness in his voice that made Willow's chest tighten.

They set the bench down with care at the foot of Henry's grave, the cedar wood glowing warmly against the cold gray stones. Betty's hand flew to her mouth, her eyes brimming with unshed tears.

"I made this for you," Eli said, stepping back but keeping his gaze locked on Betty's face. "A place to sit...to spend time with Henry."

Willow watched on, her heart swelling as the words hung in the air, heavy with meaning. She saw the way Betty's shoulders shook, the tremble of her hands as she reached out to touch the smooth wood, tracing the lines.

"Thank you, Eli," she whispered. "This is so very wonderful."

Eli nodded, his own eyes betraying a rare vulnerability. "You're welcome, Betty. I just wanted to make sure you had a place here with him."

"I have never seen anything more beautiful." Betty took him in a long affectionate hug. The sight of the grizzled cowboy showing such tenderness warmed Willow from head to too.

When Betty leaned away from Eli, she enveloped Willow, and Willow hugged her back tight. She couldn't help but feel grateful for Betty's presence in her life and the Christmas magic she sprinkled over Eli and Willow.

Betty sat a moment on the bench, stared at Henry's tombstone. "How lovely is this. It's just perfect." She sat a moment longer and then rose. "While I would love to enjoy it

longer, we do have a party to get to. I'll meet you there."
She squeezed Eli's hand. "Thank you again, dear, this is a
special gift."

"You are so welcome, Betty." Eli smiled.

As they walked back to the truck and Betty headed for
her car, Eli slid his hand in Willow's before tugging a little,
stopping her. She followed his gaze and spotted two gravestones that clenched her heart.

There were a million things she could say, but she figured to start at the beginning. "Hi, Marianne and Miranda,
I'm Willow, Eli's girlfriend," she said with a little wave. "It's
nice to meet you. We'll be seeing a lot of each other. Merry
Christmas."

Eli turned to her with a chuckle. "God, you're cute." He
pulled her in close, kissed her forehead and chuckled as he
led her away. "And they would have loved you."

Willow smiled in return, wishing she'd had the chance
to meet them.

They were back on the road in no time, and twenty minutes later, the Timber Falls Ranch sprawled before them. Its
rustic charm magnified by the twinkling Christmas lights
that wound around porch rails and draped over the shin-
gled roof. Willow had been hearing about Jaxon's legendary
Christmas Eve party for a while now, and she realized no
one was downplaying it. He went all out.

Some of the ranches' cowboys were laughing over some
unknown joke by the crackling fire pit, drinking beers. The
children, bundled up in colorful winter gear were engrossed
in their own world—lassoing fake bulls and missing most

times, while others, cheeks rosy from the cold, rolled hefty snowballs to build a snowman.

"City kids are cute, but country kids are seriously adorable," Willow pointed out. She paused to watch a little girl tug on a makeshift lasso, her tiny hands determined and sure.

Eli followed Willow's gaze and smiled. "She's a natural," he commented. "Her father is one of the best ropers I know."

A snowball whizzed past, narrowly missing them, and they turned to see a boy with a sheepish grin wave apologetically. Willow couldn't help but laugh.

"Careful, you'll start a war you can't finish, kiddo!" Eli called back with a wink, his eyes sparkling with mischief.

"Maybe later," Willow teased, bumping her shoulder against his playfully. "For now, let's get inside."

The warmth of the ranch house enveloped Willow as she stepped over the threshold. Inside the house, laughter and shouts echoed through the expansive living room, where a group of cowboys huddled with their children and better halves. They were engaged in an intense Christmas scavenger hunt.

"Got it!" a little girl squealed, triumphantly holding up a shiny red deer ornament, her father's pride evident as he lifted her into the air amidst encouraging cheers.

"Willow, honey, you made it!" The familiar voice cut through the loud voices, drawing her gaze.

There, amid the crowd of festive sweaters and happy faces, stood her parents, their eyes crinkling with delight. Her mother's arms wrapped around her in a hug.

"Hi," Willow breathed out, allowing herself to be folded into the embrace.

"We've gotten into Jaxon's fine whiskey," her father said, grinning blissfully from ear to ear as he joined in the hug.

Willow laughed, glancing to Jaxon who shrugged apologetically. "I wouldn't have expected otherwise," she said turning to her parents again. "It is Christmas Eve after all." And her parents loved fine whiskey.

Her mother gave Eli a big hug and then asked, "Did everything go well at the shelter?" Willow had told her parents the truth about Eli, the fake relationship and all of it, when she got home last night. They were happy for her, even though she knew Eli would have to prove himself worthy to them. As her parents, they'd been through lot, but Willow knew Eli would win them over soon enough.

Willow's attention was drawn toward Aubrey and Charly who were busy constructing gingerbread houses. "Everything went wonderful," Willow said, focusing back on her parents.

Eli agreed with a nod. "It's an amazing place."

"We should donate some money there," Diane said, spinning around to Cliff. "Don't you think so, honey?"

"Hmm," Cliff said. "Sounds like a wonderful cause." To Willow, he said, "You just let us know when we should donate."

"Thanks," Willow said. "I'm sure the shelter will appreciate that."

Her father finished the remainder of his drink. "Oops, looks like I need more."

Her mother rolled her eyes and said to Eli, "I might need some help getting him home later."

"That's not a problem," Eli said, laughing as her mother chased after her husband.

Willow snorted a laugh. "I love how she talks like soon she won't also need help getting home herself."

Eli gathered Willow in his arms, holding her tight. "They're having fun. Nothing wrong with that."

Willow just smiled. Everyone she loved was there, and for all that had gone wrong, it felt like life was just how it should be. As if all the bad that had happened had to, so she could find this new journey.

The laughter and competitive cheers that had been fueling the room's energy dipped into silence as Jaxon stepped forward, his presence commanding the space like a gentle but unyielding force.

Standing by the fire blazing in the fireplace, he cleared his throat, his gaze flitting across the crowd before coming to rest on Charly, who stood with a half-built gingerbread house in her hands, her brow furrowed in concentration.

"Could I have everyone's attention, please?" he called.

The cowboys and their families turned, curiosity alight in their eyes.

Jaxon offered a nervous smile, so out of character for the man known for his charming, cocky ways. "Charly," he began, his voice rich with emotion, "you came into my life like a storm—unexpected and powerful—and you changed everything."

With every eye in the room trained on the unfolding

scene, Jaxon took a deliberate step closer to Charly, and Willow could barely breath. She took a quick look at Aubrey, whose eyes were wide, showing the whites, her hands covering her mouth.

The gingerbread house forgotten, Charly watched him, her heart in her eyes. Then, to the collective gasp of the crowd, he dropped to one knee before her, his gaze never leaving hers.

"I love you. I want forever with you," he said, opening a little black box revealing an oval diamond ring inside. "Charly Henwood, will you marry me?"

In the span of a heartbeat, the air seemed to still, as if the world itself was holding its breath. Charly began crying, the surprise etching itself into every delicate feature of her face. For a moment, no one moved; even the crackling fire in the hearth seemed to pause in anticipation.

Then, as though released from a spell, Charly's lips parted, a sob that was part laughter, part disbelief escaped her.

"Yes," she whispered beneath her hands. "Yes, Jaxon, I will marry you."

The room erupted—the sound of applause and cheers. Cowboys whistled, children clapped their hands and the women dabbed at their eyes, caught up in the magic of the moment.

Willow felt a surge of happiness so potent it nearly took her breath away...*again*. When Jaxon finally moved away, she rushed forward, as did Aubrey, throwing their arms around Charly before taking a better look at the ring.

As the last echoes of celebration and congratulations faded, Eli's gaze found Willow. The radiant joy for their friends still danced in his eyes, but there was something else too—a depth that seemed to pull at her very core.

She moved to him, drawn by the magic between them. He gathered her in his arms, holding her close.

"Someday, when you're ready... I'll be the one down on one knee for you."

His declaration, soft and fierce, sent a shiver up her spine. She searched his face, finding more love than she ever could have dreamed of. "And someday, I'll say yes."

Epilogue

Seated around the massive campfire in an Adirondack chair, Willow leaned back into Eli's embrace, the warmth from his chest seeping into her back, mingling with the heat from the flames and the blanket over her lap. The Christmas Eve party had dwindled to its core, a close-knit group of cowboys and their partners. Her parents, drunk and happy, long gone back to Willow's house.

"Can you believe it?" Charly's voice, infused with joy, cut through the crackling of the wood. "A wedding at the ranch. It's going to be magical."

Jaxon, sitting with his arm entwined around Charly's waist, nodded with a smile that seemed to light up his eyes even more. "I was thinking we could have the ceremony by the creek. It's so beautiful there."

Willow felt a surge of happiness for her friends, and she couldn't help but tighten her grip on Eli's hand.

"That sounds perfect," Willow murmured with a soft

smile, picturing the scene in her mind. The reflection of the trees on the surface of the creek would make a breathtaking backdrop as Charly and Jaxon exchanged vows.

"Maybe some lanterns hanging from the branches," Charly mused aloud. "And flowers—wildflowers everywhere." She hesitated, glancing to the fire for a moment before looking to Willow again. "Imagine dancing under the stars, everyone we love around us…"

"It's going to be beautiful," Willow said. "I'll help with anything you need."

"Thanks, Wills," Charly replied with a soft smile.

Willow's glass was nearly empty. She glanced over her shoulder at Eli, his gaze still fixed on the fire, the dance of flames reflected in his eyes. "My drink's about run dry," she murmured. "Want to come with me for a refill?"

"Lead the way," he replied, helping her to her feet and then joining her.

They walked side by side, their footsteps soft against the snow, the night air crisp. The laughter and banter of the party faded behind them as they entered the house, heading toward the kitchen.

A sharp voice sliced through the quiet causing Willow to pause and exchange a glance with Eli.

"Come on, Aubrey, don't act like you don't remember." Gunner's voice rumbled from within the kitchen, laced with a frustration that seemed out of place on his usually calm demeanor. "Atlanta. That concert. It was one hell of a night."

"Are you serious right now?" Aubrey's retort carried a

mix of irritation and disbelief. "Gunner, whatever you think happened…"

Willow's breath caught in her throat, her heart pounding against her ribs. A one-night stand? With Aubrey? She shared a look with Eli, whose brows knitted together, a silent question hanging between them.

Gunner's voice ratcheted up a notch. "I know what I saw, what we did. It was you."

"Wasn't me," Aubrey shot back, her words slicing through the tension like a knife through butter. Willow could almost see the vehement shake of Aubrey's head. "You've got it all wrong, Gunner. I didn't even go to that concert."

The slight hitch in Aubrey's voice had Willow holding her breath.

"Then who the hell was I with?" Gunner's frustration was palpable, each word loaded.

"God knows!" Aubrey's retort was loud and firm. "But it wasn't me!"

Gunner snorted. "That night, your laugh, the way you moved, your goddamn moans—it's all stuck in my head, Aubrey."

"Think whatever you want, but it's not true, Gunner," Aubrey spat. "You need to get over this."

Willow's gaze locked with Eli's. Her fingers curled around his hand, as they moved toward the bathroom. "Did you have any idea about…*that*?" she asked.

Eli shook his head, his expression grim. "No, nothing. This is the first I'm hearing of it."

Willow had heard the hitch in Aubrey's voice—a telltale

sign of a facade cracking under pressure. Years of laughter and heartache shared between them granted Willow an intimate familiarity with her friend's nuances. "Someone's not being honest," she murmured more to herself than to Eli.

"I can't see Gunner lying about that," Eli said, his voice low and steady.

"Because he's not," Willow said. "I know Aubrey and she's lying about being with him. Which is so out of character for her. Aubrey never lies. Ever." Willow didn't like where her thoughts took her. "Do you think Gunner hurt her?"

Eli shook his head firmly. "No. He's a great guy. And he's trying to get her to admit it. To me, it sounds like he wants more of what they had that night."

Willow pondered. "And for some reason Aubrey doesn't."

"Do you know why that would be?" Eli asked, leaning against the bathroom counter.

Willow nibbled her lip. "No, but Aubrey can be complicated. Her feelings are complicated. Maybe she feels something...but doesn't want to." Willow's eyes searched his. "What should we do about this?"

He chuckled, before he leaned down and pressed a gentle kiss to her head, his lips grazing her hair. "We stay out of it," he said, a hint of amusement lacing his words. "But I know something we can do." He moved closer, sliding his hands up her sweater, bringing heat with every touch.

"Oh, you do, do you?" she asked, wiggling against him.

He playfully nibbled on her bottom lip and lifted her onto the bathroom counter.

"It's Christmas. And you've been a very good girl this year."

She tilted her head and let out a soft moan as he trailed his tongue along her neck.

"And what do I get for being a good girl?"

"Me." He dropped his mouth to hers in a passionate kiss, and she knew this Christmas would be one to remember.

★ ★ ★ ★ ★